I0764354

THE LANGLEY CREDENTIAL

A NOVEL

also by

RICHARD MASSEY

The Southampton Chronicle

The Gascony Letters

Municipal Tilt

THE LANGLEY CREDENTIAL

A NOVEL

RICHARD MASSEY

HAT CREEK

HAT CREEK

An Imprint of Roan & Weatherford Publishing Associates, LLC
Bentonville, Arkansas
www.roanweatherford.com

Library of Congress Cataloging-in-Publication Data
Names: Massey, Richards, author.
Title: The Langley Credential/Richard Massey | Gregory of Bordeaux #2
Description: First Edition | Bentonville: Hat Creek, 2025.
Identifiers: LCCN: 2025937963 | ISBN: 979-8-89299-031-8 (hardcover)
ISBN: 979-8-89299-032-5 (trade paperback) |ISBN: 979-8-89299-033-2 (eBook)
Subjects: BISAC: FICTION/Historical/Medieval |
FICTION/Historical/Renaissance | FICTION/Action & Adventure
LC record available at: https://lccn.loc.gov/2025937963

Hat Creek hardcover edition August, 2025

Jacket Design by Casey W. Cowan
Interior Design by Casey W. Cowan & John Bredesen
Editing by George "Clay" Mitchell & Don Money

 owe a thanks to the following people: Amy Wilson, Bryan Delagardelle, Byron Jennings, Casey Cowan, George Mitchell, Bob Coleman, Clare Matthias, and Rodney Webb. I also owe a debt of gratitude to the historians who have taught me all I know about Medieval England and France.

This book is for my mother, Mary Rensalear McClure Massey.

A Summons from Langley

The cellar, empty. All of it gone. That potent black wine that had arrived with the Christmas fleet was now confiscated, to be enjoyed by a man without the decency to ask or to pay. The king. The new King Edward. The seedling tyrant of the realm. Gregory watched his men leave, two horse-drawn wagons stacked to teetering with his precious tuns of *St. Bazeille.* He counted up the many pounds that he had just lost, and even though he knew the toll, dared not mention it to himself. He could draft a bill and submit it to court, but it would only be placed at the bottom of the pile, where it would remain as a relic of his anger. He spit and slammed the cellar shut. He turned to the street, where a crowd of Gregory's people, the merchants of the Vintry, had gathered. Shaking his head, he looked into their sullen faces. "If it can happen to me, it can happen to you, and my prediction is that it will," he said, and stormed past those who tried to console him.

A November evening with winter begging at the door. But inside Gregory's stone and timber hall down by the River Thames, the fire burned bright and wine trickled at a reputable pace. Music and wisps of frankincense mingled in the air. A dog sat in a corner chewing on its bone, and a shiny green bird chirped from its cage. The table had been cleared and the servants were eating leftovers in the kitchen. The pair of long-backed chairs had been draped with bearskins, and footrests placed at the ready.

Gregory, reclining and quite comfortable in one of those chairs, did not know the name of the song that was being played, but it pleased him. His two apprentices, Bonafice and Brun, both from Gascony, were quite good with their instruments. One played a bowed fiddle while the other a flute. Together they performed the lays and histories, the ballads and liturgicals that, together, told the tales of the world they knew, and of the one they did not. On a good night, when perhaps a few cups had gotten the best of her, Gregory's wife, Joan, would accompany them. Her voice rang slightly off key and wobbled on the high notes as well as the low. But it was still a voice that searched for the truth, as she plucked at the harp, a voice that found the stories and told them, and a voice that tremored with the sweets of joy. So, even if it did not fill the room, and even if it was not fit for large audiences or grand occasions, Joan's voice, to Gregory, was the dearest one in the world. And it was on one of those such evenings, wrapped in the familiar bliss of the daily routine, that Gregory enjoyed the proper pleasure of a merchant, with twin toddlers Herlève and Gregory fast asleep on a cushioned pallet at his feet near the fireplace.

One song ended and another was about to begin when a violent knocking shook the front door. The apprentices lowered their instruments, Joan propped her hands on the back of the chair, and Gregory sat up straight and glared over his shoulder. Householders came running from the kitchen as the dog stood and barked. For a moment they all stared at one another, exchanging fearful looks of surprise. The butler made as if to head to the door, but Gregory got up, halted him with a gesture, and himself went to confront whoever was outside. As he approached the screen separating the hall from the entrance, there came another banging, more violent and jarring than the one before. Gregory stopped, composed himself, lifted the heavy crossbar, and pulled the door open.

Crowded in the street atop their fidgeting horses were many armed men, glaring out from the brims and eyeholes of their helms, their kits of steel and leather washed in the orange light of their torches. Folded into the black and gray of their war gear was a red and blue livery, and on one sparkling brooch, the ruby inlay of the three lions. Formed in a half circle around the flagstone at the entrance to his home, Gregory looked up at them, feeling the heat of holy dread. Household knights. Royal household knights. Third and fourth sons, bastards and low-born climbers, all of them prized for their zeal in doing the bloody work without scruple or hesitation. The nameless, faceless heroes of the dark world of regal authority, they always came out once the glare of pomp and pageantry had faded. Who knew from whence they came—England, Wales, Scotland, or Gascony? A wayward criminal from Normandy or Castile? It mattered not. Once in the pay and service of the king, these wolves did as they were told without remorse or compromise.

"Gregory of Bordeaux?" one of them said.

Struggling to gain his voice, Gregory finally managed to respond.

"It is I," he said. "And what, may I ask, is your business?"

To his continuing loss, one of them pulled back the hood of his cloak, revealing himself as the Dominican friar who had summoned him to Westminster four years ago, when he had been banished from England. A taunting smile came to his face as he handed over a rolled parchment bound by the royal seal and tassel. Knowing that whatever was on this parchment could very well be the beginning of the end, Gregory reached out and took it. The Dominican laughed.

"Do not fear, Master Gregory," he said. "There are others on our list who are headed to the tower tonight, and likely won't leave until it is time to make their date with the gallows. But you? You are free—at least for now."

He gestured to his men, and all at once, they worked their reins, driving their horses onward, rounding a corner and out of view. Standing dumbfounded at the door, Gregory was expecting them to return, but when he heard the shouts and screams from around the way, he shuddered and knew they had arrived at their next stop.

"Gregory, what is it?" came Joan's voice from inside.

He closed the door and bolted it behind him. He returned to the hall, where Joan, her face a mosaic of consternation, stood with one hand braced on the table, and the other held aloft in a gesture of puzzlement.

"Those were the king's men, and that hideous Dominican, the one who sent me away last time, was with them," he said. "And he gave me this."

He held out the parchment, and as much as he did not want to read it, he knew he must. He joined Joan and his apprentices at the table, unrolled the parchment and, out loud, read the words that would surely herald a great turmoil.

Greetings to the honorable and resplendent Gregory du Mont, wine trader in the most glorious city of London. Forthwith you are summoned to the royal residence at Langley, where you are to appear before the blessed and beloved Edward of Caernarfon, Count of Ponthieu, Earl of Chester, Lord of Ireland, Duke of Aquitaine, Prince of Wales, and King of England. You are to undertake this endeavor at your own expense and peril. Failure to arrive by Martinmas will cause great distress and dishonor to His Majesty, and will be proof certain of your disobedience, the punishment of which will be swift and more than equal to the offense. Come dressed as befits your station, a common merchant, and come alone.

He looked up from the note and into his wife's eyes. She reached out and put her hand on his shoulder.

"By Martinmas," he said. "That is in two days!"

"Whatever do you think he wants?"

"I don't know, but it can't be good. Without doubt he has threatened and insulted me, but as we speak I cannot tell you why. I have done nothing to warrant his ire."

"And he does not know you."

"But he certainly knows of me, so who knows what he has been told."

Gregory did not sleep that night. Instead, he, Joan and the household prepared for his departure. Hard victuals from the larder, a gallon of wine in a leather bag, and his horse, Lady Tatenhill, readied for travel. Instructions to his apprentices, letters for his associates, and a calling-to of all outstanding loans owed to him and his wife. And finally, a kiss and a prayer for his children, Gregory and Herlève. At last, he changed into his accoutrements—his breeches, boots and spurs, the black cloak and robe, a cinched belt and knife, and the beaver and peacock hat pulled low down over his brow. With his bag of belongings slung over his shoulder, he and Joan walked hand-in-hand to the stables behind the house, where the groom held his horse by a tether. Gregory loaded up his effects and then turned to face his farewell.

"Dear wife, I promise I will return—as I always have—and we will resume our life together."

"Dear husband, I will be here waiting as I was before," she said. "Take my love with you, and let it keep you warm if ever the day or night shall go cold."

She pressed a silver trinket into his palm and closed his hand around the ancient heirloom. They embraced—promises in the silence, equals in their sorrow, and partners in resolve. He pulled himself into the saddle and gave her one last look. She clasped her hands beneath her chin and smiled, and then she bowed—a bent knee and a sweeping foot behind, and then a taut, downward arcing of the arm and hand—her solemn show of respect and devotion. In return, he doffed his hat, holding it over his heart, and in that moment, when a sinister force pulled them apart, they shared the oath of tears.

He rode out through Newgate before daybreak, as the bells of St. Martin's rang lauds, and was soon on the road to Langley. A day-long journey, he could make it there by Martinmas if all went well. But dark clouds churned in the northwest, the direction he headed, and even a blue and sunny day could not assuage his dismay. He had said goodbye many times, but things were different now. A wife, two kids, and a trade in wine and luxuries that had never been as lucrative as it now was.

In the old days, making his name, increasing his claim. Forward and upward the journey had been, the road finally leading to an undisputed seat at the table of the mighty guildhall. On his way to respectability, his vigor had always served him well. But his right ankle, the one he had broken years ago at Corby, at times ached so badly he walked with an appalling limp. He could no longer see clean and clear into the horizon, his vision turning to haze at distance. Three of his rear teeth had rotted and had been pulled, the back of his head was balding, and that trusty left hand, the one that worked the quill, yanked on the reins, and that pulled the deadly knife, just wasn't as quick and steady as it once had been.

But more than anything, he didn't have the desire. During the chronicle, he yearned for the road, and in Gascony—not that long ago—he relished the rigors of travel. But not now. He wanted to be home with his wife, to hear the cries and murmurings of his children, to play chess with his friends at the Purple Pot tavern, and to argue over taxes and tolls at the guildhall. *I am thirty-seven, and I am too old for this.* Yet there he was, riding into a storm, hurtling headlong into peril. As the clouds went bright with lightning, and as a gust of wind nearly blew the hat from his head, a grim smile settled upon his face. *I will make the king's acquaintance, but I will not present to him my trickeries.* He made the sign of the cross and urged Lady Tatenhill to go ever faster. The murderess mare honored her master's request.

He slept in a village barn on the outskirts of Langley. He broke his fast with a piece of unleavened bread and a hunk of hard cow cheese. He made the sign of the cross, mounted his horse, and rode out into the morning drizzle. Langley soon appeared on the dark horizon, its elegant stone and timber reaches sprouting up from a lush green field. Gregory pulled his horse to a stop, took a deep breath, and considered what lie ahead. *I have made it here before Martinmas, so that is a good start.* But after that, he had nothing but questions, nothing but speculation, all of it hinging on that terrible summons and the threatening way it had been delivered. He coaxed Lady Tatenhill into a quick canter, down the lane to the gatehouse. He identified himself, presented his summons, and was granted entry to the grounds. A groom took his horse to the stables, leaving him on foot, standing there with his handlers, agape at the sumptuousness surrounding him.

Wafting out came the scent of spitted pork from the roasting house, and the yeasty aroma of fresh bread from the bakery. The place buzzed with ushers and valets, sycophants and servants, all of them inspired by the reward of royal favor. The woodwork precise, the stonework embellished with fittings of marble, and high-pitched roofs adorned with Cornish tiles, and a manicured landscape. The louvered long house and the chapel, the stables and the sprawling kitchen, barns and mills, gardens and courts. Beneath the hall, or so Gregory had heard, was an enormous wine cellar with only the finest vintages from France and Spain. Were it not for his circumstance, Gregory would have loved Langley, but being what it was, he saw beneath the outward opulence. This was the seat of power, a warted, troubling power whose commands must be obeyed. Soon he would have his directive, Gregory just knew it, and thus he savored the irony of an ugly future being born in such a beautiful place.

And so, he waited in line, a chaotic press of anxious petitioners hoping the king would grant them whatever relief they sought. These were common folk, and from the looks of them, from all aspects of society—masons and carpenters, miners and metalworkers, tanners and leather men, cobblers, hatters, painters and bakers—and merchants, all manner of merchants surely here to claim some right or privilege that would put more coins in their coffers. It was yet early, and with a crowd in front of him and yet more filing in behind, Gregory sighed and resigned himself to a long day, much of it, he presumed, to be filled with small talk amongst strangers. But his wait did not last long. One of the king's valets, a young nobleman, approached him, gave him a derisive look from head to toe, and said, "Follow me. The king will meet with you now."

Gregory followed the valet into the great hall, its walls decorated with embroidered hangings, dozens of mounted shields, and a grand painting of four knights in search of a tournament. The floor was lined with tile and priceless rugs from the Levant, an explosion of mesmerizing color, and the table, the longest Gregory had ever seen, was set with glass lamps that emitted a soft and dazzling light. The aroma of incense, and that of the wood that crackled in the ornate and cavernous fireplace, filled the air. The raftered reaches soared to the heavens, and the hall's windows, fitted with glass and sculpted mullions, were flecked with morning drizzle. In one corner sat a team of Dominican scribes, their desks and tables under a snow of official documents. And in another corner sat a pair of minstrels, one strumming lightly on a nine-stringed lute, and the other playing a magnificent set of bagpipes with carved drone and chanters. This was the hall of Gregory's dreams, and for a moment, he forgot all about that nasty summons, and instead enjoyed the wash of wonderment that had overcome him. But his revelry was fleeting. On the far side of the hall a door opened, ushers formed a line, and one of them bellowed, "Bow down to his royal majesty, King Edward!"

Gregory bowed lower and with more deference than he'd ever done before, nearly cramping his hip in the process. When he raised his head, looking across the hall, he saw the king, seated in his country throne, crowned and draped in an immaculate ensemble of green Lucca silk and Norfolk wool, all of it stitched with pearls and run through with thread of gold. He sat tall and imposing in his throne. With an icy nonchalance he held out his right hand, the one bearing a huge gold and gem encrusted ring. Gregory scurried down the length of the hall, knelt before his sovereign, and dutifully kissed that ring. The king bid him to rise and motioned for him to take a seat down at the middle of the table, where Gregory noticed a tankard of wine and a sparkling chalice of silver and glass. He took his seat, yet dared not look directly at King Edward, now whispering in the ear of one of his valets. His hushed conversation finished, Edward leaned back, made a magnanimous gesture with his hands and, with a smile, said, "Please, merchant, drink."

Gregory did not usually take full wine this early in the day, but how could he say no to the king? And besides, it looked as if Edward might have already been in his tuns, so when an usher poured into the chalice true and full, Gregory lifted it to his lips and took a sip. Excellent and familiar, so he took another sip. As it washed across his pallet, he recognized it as a St. Bazeille. He nearly coughed it up with the revelation that this was his wine, seized from him just a month ago. The royal household had the "right of prise," the right to claim a certain allotment of cargo—free of charge—from any ship. And it was this right, abused by the old King Edward and even more so by his son, that had been invoked when liveried men arrived at his cellar and had taken as they pleased. Gregory had lost a small fortune that day, and all he could do was complain privately to wife Joan and his apprentices. It was hard for him not to show his disgust, not to betray his emotions with a frown or the slanting of his eyes. But he maintained a straight face, took another sip—of his wine—while refusing to give King Edward the petty pleasure he so desired.

"This is good, no?" the king said, raising his chalice.

"Indeed, it is," Gregory said.

"This comes to us by way of La Réole."

"Oh, I am well aware of its origin."

"A beautiful city, La Réole. Have you been there?"

"Twice, I believe."

"The wines imported from there are of the highest quality. Do you agree?"

"Yes. Only the best vintages leave its quay."

"And you should know. From what I hear you do good business all along the River Garonne."

"Some years are better than others, but on the whole, it is good. Let us pray the French do not get their hands on the trade."

"Oh, they will not, dear merchant. If there is one thing I will do as king, it will be to keep Gascony, and its wine, within our grasp."

Upon his return from Bordeaux, Gregory had been asked to write a detailed account of his entire time in Gascony. He did as he was told yet keeping to himself a secret here and there. He choked on a morsel of regret thinking that Edward must have read that account, that he knew it well, and that he might have even found a hole or two in the telling. Gregory, you see, had omitted his visit to La Réole, when uncles Hugo and Helias had granted to him the wine franchise. He also failed to mention his visit to the Pyrenees, when he had made his own copy of Marco Polo's book, *Di Mirabilibus Mundi.* At the time, he viewed this through the prism of privacy. The royal household needed to know what he'd done, officially, but the king's men didn't need to know everything. His business, after all, was his business, he had reasoned. But sitting here in front of Edward, he knew he had made a mistake, that mistakes could be costly, and that a man like Edward could make him pay.

"You served my father, and served him well, in Gascony," the king said.

"He was my king, your majesty. It was my duty."

"And now I am your king. So is your duty to me as strong as it was to him?"

"It can be no other way, sire. You are my king and I am your subject. I serve as it pleases you."

The king took a sip of wine. He snapped his fingers. The minstrels quit what they played, but soon enough began a mournful song of foreboding notes down in a low register. Funerary, it was, and the somber turn was not lost on Gregory. He took a sip of fortifying wine, and after setting the cup back down, propped his elbows on the table, put his chin on his locked hands, and sheepishly waited for what would be next.

"Alphonse of Bayonne," the king said, with a cunning grin. "I knew him. Even in light of his transgressions, it saddened me and my father when we heard of his death."

"My apologies, sire, but at the time, I meant not to darken royal hearts, but to burnish them by my loyalty. Alphonse, as you know, had been condemned to death as a traitor."

Edward tilted his head in a pout. He turned the ring on his finger. Such a handsome man he was, as long and comely as the courtiers had said. Fair of hair and bright of eye, young and clean, even the many jewels he wore could not outshine him. Easy in his virility, charisma his in abundance, new Edward basked in the comfort of his many gifts. Favoring his father in the verdant days, even in repose a glorious king. Yet Gregory saw it, deep within Edward's core, way down deep in the damp chasms—the slow boat of cruelty gliding across black waters, the crashing waves of rage, and the brackish stream of vanity.

"Had Alphonse still been alive when my father died, I would have pardoned him," he said. "But I never had that chance. Drawn and quartered at Bordeaux, correct?"

"Yes," Gregory said. "As a traitor to your father. And defiant to the end. He refused his last rites even though they were offered."

A fleeting expression of bewilderment, or some other facet of discontent, must have crossed his face because the king leaned forward in his throne, effected a counterfeit smile, and said, "Don't look so glum, merchant. Alphonse is dead, as he should be, so you have nothing of which to be ashamed. But please, let us speak of something more pleasant. I recently started reading a most curious manuscript. It is the tale of a Venetian merchant who travels to Cathay and who serves in the court of Kublai Kahn. Are you familiar with this story?"

As if chastened, Gregory looked down at the table, fearful of what he might see if he looked into the king's eyes.

"Indeed, sire, I am," he said.

Gregory gasped and put a hand to his mouth when one of the king's Dominicans approached the table carrying the very edition of *Di Mirabilibus Mundi*—the one with the gemstones plucked from the cover—that Gregory had purloined from Fumel back in Marmande. This codex was supposed to be in the possession of the Earl of Southampton, and that it wasn't meant something terrible must have happened to him, but Gregory would have to save that speculation for later.

The Dominican set the book on the table, in front of the king, who opened it to a page marked with a slip of wool.

"If you are familiar with the book, then are you familiar with this particular copy?"

"Indeed, sire, I am."

The king scanned one of the pages, and then looked up with an expression of disgust. "Yes, in Gascony you served my father well, but did you not also serve yourself?"

"A man must sustain himself if he is to satisfy the wishes of others," Gregory said.

"Sustenance is one thing, but gluttony is another."

"Gluttony, sire?"

"A book of some renown, and a wine permit that makes you rich in London. Both begotten on my father's time. True, is it not?"

Gregory stammered, but before he could collect himself, Edward continued.

"Worry not, merchant, what is yours will remain yours, but as the rightful king, I am entitled to all that was my father's. And by my reasoning, you owed him a debt, a debt that is now mine to collect."

"But you have the manuscript, which was never mine," he said, "and the wine franchise was granted to me under the ancient customs of Gascony, customs that have long been recognized in England by your dynasty."

"You were in Gascony for a year?"

"Yes, sire."

"Then that is what you owe me—time. You took a year from my father to do as you wished, so I will take a year from you in return."

"What will the year entail, sire?"

"I could lock you in the tower and give you nothing but tepid water and gruel. But that would be a waste. And perhaps exceedingly unpopular in London. No, a man who can arrest and execute Alphonse of Bayonne is a rare man whose talents cannot be squandered. Instead, you will ride forth as my envoyé, for there are many in the realm who have yet to receive my command."

Edward took a long quaff of St. Bazeille, then held out the chalice, the bowl resting in his palm, the stem held between his middle and index fingers. A feral glee overcame him as the lamplight danced in the points of his crown. Gregory wanted to stand, pound his fist against the table and decline. Instead, he did as he must.

"I will undertake this task to the utmost, your majesty," he said.

"I know you will—Gregory of Bordeaux—for you do not want to face the consequences of failure."

An Evening at the Red Rooster Inn

Gregory found lodging at the Red Rooster inn on the road to St. Albans. The king had unceremoniously dismissed him from Langley, but not before the Dominicans had given him a leather satchel crammed with documents. Shaken by his *tête-à-tête* with the king, and unsettled by the many questions yearning for answers, Gregory had fled Langley, anxious to put a hard ride between him and what he had left behind.

Thinking someone might be lying in wait, he had first headed south to London, but soon circled back north on a drover's road to find himself on the outskirts of St. Albans, ambling up to the inn as the day was going dark. He stabled his horse and paid for his room. Sitting on a three-legged stool with the satchel at his feet, he went through the documents one by one, sitting them in a neat stack on the rickety bed in front of him. Rolls, charters, indentures, writs, a codex and a psalter. Gregory allowed himself a long sigh of self-pity. This pile of ink and parchment, all of it bearing the imprint of the king, represented an enormous amount of work, work Gregory did not want to do. But he had no choice, so when a servant appeared at his door with a tankard of ale, he took it, poured himself a cup, and began the process of deciphering this elaborate royal riddle.

Canterbury and Norwich. Feuding guilds and an alewife. A bell maker and a goldsmith. The Cinque Ports, the south coast and the County of Ponthieu across the channel. Out west to Gloucester and Devon, to the tin and lead mines, and on north to Nottingham. And then he came across a word that made him stop reading. Not just an ordinary halt, but the hard wall of dread, or the sinking sands of dismay, or even the distant yet approaching flood along the river of the forlorn. Ireland. That hulking isle in the midst, where men went to die, or to become a hideous something of which they had never dreamt. He shook his head as he looked up from the trove of documents.

He lit the second candle, filled another cup of ale, and with the specter of Ireland now looking over his shoulder, continued. Holding the parchment close to the flame, Gregory was pleased to discover a certificate, a direct testimonial from King Edward himself giving Gregory broad authority to execute his duties. Reading deeper, Gregory realized the extent of his newly gained powers—Edward had made him a clerk in the royal wardrobe. Gregory knew he would enjoy, and need, the authority, but he was sure those he'd encounter along the way would think differently, especially those jealous of their calcified privileges.

While the king had given him authority, by the same document he had taken it away. His appointment only lasted until next Martinmas, the terms of which were spelled out in meticulous detail as a post-script on the certificate, which functioned as a letter of safe conduct giving Gregory clearance to travel "anywhere in blessed King Edward's realm without taint of trespass, to enquire of those he sees fit, and to demand of anyone the goods and services needed for the fulfillment of his allotted duties."

The contents of the satchel gave Gregory enormous clout, but if he could use that clout, so too could it be used against him. The king, just four months into his reign, already had a formidable host of enemies, from the loftiest of earls down to town burgesses, from simple parish priests up to influential bishops. Though William Wallace had been executed two years ago at

Smithfield, the Scots still remained a problem. And then there was France, trouble for any English king. If all this was a lot, none of it compared to King Edward's Favorite, a Gascon knight banished by the old king but soon recalled once new Edward had succeeded to the throne. Much was said of the relationship between the king and his Favorite, and none of it was good. Love beyond friendship and brotherhood, twin siblings in arrogance, and a blatant resentment of the old lords insulted by the invective heaped upon them by mere boys. And to gall them all, the king had made his Favorite the Earl of Cornwall, an unexpected move that had rocked the peerage. Indeed, the king, for a multitude of important reasons, was in some circles unpopular, and in others, despised. As one of his clerks, Gregory knew he would be deeply unpopular, and perhaps even despised, as well. And that's what perplexed him. If the king needed him for royal duties, why had he been so threatening with the summons, and why had he been so rude to him at Langley? Why mention the wine franchise at La Réole, and why mention *Di Mirabilibus Mundi,* while at the same time giving him such a sterling credential—the Langley Credential—with which to complete his tasks? *If King Edward wanted a loyal and eager servant, he did not go about it the right way.*

Gregory opened the shutter, put his arms on the windowsill, and drank his ale as he gazed out into the night. The sky an exalted yard of stars, a hint of frost on the breeze, and an owl hooting somewhere from his roost. He thought about his wife, knowing that she worried over him. She was probably already in bed, the canopy closed, but awake and restless beneath the light of a small lantern. She would be hoping for his return, but also plotting for the benefit of the household if he did not. The thought of it made him sad, but he could not resist a stirring of pride. While he was gone, regardless of how long, the home fires would be burning. Under the circumstances, a man could ask for nothing more, Gregory reasoned, so he counted his blessings and took another sip of ale.

He tried to sleep, clasping his hands behind his head and stretching out across the bed. But too much weighed on his mind, and in addition to that, from the tavern below came the boisterous noise of a celebration. Singing and laughter, and from the thud and creaking of wood, he could tell that people danced. Weary of the darkness that enveloped him, and anxious to spend a pinch of the substantial sum of silver the king had given him, Gregory scrounged through his effects, collected his scrivener's kit and a piece of parchment, shouldered his sheriff's satchel, and headed downstairs to the tavern.

He ordered a tankard of ale, found a table in the corner, and for a moment lost himself in the revelry unfolding around the hearth fire. One man played both the pipe and tabor, using one hand for the pipe and the other on the drum, while another made merry with a tambourine. At a long table sat an assortment of men, all of them rough-cut common folk, hoisting their cups and singing a rowdy song, its refrain a falling frolic of rhymes, in their thick Yorkshire accents. All of them about to be drunk, and all of them cheering the kick line of wenches hitching up their robes and flashing their knobby knees. Not quite sloppy yet, this fête would endure indefinitely. With a subtle nod and an easy hand, Gregory pushed a small pile of pennies into the palm of the taverner, making sure this moment did not end before its time. As the party turned inevitably upward in spirit, Gregory set his table with quill, inkwell and parchment. When the taverner arrived with his tankard and a new candle, Gregory was at last ready to assert his royal prerogatives. As a clerk of the wardrobe, he wrote a letter to his old employer, Richard Beaufort, the Earl of Southampton.

To my dearest and most esteemed lord of Southampton, I write to you as a most humble and agreeable liege. It has been a year since we have had occasion to acquaint ourselves with our most recent doings. As told in London, your ships captured the French pirate Le Chien Terrible, and that you had him executed. Since that most grand event, I have heard nothing of you or your travails. I might be to blame, as I have been too busy with my own affairs to enquire into the affairs of others. My apologies for seeing only the fattened pig before me, and not the greater world in which we live.

I must tell you that things have changed for me. Summoned to appear at Langley, I am now in the employ of our most blessed and cherished king,

Edward of Caernarvon. Appointed as a clerk in his wardrobe, and given broad powers of requisition and inquest, I have been assigned a long list of tasks, the completion of which must be proven before I can return home to London. While I hasten to the service of our beloved king, I prefer the warm bosom of my family.

I have recently seen the manuscript I procured for you while in Gascony. Its appearance at Langley, in the king's possession, was cause for much distress, as it was supposed to be in either your possession or in that of Mariano Taccola, its original owner. I ask of you, why is Di Mirabilibus Mundi no longer your chattel? If this was a gift you gave, then I should feel a great relief, but if it was taken from you as a blackbird takes a robin's egg, then I should fly forth with enduring harm.

Our new king is young yet and does not know the ways of the realm as did his father. In London we see the difference. They say he likes his dalliances and his favorites, but that proper rule is not one of his interests. The merchants are not happy, for he has made quick work of his right of prise. What the merchants do not know, beyond our speculation, is what the peerage thinks of young Edward. I ask you, are the earls and barons behind him, or, as they say in London, are they in opposition? As a loyal servant of the old king, on which side do you now stand?

I expect to be on the south coast by the Feast of St. Gregory, when perhaps we can meet in person. It would please me to see you again, and it would please me more to gain answers to my questions. Please send word to Warren that I am back on the hoof and that I should appreciate his service.

Your humble friend and liege,
Gregory de Bordeaux

Gregory knew this letter could get him killed, but he also knew it could galvanize Southampton's support, which he had always had and hoped to maintain. While Gregory didn't know what the king really had in mind, he knew it wasn't the simple running of errands. Edward could send orders to his sheriffs and have them do what was being asked of him. No, something else was at play, and the Earl of Southampton just might know, or come to know, what it was. He folded the letter into a square, sealed it with drips of wax from the candle at his table, pressed it with his personal signet, and then tied it off with a piece of gut. He tucked it into his satchel, lifted his cup, and took a long drink of ale.

The revelry over by the fire was finally starting to wind down. A couple of men had passed out, and several of the women had retired upstairs with their suitors. But the pipe and tabor still played, and a motley quartet struck up a desperate rendition of a song every commoner in England knew word for word, "Saying Goodbye is Never Easy." Gregory, having heard the song many times in the taverns of London, knew it well. So, he poured the last of his ale into the cup, held it out in front of him, and joined them when the song reached the second stanza. The singers turned to him, surprised and heartened by the new voice at last joining the lay. Gregory smiled as he sang, stealing this little moment of pleasure while he could. Dawn would come soon enough, and it was a long ride to Norwich.

A Fine Market Day in Norwich

After five days of riding, he arrived by way of the Windham Road to the Norwich city gate. Rattled by travel, his stomach grumbling, he wanted nothing more than to find lodging, treat himself to a day's rest, stuff his gut with roasted pork, and perhaps drown himself in a tun of wine. But he knew that was fanciful, the thought of pleasure, when he was in Norwich for just the opposite.

He produced his Langley Credential at Norwich and was admitted to the city. Gregory noticed a young boy running ahead of him, looking over his shoulder from time to time. An obvious spy, and it was then that Gregory knew his arrival here had been expected. That could only mean trouble. He shook his head, made the sign of the cross, and guided his horse into the realm's second largest city, its walls still under construction, its old castle keep perched high atop the hill, and the cathedral's tower a splendid anchor in the sky. The riches of sea trade fueled its teeming streets, and its many beautiful churches exemplified its sanctimony. Gregory compared much of what he saw and knew to London, and in that light, Norwich was not much.

Still, he could not squelch the feeling that he had arrived somewhere, a place perhaps bloated on its self-importance, but also worthy of such conceit.

As it had decades ago, a nasty dispute had again taken root here in Norwich. Not between the city and the monks, but between the mercers, those who traded in textiles, and the grocers, those who traded in food. The rancor had spread, too, as all manner of merchants and craftsmen tied to the mercers took their side, and everyone tied to the grocers took theirs. The feud dated back to the reign of the old King Edward, when the mercers and the grocers, both looking to flaunt their status, squabbled over their placement in a royal procession in London for the Feast of All Saints. Both groups had wanted to be first in line after the Londoners, and when agreement couldn't be met, an ugly row ensued right there in Cheapside. Gregory, who had been in that liveried procession with his fellow vintners, had witnessed the fracas, and had been among those telling the Norwich merchants to go back home, where, at their own pleasure, they could gorge on their vanity. And gorge they did, the feud devolving into riots, pitched battles in the streets, and moments of calm followed by violent upheavals. Nothing, Gregory mused, that did not happen in other towns. But it had affected the revenue that came back to the king's household, and for that one reason, the turbulence in Norwich was a problem. By writ, Gregory was here to put an end to the feud, to broker a lasting deal between the partisans, and to make the silver flow again. A fool's errand, he knew, but one he would undertake with the threat of royal reprisal in his favor.

He smelled the tanneries, with their piss pools and stink, the shit and funk of Hog Hill, and the rot of human refuse. Judging by the power of its odor, Norwich was much bigger than he'd thought, and it was that little revelation that fueled his doubt, that fed his insecurity, and that told him he did not have a broom big enough to sweep away the mess in front of him. Onward he went down Newport, through the French borough to St. Peter's Church, where to the north and south and all in between stretched the famous market of Norwich, pulsing in the shadow of the great castle mound. To the south they sold livestock, grain, and a grand assortment of cheeses, while to the north were the stalls for cloth, leather goods, metal works, fish and butchered meats. Stall after stall, spices and fowl, shoes, boots and saddles, linens, drapery, and the desperate calls of the haberdashers. A rotting corpse hung from the gibbet, and a miscreant stood helpless in the stocks.

Gregory pulled his horse to a halt and absorbed the immensity of the scene. On any other day, he would stable his horse, walk through this fabulous market, and find for himself a luxury item—a carved trinket for his mantle, a comb for his wife, or a scented candle for his table. He would munch on a meat pie, sip on an ale, and make small talk in the crowd. He might watch the puppets, listen to the minstrels, and otherwise enjoy the benefits of commerce. But this was not that day. The kid he had seen at the gate had now finished his rounds, and slowly, and then all at once, the boisterous market had gone silent. All eyes turned on him, those of the local gentry and the country peasants, those of the merchants and craftsmen, and those of the city bailiffs. Gregory was a bit surprised that even the monastics were in attendance, as knot after knot of Benedictines, Dominicans, Franciscans, Austins, and Carmelites, their tonsured heads shining in the autumn sun, joined the crowd. So, there he sat, on his great warhorse, Lady Tatenhill, staring back at what appeared to be the entirety of Norwich society.

The bell at St. Peter's rang sext.

"Go back to your dung heap in London," one of them said, once the bell had stopped sounding.

"You are a gelded ass," said another, eliciting a scattering of laughter.

Shaking their fists and spitting at the ground, and making obscene gestures with their hands and faces, these people of Norwich were a surly lot. Gregory did not give them a reply, he just looked at them from beneath the brim of his beaver and peacock hat, making sure his gaze conveyed menace.

One in the crowd, plump and draped in a fine ensemble of blue wool, black buckled shoes and a black buckled hat, stepped forward, propped his hands on his waist in a show of defiance, and was soon joined by many others.

"Gregory of Bordeaux, is it?" the man said.

"Yes, and who, may I ask, are you?"

"I am Reginald Hoccleve, of the mercers, and you, sir, are not welcome in Norwich."

"Perhaps I am not welcome, but still it is my duty to be here," he said. "You might find it in your interests to treat me hospitably, for I am here to repair what has been broken."

"Broken? Look around you. Nothing is broken. Norwich prospers."

Gregory had planned to go unnoticed to the cathedral priory, on the other side of town, take lodging there, and go to work from the serenity of the chapter house. He had wanted to approach the Norwich guilds as close to Christmas as possible, and to meet with them in the priory. A Godly setting and proximity to the holiest of days would give the proceedings the stamp of goodwill and increase his chances of success. Or so he had reasoned. But with his identity known, as well as his intentions, that plan no longer made sense. On the spot, and from the looks of the crowd, in immediate danger, Gregory figured it would be best to hold nothing back. He was, after all, a royal envoyé, thus outranking virtually everyone in Norwich, including Reginald Hoccleve.

"Perhaps Norwich prospers, but you are disturbing the king's peace, and your continued belligerence is unseemly, not to mention detrimental to the royal coffers," Gregory said. "I have come to offer a solution, to mend the rift between your town and our dear king. But if that is not what you desire, then there are other remedies to which I can resort."

"Such as?"

"I can levy an extraordinary fine that you and your rivals would not want to pay. A punitive fee that will bleed this market dry."

"So, you threaten us with ruin?"

"Yes, if that is what you wish. Do you dare oppose the king's command?"

"It is not the king we oppose, but his fraudulent designee," he said to the howling approval of the mob.

"Fraudulent? I have royal letters beyond your reprove, Monsieur Hoccleve."

"That is not what I hear," he said.

Hoccleve turned, and with his hands moving outward, motioned for the crowd to part. At the far end of the market, Gregory saw the old stone and timber tollhouse, the seat of local government, with a group of men waiting at the door.

"Follow me, Gregory of Bordeaux, and you shall be enlightened," Hoccleve said, a slight jingle in his voice.

Gregory could turn and make a run for it, back down Newport and out through the gate and into the Norfolk countryside. But then he would be a fool. And word would surely leak back to the king that he had shirked his duty at the first sign of trouble. And besides, some of the roughest men and boys in the crowd had surrounded him, and Gregory was not so sure he could turn and flee before being dragged from his horse. So he trotted Lady Tatenhill in behind Hoccleve, enduring the harangues from the populace as he approached the tollhouse.

He dismounted and tethered the horse and met those who waited for him—the bailiffs of Norwich, hard city men in town garb, an assortment of merchants, all clothed in their riches, the sheriff of Norfolk-Suffolk, he of the large gut and gray hair, and above all, a splendidly pompous, runt of a man in robe and mantle of sienna, who introduced himself as John Debenham of the grocers, the second piece of the two-guild feud. Too short to look Gregory in the eye without tilting his head upward, he made belligerent ceremony of the act, and in a voice much deeper than his stature would suggest, and with a spray of spittle, said, "Show us these letters you speak of!"

Gregory wiped a bead of Debenham's spit from his chin, stepped into the tollhouse, set his satchel on the table around which many were crowded, and retrieved the Norwich writ. Debenham yanked it from his hand and gave it to the town clerk who, seated at the table, opened it and began reading. Tracing a finger across the parchment line by line, it didn't take long for a thin smile to greet his lips, and for a fire to light in his eyes. He looked up from the document and around the table at his host. Holding them in a moment of suspense, he stood up, brandished the writ over his head, and when they could stand his silence no more and begged him to get on with it, he shouted, "He has come to fine us one thousand five hundred marks!"

The room erupted with vituperation and invective, with Hoccleve and Debenham red with rage, gesturing angrily with both arms outstretched, their volcanic exaltations rippling out into the marketplace, where two thousand voices sounded a shrill clap of anger. Gregory, knowing full well the philosophy of fines and how they were used to punish and control, stood motionless in the maelstrom, aware that he had first lost the advantage, and then had lost all control. Debenham turned to him, shaking his fist in his face.

"You dare come to Norwich with this disgraceful fine?" he said. "You threaten us with penury, thinking us ignorant and servile. But it is you, Gregory, who is swine. In your haste to bring Norwich to heel, it appears you have arrived too late!"

Confused, Gregory looked to Hoccleve who, having moved past his outrage, broke with a smile of warning and laughed.

"Master Debenham is right, Gregory," he said. "Shortly before you arrived, the mercers and the grocers agreed to a peace."

So, now it was Gregory's turn to examine a document. The same clerk who had read his parchment now produced a parchment of his own. He slid it across the table. Gregory took it, pushed it flush with an outstretched hand, and as the Norwich men crowded him on all sides, he read what had been proffered. Indeed, the mercers and the grocers had agreed to a peace, in order to "appease the most blessed King Edward, and to return dignity to the ancient and noble city of Norwich." Affixed with an assortment of seals from an assortment of witnesses, the indenture pledged all the right sureties in the event of default. Gregory, of course, knew everything would be in legal order. But what he wanted to see was the penalty that Norwich had agreed to pay. And finally he arrived at it, a paltry sum, at least compared to the king's fine, of just 200 marks—the equivalent of 155 pounds—to be paid in two annual lump sums during the feast of St. John.

"Only two hundred marks?" Gregory said, looking into the eyes of Hoccleve and then Debenham. "Surely you are happy, and delusional, with too much Malmsey wine. The king will be furious that you have not matched his proposal."

"Perhaps, but we are acting in good faith," Hoccleve said, "which, I might add, is more than we can say of you."

Under different circumstances, Gregory would certainly make a counteroffer, and even if he did not push for the full 1,500 marks, would push for much more than 200. But he wasn't thinking about the difference between this amount and that. His concern was how he was going to get out of Norwich alive. Glancing over Debenham's shoulder and out through the toll-house door, he saw that the crowd had inched ever closer, and that a group of men had encircled Lady Tatenhill, with one of them holding her tether. As much as it pained him to relinquish his merchant's pride, he did so with the justification that this was not the time to drive a hard bargain. Instead, he looked at Hoccleve, made an expression of deference, and said, "Hand me the ink and quill, and I will affix my signature and seal."

He bent over the parchment and did as he must, thus finalizing this terrible deal that would surely infuriate the king. He could only imagine the look on Edward's face, and the words that would come out of his royal mouth, when this indenture arrived at Parliament, where it would surely be approved by a rank-and-file eager to show their sovereign that his power would not go unchecked.

"Monsieur Hoccleve, Monsieur Debenham, our business is done, and I must be on my way to Canterbury," Gregory said, as cordially as he could.

"What, do you think you can simply leave?" Hoccleve said.

"While I have enjoyed Norwich's hospitality, and while I am touched by the reception I have received by these many fine people, I think it best that I use the remaining day to make ground on Canterbury."

Reading the assortment of faces glaring back at him, Gregory knew they had no intention of letting him leave. As they had told him earlier, his royal appointment had not gone through the exchequer, nor had it been authorized by Parliament. As Debenham had told him, he was a "creation of the king's misguided largesse," and by that reasoning, was a fairly worthless man. If anything were to happen to him, at least here in Norwich at the hands of the mighty guilds, the penalty, if any, would not be too severe.

"Now that we have our own agreement, and that we have shown our obeisance to our dear king, you are of no use to anyone, least of all us," Debenham said, his bantam stature charged with authority.

Gregory saw the hand reaching out to seize him but evaded it by jerking his shoulder backward. He then leaned in with a sweeping right elbow, and caught his assailant, the Sheriff of Norfolk-Suffolk, plum across the chin. The old man fell to the floor as Debenham and Hoccleve cried out in alarm. Gregory turned to the door, still open, and to his holy dread, beheld the commotion taking place outside. Lady Tatenhill, in a sublime convulsion, had yanked the man holding her tether to the ground. She finished his face with a front hoof, and then erupted in a half turn, her back legs springing out and cracking skulls as she went. Gregory dashed out the door, and in the tumult, and as many hands grabbed at his cloak, managed to mount the horse, and nearly fell off as she bucked and whinnied. Debenham, delirious with anger, latched onto Gregory's leg. He shook it free and, cocking his knee, drove his boot back down over Debenham's hatted head. And then he worked his spurs, with no concern for the pain he caused, driving them deep into Lady Tatenhill's flanks. Squealing in agony, the great horse lurched forward, trampled a trio of men, and then found space as the crowd—witness to the carnage she had wrought and awed by her eagerness to murder—respectfully parted, forming an avenue of escape.

She sprinted eastward out of the market, past castle mound, past the alehouses and butcheries at Tombland, and then northward to Barragate. As she passed, tiles slipped from the roofs, black birds flocked out from the eves, and stone cobbles were split asunder. The timber canyons of the city rang with the hearty bellow of thousands. They had seen much more than expected on this market day, when Gregory of Bordeaux had come to town, so they hoisted their cups in commemoration.

Gregory looked over his shoulder. No one was in pursuit. But that didn't matter. He drove Lady Tatenhill until he was closer to Yarmouth than he was to Norwich. As the day began to fade, he pulled her up to a fast-running creek so she could drink. Placid she was, quenching her thirst, regaining her demeanor, indifferent to what she had just done. By his count, Lady Tatenhill had killed five men, had maimed many others, to get them out of Norwich alive.

Gregory dismounted, stretched his shoulders, and winced at the shard of ache stabbing at his old ankle. He turned to Lady Tatenhill, who neighed and looked back at him from behind her spiked leather face mask.

"This is going to be a long and difficult journey," he said, and stroked her on the neck.

IN CANTERBURY, SAPPHIRE AND SIENNA

Great Yarmouth. Gateway to the North Sea and the Low Countries. Gregory arrived at Vespers, flashed his Langley Credential, and was soon at the port, where he secured passage south to Dover. The ship was to set sail at dawn, giving Gregory a night in a town where he knew no names, and, hopefully, where no one knew his. He found lodging in the dank basement of a warehouse on the waterfront, sharing his space with sacks of wool, barrels of wine, and casks of salted herring. Not much for accommodation, but it was convenient and obscure, and with the Norwich calamity still at the top of his mind, exactly what Gregory needed.

A servant boy took Lady Tatenhill to the stables and returned with a heaping trencher of spiced pork offal—heart, liver and entrails, feet, and a juicy hunk of tongue. Gregory feasted, washing it down with a tall cup of terrible English wine. He dug into his pack and fetched his ink well, quill, and a tired piece of parchment that had been recycled several times. He lit a candle, a hunk of Frankincense, and placed the parchment flat against the top of a cask. He sharpened his quill, dipped it in the ink, and made words out of love.

Dear wife, my blessed Joan of Devon, my sustaining fire, my sustenance for health and joy.

I miss you as the fish misses the river, as the sun misses the day, and as the hilltop misses a gentle northern wind during the first rain of spring. Circumstance has brought me to Great Yarmouth, to the salt and brine of the sea, far from our happy hearth in London and the fulfillment that I find there. As we had guessed, our beloved king has asked of me a great task, to do his bidding before those yet fortunate enough not to have met his royal highness. He has me traveling here and there, on missions of many colors, under the robe of official right. The king has appointed me as a clerk of the wardrobe, which during a different time, would be cause for great celebration. But our new lord is a different man, as you well know, and his way is as baffling as it is unwholesome. I should be unpopular everywhere I go, as is the king, and fear that my travails will afford great compromises to my safety. The king claims that I owe him a year, and that the inconvenience he has caused is warranted by my deeds in Gascony, when I served his father to the utmost. But I surmise that all of this is about more than a simple debt of time. What he truly has in mind I do not yet know. These errands, if that is what we can call them, will surely lead to something, somewhere, that will only become apparent when at last I arrive. Though the king told me to come as a commoner, I, as you know, did just the opposite. I have my knife, my mail, and Lady Tatenhill has already been better than the challenge during an unfortunate episode in the cursed city of Norwich. I now sail to Dover, from which I will send this letter, and will then make haste to Canterbury, the site of my second errand. Please write me a letter and send it to Southampton, where I hope to be not long after Christmas, and tell me of all that has transpired since my abrupt departure.

Give Gregory and Herlève a kiss from me and do pray for the sanctity of our union and our home. Be discreet in your dealings with our friends and family, but do not hesitate to drive your bargains with force, or to lodge your writs at court with a punitive zeal. When on the morrow I am at sea, standing under sail and rolling with the waves, my thoughts will be of you.

I will embrace the danger and the difficulty, knowing that we have done this before, and that the story has always ended to our benefit.

Your loving and dutiful husband,
Gregory du Mont

He folded the letter, secured it with hot wax and his personal seal. He kissed the parchment, placed it in his pack, and took the last swig of wine. He put away his effects, blew out the candle, curled up in the corner beneath his cloak, and went fast to sleep.

The north wind was not asleep this day. Billowing down from the hinterlands, the gusts filled the canvas sail, propelling the huge and laden cog southward to Dover at a terrific speed. Crewed at every point with excellent sailors, the ship cut through the sea with ease, racing past the smaller cogs, slashing through the eastward cargo lanes, and rolling over the dips and swells. Jammed with the bounty of Norfolk, the cog was bound for Bordeaux, where its goods would be traded for the coveted Easter wines of Gascony. Gregory had to laugh at the irony. The ship that took him to the safety of Dover was owned by one of his competitors.

He stayed on deck all day, enjoying the good wind and water, making small talk with other passengers, and otherwise savoring this crisp autumn day of sunny blue skies. Out east, the ships tacked toward the Low Countries, to the riches of Antwerp, Ghent, and Bruges. And to the north, the fish fleet casted for cod and herring. Gulls circled and cried, dolphins leapt at leisure along the starboard side, and all along the deck, the seaman worked the rigging. The day, begun well before dawn, had grown long and wearisome. But as Gregory's energy was just about to fade into sleep, an enchanting carmine sunset peeled across the sky. Sitting against the gunwale, he rose, looked to the east, and saw the faint silhouette of France peaking above the waters.

He turned to the west and shook his head in awe. There stood the towering white cliffs of Dover, brusque and foreboding, but welcoming all the same.

While Gregory made easy work of climbing down the rope ladder and into the rowboat that would take him ashore, loading tackle had to be used to hoist Lady Tatenhill up, out, and in. A few pennies into the hands of the boatmen were enough to ease their toil, and soon enough, Gregory and his steed were back on land and heading into town. High on the horizon sat Dover Castle, with its sprawling network of ditches, walls, and towers. The biggest in all the land, an impregnable fortress that safeguarded the hopes and dreams of all the English kings. But Gregory wasn't going there. He had no time for its surly garrison, its conceited warden, or its halls filled with traps and intrigue. All he needed was a quiet night on a pallet near a fire, and perhaps a cup or two of wine and a crust of bread and cheese before he slept. If he drove his horse just fast enough to the town center, he just might find a merchant or a holy house for lodging tonight. But even if that didn't happen, and he found himself beneath a tree out in the county, that would not be grounds for discontent. He had spent a day at sea rather than a week on the road, respite that would count in his and Tatenhill's favor.

He entered Canterbury through Riding Gate, down Watling Street and up Pillory Lane to St. Mary's, where he flashed his Langley Credential and stabled his horse. Coming in on the great Dover Road through a verdant valley in the Downs, he had slept at a farm the night before, rising with the rooster, rousting the wrens, and heading out with the crow.

This most ancient of English cities, Canterbury, with its mighty archbishopric and cathedral, and its august rollcall of saints, was not only the beating heart of Kent, but the site of a royal mint. Having risen and fallen on a few occasions, the city proudly displayed its survivor's bones of Caen, ragstone, and flint. Blessed with a river for commerce, brawny gates for protection and tolls, and a bountiful countryside to fatten its larders, Canterbury, though dwarfed by the likes of London, Norwich, and York, had a conspicuous seat at the top of the kingdom's hierarchy.

Gregory didn't have business in Canterbury. Rather, King Edward had sent him on a mission just south of town. But how could he come to this part of the world and not partake in a ritual that had catapulted little Canterbury into the utmost heights of renown, a ritual that had made the city famous throughout Christendom? He couldn't, and that's why Gregory walked, with a bit of a skip in his step, to the cathedral which housed the extravagant shrine of St. Thomas Becket, the former archbishop who had been murdered near the altar more than a century ago.

Said to have been slain on the command of the old and most cantankerous second King Henry, Becket was quickly canonized. His tomb became the focal point of Christian piety, the destination du jour for pilgrims from across England and the continent. From the lowborn to royalty, each year thousands flocked to Canterbury for their chance to venerate Becket, to lavish him with gifts, to receive his intercession, and to be cured of the ills that impaired them. Two generations after his assassination, his remains were moved from the crypt beneath the cathedral to an elevated shrine in Trinity Chapel. The cathedral and the city had grown fat on the pilgrims, as an industry had sprouted up around Becket's martyrdom. The inns were packed, the taverns, too, and many who had come empty handed would leave Canterbury with a souvenir badge—which they paid for, of course—of the great archbishop with his cross and miter.

Gregory entered the cathedral through the south door and a monk sprinkled him with holy water. Eastward down the soaring, vaulted nave he went, past the choir, beyond the altar and up a flight of stairs to Becket's hallowed resting place. Deep within the crush of pilgrims and its fog of odors and unfortunate secretions, the going was slow, the jostling relentless, and the small talk tedious. But Gregory enjoyed the procession, filled as it was with all walks of English life—the jolly peasant, the haughty knight, the self-possessed merchant, ecclesiastics from throughout the holy hierarchy, and the prim and preening noble. A thousand faces, a thousand voices, and a thousand reasons—Becket's righteous cacophony on this frigid December morn.

His coffin—gold and silver and encrusted with gemstones—sat on a marble plinth supported by stone pillars with sculpted floral capitals. Heaped at the base of the shrine, some of it on the mosaic floor and some of it piled on pedestals, were glinting ingots of gold and silver, carved alabaster, chalices and jewelry, coinage and plate. Cloth of gold and strands of emeralds and pearls, woven into finely embroidered drapery, hung from beams all about the chapel. The collective outpouring of wealth and gratitude, the shining residue from decades of reverence, spilled out from the coffin in a dazzling splash of light, as if God himself had vomited out this spectacular horde of treasure. The eastern sun, creeping through the corona and the towering pains of stained glass surrounding the shrine, washed the chapel with an angelic glow of sapphire and sienna. Peering out from this colossal array of finery was a giant ruby, burning red as blood. And it was that ruby, drinking in and claiming the surrounding splendor, that beckoned Gregory forward.

He took to his knee, made the sign of the cross, and basked in the sublime peace that had overcome him. He no longer heard the other pilgrims, and nor did he see them. Before him rose a radiant haze of joy, a benevolent flame flickering out from the dark. The pain in Gregory's heart went away, as did the ache at his ankle. His doubts turned to certainty and questions no longer needed to be answered. In an astounding moment of clarity, when a chime had sounded the perfect note down deep in his soul, Gregory knew what was needed—that Saint Thomas Becket be on his side.

Glorious Saint Thomas, bishop, priest, and martyr for the faith, pray for us. You who are a determined leader of the children of God, give us courage to face the circumstances of our lives, and the wisdom to follow the light of your example. Like you, may we be faithful unto death, and may we always serve God's Holy will. Saint Thomas, many were brought to you for healing and guidance, both in your life and after your death. If it pleases you now, hear and accept my humble request for the health and happiness of my dear wife, Joan, our children, Gregory and Herlève, our household, the whole of London, and for the prosperity of my old friend, Warren of Lichfield. May I see all of them again. My horse, Lady Tatenhill, is fast, but she could be yet faster. As you stand before God's Holy Throne, intercede for us so that we may enjoy the gifts of the Almighty. Amen.

Gregory opened his eyes, breathed in the soothing aroma of incense, and rose from his knee. He took one last look at that blinking ruby, turned, and along with many other pilgrims, headed back down the nave to the west door, out into the cathedral precinct, and then into the city at Rush Market. He found the Lion Inn on High Street and secured lodging there. He ate a spiced onion-and-leak potage and a regrettable thigh of fowl. But if the food was not good, the same could not be said of the ale. He ordered a flagon and, before long, found himself with pilgrims from Oxford who had abruptly sat at his table. An agreeable lot, so he paid for one flagon and then another. All of them had been to Becket's shrine, and all of them were enthralled by the treasure they had seen, and the divine presence they had felt, on the yonder side of the high altar. Yet even in the afterglow of the experience, and even as he laughed and then sang with his cordial Oxford host, Gregory was troubled by one nagging question—had Saint Thomas been listening?

Brewster Maude and the Drawbridge at Chilham Castle

Gregory arrived where he thought he was supposed to be, but when he got there, all he saw was the burned-out hulk of an old, thatched farmhouse. A fresh fire, too. The charred wood still stank of the inferno, and the detritus that always accompanies such a disaster had not been cleared. He looked all about, but other than the yellowhammers piping in the bush, no signs of life.

The king had sent him here to buy ale. Lots of ale destined for Brabant across the channel in the Low Countries. A gift, Gregory presumed, for the king's allies, as the ale from this place was reputed to be among the best in all of England. Surveying the devastation, Gregory could not understand how that could be. Even had all been well, Gregory would still have had his doubts. A farmhouse on the outskirts of the village of Chilham, Gregory had seen nothing but the small plots of peasants and freeholders, the undistinguished, if exceedingly idyllic, landscape of a typical manor. *If the king had wanted ale, he should have sent me to St. Edmunds Abbey in Bury, where they brew enough to besot the whole of Suffolk.* But here he was, at a blackened homestead near the pea fields, talking to himself when that was the last thing he wanted to do.

He heard a sound, the gentle step of feet on old autumn leaves, and turned in that direction. A woman, her young and handsome face framed in a blue veil, stopped and made a gesture of welcome.

"Good day," she said.

"And good day to you. I am looking for a brew house, but it seems I have arrived at the wrong place."

Others had followed the young lady down the path from which she had come, and in a long instant, Gregory was faced with what he guessed were the locals, those who had watched him arrive and who were curious as to who he was. With the bad experience of Bajamont in the back of his mind, when he had lost his beloved Black Saddle at the hands of Peasant Paul, he made sure to give a respectful nod to these people. Things could go poorly in but a blink, even for a clerk of the royal wardrobe.

"This used to be the brew house but, as you can see, there was a fire—lightning—and everything was destroyed," the woman said.

"And the brewster, Maud, whatever became of her?"

"Oh, she is certainly alive, but she is despondent over the disaster and is staying with her brother," the woman said.

"Can you take me to her?" Gregory said. "I am on urgent business for the king, and a demand has been made on Maud's services."

The villagers exchanged looks of puzzlement, and even glances of alarm. The restive silence settled on the woman, who, by the deference shown to her by the others, appeared to be the de facto leader of this turf-stained group of ploughmen. She plucked up her resolve, planted her feet anew, and put her hands on her hips.

"What is this business you speak of?"

"Our blessed king has ordered the brewing of ten casks of ale and has demanded that the task be completed by Christmas. That is, leaving by barge from the quay at Canterbury."

"But Maud has lost everything and cannot possibly do what you ask in such a short period of time."

"Yet she must try, for it is the king's will. Take me to her and do keep in mind that Maud will be well rewarded with silver should the ale arrive in time at the seaport at Sandwich."

The mention of money had done its work. The woman's posture softened, and the shine of hope sparked in her eyes.

"Follow me," she said, and headed back up the trail.

Maud sat at a stool near the hearth fire in a thatched, one-room cottage. Gregory removed his hat and ducked his head beneath the door beam as he entered. She turned to him, and in that moment when their eyes first met, Gregory saw the anguish in her heart, the bewildered soul lost in the bottomless well. Gregory could not blame her. The ruins of her farm were substantial. From the footprint of the burnt remains, Gregory could tell that there had been a multi-roomed house, a large barn, a row of workshops, a detached kitchen, and even a stable. The hard-won accomplishment of a lifetime, and all of it gone. So, Gregory made sure to approach her with care, to perhaps sow a shoot of dignity and thus gain her trust.

"Maud," he said, in a soft voice and with a slight note of sympathy.

He kept a respectful distance as the woman who led him here squatted at Maud's side and hashed out a short, hushed conversation. Maud's face brightened, she began to nod with concurrence, and in a fit of excitement, rose from her seat, bowed low, and welcomed Gregory to the fire. There he took a seat with her, warming his hands, waving off the crust of bread that had been offered, but gladly taking a cup of watered ale. For a long while the two of them did not speak. Rather, they searched each other in silence, finally converging at a meeting place that both of them could abide—they liked each other, their mutual admiration obvious in a pair of warm smiles.

"You have lost everything, but I can help you rebuild," Gregory said. "Though your material possessions are gone, your reputation as a master brewer remains. And if we work together, that can be your redemption."

Gregory's hopeful words teased out a look of relief in Maud's haggard face—a bit of color returned to her cheeks, the redness in her big green eyes raced away, and the sad, sour lines of grief turned in retreat. Her stained veil, a light blue cloth of once-sumptuous make, gave portrait to a proud woman, a woman, Gregory guessed, who would eventually push back against the disaster that had befallen her. Gaining her gumption, and charging the room with energy as she did, she peered into Gregory's eyes with an intensity that must have been hers before the fire, an old certainty that had brought him here in the first place, and said, "What do you propose?"

"First let's speak of what the king proposes," Gregory said. "According to him, you make some of the finest ale in all of England, and to that end, he is willing to pay twice the market rate. Three pounds per tun, and he wants five tuns. So, fifteen pounds to you. Surely enough to rebuild what you have lost."

Gregory didn't have to wait long for the swell of elation to overcome her. Maud, rejuvenated by what she had just heard, burst up from her stool, wrapped the young woman in her arms, and in tandem the two of them went kicking and skipping across the room, making a wide circle and then another. Watching them, and laughing as he did, Gregory knew these two women were the closest of kin, mother and daughter, and to witness their moment of euphoria filled his jaded heart with gaiety. A gutsy cheer rose from outside. Gregory turned. What appeared to be the entire village stood just outside the door.

Gregory allowed the frolic to last for a while. Maud needed the release, as did the village of Chilham. But Gregory was here for business, and while Maud was now giddy with the opportunity in front of her, much work—and surely a penalty in the event of failure—needed to be done. As the celebration began to die down, Gregory killed it all together with a sober telling of the circumstance.

"Maud, you have lost it all, so how will you fulfill the king's order?"

Maud, still in the arms of her daughter, gave way to deflation. She exchanged a meek look with her daughter, turned to Gregory and said, "Yes, there is that."

But her daughter, quick to thwart despair, bent her knees and held out her arms in a declaratory gesture.

"I have an idea!" she said.

"For the sake of Maud and myself, please, tell us what it is," Gregory said.

"Lord Wylughby, he has everything we need. He has his own brew house, and his granary is plump with malted barley."

"Are you sure of what you say?"

"I am his brewer and have been for some time. He has laid in stores for a big Christmas feast and is expecting visitors from Ashford."

A grin came to Gregory's face as he shook his head in mock disbelief. Deep within the trove of documents given to him by the king was a short history on the keeper of the local castle. His name was Alexander Wylughby, and in the vast and entangled feudal hierarchy, he was much closer to the bottom than he was to the top. Lower gentry at best, Wylughby had lucked into a marriage, gained title to the manor at Chilham, and there sat as a happy widower, a piss-pot potentate whose dandy conceit far outweighed his talent and ambition. He did not participate in county government, being content with collecting his taxes and rents, and little more. Never had he been knighted, and nor had he been invited to Parliament at Westminster. Most importantly, he owed a royal debt—for thirty pairs of shoes, twenty shovels, five saddles, four wheels of cow cheese, three barrels of salted cod, one coat of mail, and one warhorse—for the provisioning of old King Edward's last campaign to Scotland. The supplies had never been delivered, so a debt had been lodged at the exchequer. By Gregory's estimate, a total of nine pounds, nine shillings and five pennies—not an exorbitant amount, but surely enough to ruin Wylughby's Christmas and Easter. He would be easy pickings, Gregory thought, if indeed it came time to drive a hard bargain.

As he weighed Wylughby's plight and how his circumstance might be used against him, Gregory realized it wasn't really about the ale. The best in the land? Probably not. Maud and her daughter, even if talented, were probably no different than the countless alewives throughout the realm. Two varietals, strong and weak, one batch for the people who had money, and another for those who did not. The king had sent him here for the debt, the ale being a convenient excuse to send a royal servant to this otherwise obscure corner of Kent. And if the ale had been nothing more than a clever ruse, it was still the stated reason for his presence here. So, ale would be brewed in Chilham, and ale would be delivered to that shadowy host waiting down river in Sandwich.

"Let us go and meet this Lord Wylughby and find out if he is in the mood to do business," Gregory said, to the cautious delight of Maud and her daughter.

Gregory arrived on the outer bank of the ditch, looking up to the third-floor window of the Chilham castle keep. A squat, octagonal pile of stone surrounded by a low wall, this place was locked up, closed off, and otherwise separate from the village over which it loomed. At the head of dozens of villagers, Gregory hoped he was a sight to behold—seated high and proper on Lady Tatenhill, his mail coat glinting from beneath his robe, holding the Langley Credential high above his head, shouting out Lord Wylughby's name, and imploring him to respond. It took some doing, but the shutters flew open, and Wylughby, a red, rotten apple of a man in a feathered hat and wool, at last appeared in the window. He held out his arms and shrugged, as if to suggest that he was confused, and most certainly annoyed, by the sudden ruckus at the foot of his sanctum.

"Come down from your tower, Lord Wylughby, and entreat with me," Gregory said. "I am on the king's business, and do not have time to dally."

"And who has ripped me away from my morning prayers?"

"Gregory of Bordeaux, and God will surely forgive you for cutting short your time with him."

"Before I come down, I must ask, what is your business?"

"I have come for three tuns of ale, Lord Wylughby, for King Edward's retinue."

"Ale? Three tuns? How is this my concern?"

"Because I have deemed it so," Gregory said. "Now come down and open the gate so that we can negotiate an appropriate agreement."

Wylughby leaned on the windowsill with both hands, took a deep gulp of breath and shouted, "I refuse to open the gate! If you need ale, talk to Maud!"

"From your vantage point, I'm sure you had a good view of the fire. Maud is destitute and you know it. Face me while the terms are still good, for if you wait too long, they will not remain that way."

The venom in the retort must have been just right because Lord Wylughby pulled the shutters in, and not long afterward, bellowed the name of one of his servants. The drawbridge began to open—the wood creaking, the old chains clanking—rising, the murmurings of the villagers. Gregory cut a side glance at Maud, who returned his look with a devious grin. Flanked on his left by a man-at-arms, on his right by a young archer, and backed by his assortment of householders, Lord Wylughby, inch by inch and foot by foot, came into full view as the bridge lowered into place. And there sat Gregory, perched in his saddle, trying to look lethal with his head crooked downward in a glare, the shine in his eyes a set of stars in his billowing black finery.

"Greetings, Lord Wylughby," he said. "I must commend you for stepping away from your prayers to meet with me, a messenger who has arrived unannounced and who bestows upon you an unexpected burden."

Wylughby, arms across his chest, a hand rubbing his chin in an exaggerated act of contemplation, and with an old, seasoned frown on his face, looked skyward before leveling with Gregory.

"Ale? You have rousted the village and ruined my day for ale?"

"The king's ale, Lord Wylughby, and it's bound for the Low Countries where Edward has allies."

"But the king has sent no such request—"

"—Yes he has," Gregory said. He fished into the chest pocket of his robe and pulled out the rolled parchment. He held it aloft. "Indeed, it has arrived today."

Wylughby motioned to his man-at-arms, a burly lad in a full kit of mail, helm, axe and sword. He walked across the bridge, plucked the writ from Gregory's lowered hand, and took it back to his master. Wylughby unrolled and read it, a core-and-seed smile settling in his face.

"By this writ the obligation is with Maud, as I told you earlier."

"Under the current circumstance, she cannot do what is needed at her brew house, so I kindly ask you to allow her to do it using your chattel."

"Three tuns is an enormous amount of ale," he said. "As much as it troubles me to deny your request, and to cause distress for our dear king, deny it I must—unless other arrangements can be made."

"Such as?"

"Since it is my property that is the key to your proposal, perhaps it should be me who is credited with satisfying the king's demand."

"And cut Maud out of the deal? To jilt her on the fifteen pounds?"

"Why yes," he said. "She is a peasant woman, while I am her lord. Surely you understand."

"No, I am afraid I do not," he said. "I have come here looking for a bargain—we will recompense you for your services—but Maud's name must be on this, not yours."

"Then you will not have your ale, and Maud will not have her reward. Now that our disagreement has been settled, you would serve yourself well to leave Chilham while there is still enough light in the day. If you persist, I will say the word and Andrew and William will make short work of you."

The archer looked at Gregory and spit, and the man-at-arms crooked his hand around the hilt of his sword. This overt threat of violence did not serve as a deterrent. Rather, it stirred the villagers, Maud chief among them, with a dash of defiance. For a hot moment, it felt as if this standoff would devolve, from ale to blood, from the promise of riches to the long truth of no pennies. But Gregory stayed the unease with the raising of a hand. Reaching down into the dignity of his officialdom, he found a new voice, one that frightened even himself, and spoke so that all could hear.

"Lord Wylughby, you owe a substantial debt to the king, and until that debt has been paid, you do not have the standing to negotiate on terms of your choosing," he said. "If you do not allow Maud to brew the king's ale on your domain, then I shall call the debt due, and do so today."

The quick burn of comeuppance overcame Wylughby, and Gregory allowed himself a cruel smile as the flames of reality engulfed his rival. Royal debts were never forgotten, and they always resurfaced at the most inopportune of times. Gregory knew this all too well, as it had just recently happened to him. So, he relished Wylughby's wilting chagrin, the sudden timidity of his retainers, and the shrinking stature of his household. Victory was on the brink of being had. But if Gregory knew anything, it was that pride and privilege, the twin siblings of all the old lords, were difficult to vanquish. And thus it was with Wylughby, who recovered, took a few steps to the middle of the bridge, and said, "I demand that we take this case to the Sheriff of Kent! It is he, not you, nor I, who will determine the outcome."

A tortuous groan arose from the villagers while a quip of joy sounded among Wylughby's lot. Gregory felt deflated, but he dared not show it. Sheriffs, almost to a man, were residents of the county to which they had been appointed. What this meant is that Wylughby probably knew who the sheriff was, and as peers in the same local gentry, were probably friends. At the least, they were associates, while Gregory stood on the outside as the stranger in black. A complication, no doubt, but Gregory could not let it get the best of him.

From where he was, and from his high seat in the saddle, Gregory saw over Wylughby's host and into the castle's inner bailey. He spied the stables, seeing the rumps and heads of a few horses. He frowned, waved a dismissive hand, and said, "I would ask you to go fetch the sheriff, but, as I see, all you have are nags and carters."

Before Wylughby could respond, Maud crooked her head in Gregory's direction.

"The sheriff resides in his manor this side of Faversham," she said.

With the good news lifting his spirits—Faversham was not too far away—Gregory locked eyes with Wylughby and said, "Do not bother with your horses. I shall go fetch the sheriff and bring him here."

Lady Tatenhill needed little coaxing. The coarser thundered out of Chilham, found the high point between the ruts in the road, and made haste northward to Faversham. The cold December road ran through the majestic rolling downs, beneath beech and elm, over rickety wooden bridges across the steep banks of sluggish streams, and out across the emerald county fields. Hamlets and farms, ruins and hedgerows, the beauty of Kent welcomed Gregory with its ancient charms. Even in the race to claim the sheriff's ear before Wylughby did, he pulled his horse to a stop, atop the highest hill he had yet to traverse, and looked all about him. A chalk cliff in the distance, a wooded ridge, and a deep valley of brambles and broom. The sun fading in the west, winter wagtails perched in the bush. The golden air pleased him, and he savored it for the duration of a piper's song. But his business beckoned him. He worked the reins, and Lady Tatenhill, her breath a burst of fog, charged farther north to where, Gregory hoped, the issue of ale would be settled.

The moated manor had yet to be shuttered for the evening. Firelight showed in the hall's glass windows and a healthy plume of smoke rose from the chimney. Breaking the silence of twilight, a group cackle of laughter, that which punctuates a successful joke, stoked the mirth of many. Gregory hated to arrive unannounced and to barge into a private gathering. It was never a good look and would always count to his detriment.

On the outer bank of the moat, its waters streaked with sunset, he asked himself if there was any way one of Wylughby's men could have arrived before him. *The locals always know the shortcuts, but a shortcut is no match for my Tatenhill?* With that doubt in mind, he approached the gatehouse, stated his name, produced his Langley Credential, and waited for admittance to the sheriff's great hall.

Gregory could not tell exactly what they were saying, but it was evident from the many voices within that his arrival had triggered a new and spirited conversation. As the muffled sound of debate continued, the gate opened. Gregory crossed, dismounted, and under the watch of two men-at-arms, approached the oaken door, its arch carved with saints and sinners. Though the glass was opaque, Gregory saw the silhouettes of faces in the windows, and knew that they were curious, even unsettled, by the surprise visit from a man bearing the king's letters.

The door opened. A valet ushered him in. The cream of Kent County appeared to be in this hall. All of them dressed in their finest ensembles of fur trimmings and wool, all of them participants in the unspoken contest of accoutrement. The splendid trying to impress the splendid, a clique of vanity, the elites celebrating themselves inside this timber cavern of opulence. The table had yet to be cleared, so Gregory saw that a gluttonous feast had recently been had. Carcass of pork and fowl, of fish and beef. The tableware smeared with sugars and sauces. The roots and vetches of the land, and the browned loaves of the estate. Goblets and chalices, cups, bowls, and tankards. If here ran a river, it would never run dry. At the head of this fulsome heap sat a young man, flanked on his right by an older, homely woman, and on his left by a ruby-cheeked damsel.

Gregory doffed his hat and bowed.

"Greetings, Sheriff de Faucomberge," Gregory said. "Perhaps I have come at an inconvenient time, but I assure you, my business is worth the disruption."

He returned to Chilham with the *posse comitatus.* The sheriff, the coroner, the tax collector, justices of the peace, and a clutch of county men who had all seen jury duty. Gregory did not have to work too hard to convince them to come. Chilham was near, and for a chance to gain royal favor, and with the promise of entertainment, they gladly mounted their horses, the morning after their feast, and went south.

There was, of course, the issue of emeralds and pearls. Gregory had a few of each on his person, the secret stash given to him by the king. In private, he had offered a few to the sheriff. "To buy oats for your horses," Gregory had said. The sheriff responded with a sly smile and a covetous hand, and from that moment on, Sheriff de Faucomberge of Kent was Gregory's man.

Arriving as they did with the commotion of many hooves, the villagers heard them and poured out of their thatched and whitewashed homes. And in the high window of the tower keep, that outpost of authority, that old seat of rulemaking and control, appeared Wylughby and his man-at-arms. Peering down on the impressive host now arrayed at the drawbridge, Wylughby looked as if he had pricked his skin on a thorn and had then choked on a prune. Exactly what Gregory wanted to see.

"I have returned, Lord Wylughby," Gregory said. "Perhaps now you will assign more credence to my request for your cooperation."

"And what lies have you told them?"

"He has told us no lies," the sheriff said. "He is on the king's errand, and if you do not want me to blacken your name the next time I send my missives to Westminster, you would be best to do as you have been asked. Now open up, and let the alewife make her brew—or I will press the king's claims forthwith."

Wylughby sighed. He looked to his man-at-arms for comfort, but only received a clumsy, half-hearted shoulder hug for consolation.

"I will be down shortly, and Maud can use the brew house for as long as she needs it," he said.

Gregory looked over at Maud and conveyed his triumph with but the slightest crimp of his lip. She returned the gesture with a quick curtsy, and in that moment, when she knew she would have her way, Gregory found her beauty restored. A country lass of the first order, with blue eyes, a proud Saxon brow, a blonde lock loose from the veil, and about her an air of plumb blossoms and primrose. He had seen this years ago, in Corby with Margery Alesworth. The mere memory of her filled him with mournful delight. He sat on his mighty war steed as the sheriff and all the others poured over the bridge and into the castle grounds. Wylughby, cloaked in his wool and fur and buried beneath a billowing blue hat, protested as he must. Maud stopped and turned.

"Are you coming in?" she said and gestured for him to join them.

"Yes, I will be there momentarily."

He looked down the road from whence he had come, and for a moment hoped that Margery would appear around the bend. Alas, he knew that would never happen, but he held onto the daydream for a while nonetheless. He turned to the commotion ahead of him, the hubbub of the great brew fest about to unfold. He coaxed his horse forward. Lady Tatenhill snorted, tossed her mane and pranced across the drawbridge.

A MOST PERILOUS ALE TASTING AT SANDWICH

Gregory folded out his Langley Credential at the quay at Canterbury. The toll clerk waved him on through. The barge on which he stood, worked by a team of watermen with poles and oars, floated on past the great cathedral city and out into the current that would take it to the seaport at Sandwich. Clear of people and places, and for now his duty done, Gregory breathed a sigh of relief and took a seat on a wooden box at the front of the barge. The river, green in the afternoon, rolled before him. Near a clump of sedge, a cormorant searched for fish, and on the southern horizon, a stand of elder. He removed his hat and ran a hand through his thatch of hair. Bitten by the cold, he put his hat back on, pulled his cloak tight, and gazed into the bleak December sky. Bloated with leaden clouds that promised rain and sleet, and perhaps even snow, Gregory told himself that it was the season for such weather, and that the fires burned hot in Sandwich.

The barrels of ale, packed high and tight, appeared to be a regular shipment of cargo, similar to many pieces of commerce that had been shipped down the River Stour. But to Gregory, all of it was curious. Brewed for the king, destined for the Low Countries, and procured through an instrument of debt, this ale was a royal gift meant to impress whatever allies the king wished to flatter. But if they only knew what was in this ale, perhaps they would not be so keen to imbibe. The standard cereal had been used, of course—malted barley. But something else had been put into the mix, a secret ingredient of which Gregory had sworn never to tell.

Inside the brew house, with the door closed so no one could see, Maud had hiked up her robe, squatted good and low, and pissed in a pot. When she was done, she asked Gregory to do the same. Though surprised, he did as he was asked, giving voice to neither question nor doubt. Troubling to him was Maud's recitation of some strange incantation that Gregory could not decipher. He let his unease pass, consumed by the moment at hand, thrilled at playing his part in the delivery of a dark art. To the urine, bubbling in its pot and congealing into a syrup, Maud added a large dash of brown dust, dipped out with a spoon from a worn leather pouch kept deep in the folds of her robe.

"What is that?" he said, with the grin of collusion.

She looked at him, wondering if she should tell him or not. Gregory could sense that she would not tell, but he did not allow her to decline.

"Tell me, so that together we can share a secret."

Maud, hands on her hips, relented.

"Lavender and rose, almond and saffron, mandrake and poppy—and the bones of three large rats hung by their tails and roasted, while still alive, over an open flame. All of it ground under a full moon a week after the marigolds have bloomed."

"And how, may I ask, did you arrive at such a recipe?"

She laughed and then turned serious.

"I have already told you enough," she said, and went back to her work.

She set the elixir on a small flame off to the side, stirring it three times. When it came to a soft boil, she pulled it so that it would cool. Through the night she went, firing the wort, and to each batch adding a ladle of the secret concoction while at the same time uttering a garble of words, none of which were in the five languages Gregory knew.

The entire village had come out to help her fulfill this enormous order, fetching water from the well, hoisting the malt, stacking the fuel, positioning the barrels and, at the end of two restless days, hauling the ale down to the river and loading it on the barge. Maud stood on the bank and watched Gregory leave. Just as the barge cruised out of view, they waved to each other one last time. It saddened him to leave, knowing he would probably never see her again. But he had helped make her wealthy—the indenture already signed and sealed and on its way to Westminster, the payment already made with a slim ingot of silver stamped with the king's arms.

With a fortifying sense of self-satisfaction, he turned to the watermen, made a stiff face and said, "Lads, steer this barge to Sandwich and do not delay!"

At the end of a long day, the patchwork silhouette of Sandwich appeared—ships bobbing at the quay, loading tackle splayed along the riverfront, city walls and a bell tower. Gregory showed the toll clerk his bill of lading, flashed his Langley Credential, and ordered the watermen to pull the barge up to the quay. A large group of fine horses, attended by a team of servants, stood outside a tavern, from which came many boisterous voices. Gregory paid the watermen well, as the king would have wanted him to, and absorbed their profuse gratitude. This rough company he would like to keep. On their journey down the river, the watermen had sung peasant songs, jovial and hopeful at one turn, mournful and longing at another. He had made small talk with them, had broken bread with them, and appreciated their earnest trade. But it was time to say farewell to these common folk and go and greet the drunk lords now causing a stir inside the tavern.

He steeled himself for the worst, not knowing who exactly he was about to meet. But judging from their horses, the beautiful gear they wore, and the seriousness with which the servants watched over them, Gregory was certain they were nobles, the king's nobles, and that they would talk to him, and treat him, as they pleased. He walked into the tavern, made eye contact with the worried proprietor, and then turned his attention to the far corner of the room. Crowded around a long table near the hearth fire, a gang of knights, cups and tankards before them, empty trenchers and bowls littering the board.

In the long shadows of the smoke and firelight, this band of armored fools, keepers of secrets and lies, appeared as they truly were—lawless dogs yet well trained for the hunt. Deep into a story, these knights did not notice anyone but the person telling it. So, before they became aware of him, he took a good look. His heart sank when he recognized the person weaving the yarn that so enraptured his fellows. This man, draped in his road-worn regalia—a blue and red checkered jupon, a sweeping blue cloak, and the luster of plate and mail—was one of the men who had arrived at his house a month ago to serve him with the summons to Langley. From the documents the king had given him, Gregory knew who he was. Henry de Thornhill, the latest progeny of a family that came over with, and was rewarded by, William the Conqueror more than two hundred years ago. The pedigree, the stone-bound tranches of prerogative and favor, marked this man as a baron in waiting, an exceedingly dangerous thing just north of his teens who didn't need a Langley Credential to shoulder his way through the kingdom.

If it had been up to him, Gregory would have turned and left before they saw him. But his duty demanded that he do just the opposite. He waited until the story was over, keen not to rob these men of their narrative, and to sidestep a clumsy interruption. The crowd roared with laughter. The fleeting moment of crescendo subsided, and the men went back to their ale. Gregory knocked loudly on the door sill, and all at once, these young knights, all of them unstoppably deep into their cups, turned his way.

"I am Gregory of Bordeaux," he said. "And I have brought the ale from Canterbury."

"Bordeaux, you have arrived!" said de Thornhill, and raised his cup. "It is good that you are here, for the taverner fears he is about to run dry! And if indeed he does, then he will have a riot on his hands!"

The comment drew cheers from his men. As they howled with the prospect of more drink, Gregory approached the table. Mindful of his manners, he doffed his hat and bowed.

"Greetings, my lord, it is good to once again meet your acquaintance," he said.

"Oh, is it?" he said. "The last time I saw you, you were as frightened as a child without a mother's teat, sucking at the knob and not the nibble."

"Indeed, but I have regained my composure since that time," he said. "Working for the king, as you know, does wonders for one's assurance."

The rugged men all about Gregory stared at him in silence, drinking in the presence of the newest member of the group. As they adjudged him, Gregory did the same in return. While some of these men were older, greying at the temples and ornamented with senior scars, others at the table were just lads, still pimply faced and with beards and mustaches of fuzz. All of them with the shine of rambunctiousness, fueled by the ale they had consumed, and emboldened by the fact that there were many of them and few of everyone else. Gauntlets and knives, helms and mailed coifs, sword hilts and axe blades—the arms and armor of this host were vast, the volatile authority of their presence unmistakable. Gregory was sure the town fathers of Sandwich would be relieved when they were gone, as would he when his business with them was done.

Their leader pointed to two of his man, growled out their names and told them to fetch one of the casks of ale now bobbing at the quay.

"Do not drink it all," Gregory warned. "It is meant for the king's allies across the channel."

"Do not worry, Bordeaux, we will not drink it all, but we will have enough to know if you have done as the king has asked," the leader said. "Reputed to be the best in the realm? I have drunk it all so I will know. If you have brought us mule piss, then we will make you regret that you came here."

"But what if it is the best you have had?" Gregory asked.

"Then you will wake to a glorious Christmas day."

The two knights returned with a barrel over their shoulders, and plunked it down, right next to the table. They summoned the taverner, who tapped the bung hole and drained a gush of amber liquid into a much smaller bucket, affixed with a ladle. With a wooden mallet, he hammered the plug back into the barrel. Their leader, a predator's smile crouched in his face, looked at Gregory as he dipped the ladle into the bucket and filled his cup. He raised it, dipped it in Gregory's direction, and said, "For your sake, Bordeaux, this better be good."

He took a long gulp, a harrowing gulp that drained the cup. He swallowed hard. But for a long while his expression betrayed neither approval nor dissatisfaction. And then, with the narrowed eyes of many knights bearing down on Gregory, the retinue's leader slammed the cup to the table. He filled it with another ladle and took a second drink. His Adam's apple chugged, a drip ran from the corner of his mouth and down his chin. And again, he slammed the cup to the table. Looking at Gregory—a lad's grin revealing a pair of missing teeth—he said, "It is the best I have ever had! We take it with us to Brabant! And when I am done there, I will join you in Ponthieu—should you need assistance enforcing the king's will."

His men whooped and cheered and went to filling their cups with Maud's mysterious brew. Gregory smiled and nodded his head slowly and with confidence, suggesting to his host that the ale's quality should have never been in doubt. Indeed, he filled a cup of his own, and was pleased with what he tasted. A top note of flower and of fruit, and a dank bottom of inebriating power. The turning point having passed, the man in the corner with the pipe and tabor launched into a spirited country lay. The youngest of the lot leapt onto a table, kicking out his feet in a wild, rhythmic stomp. The taverner, sensing that the crisis had been averted, gave Gregory a gesture of welcome, and had a servant boy bring him a stool. And so, the hours passed, the contents of the barrel disappearing into the yapping maws of these sloppy knights and squires. Out in the town the Christmas bells rang, but inside the tavern the revelers were oblivious to the solemn birth of Christ.

Gregory partook, but sparingly. These were not his people, and he would be in peril if he were to lose himself in them. Besides, if his tongue were to loosen, he might tell them that the ale's secret ingredient included mulled urine, roasted and ground rat bones, and a dash of mandrake and poppy. And that, he told himself over and over again, was something he didn't need to do.

Sauced Canard and Stuffed Crêpes (The Colossus of Abbeville)

Gregory walked his horse down the gangplank. They trudged up the muddy quay. He turned and took a last glance at the sluggish River Somme before turning his attention to the town before him, Abbeville in County Ponthieu. Compared to all that Gregory had seen, nothing spectacular. A typical jumble of stone and timber crowded near the bank, a line of warehouses fitted with cranes and loading tackle, and a congested *place* at the foot of the church. He looked up to the great belltower. A thin smile crept over his face when he noticed that it was empty. Perhaps they rang the hours in Abbeville, but not from there.

He motioned to a servant boy and paid him a few farthings to take Tatenhill to the stables.

"*Garçon, faites bon usage de ce que je vous ai donné*," he said, and pressed the coins into his hand.

Just as soon as the boy had left, Gregory smelled something wonderful on the wind—was it a fresh yeasty dough and sauced canard? Was their cider from the nearby orchards, an assortment of cow and goat cheeses, and all manner of stuffed crêpes? It had to be so, for this was Abbeville, the stout little capital of the king's County of Ponthieu. He realized from which direction the tantalizing aroma had come, a rickety stall on the far side of *la place* where old men sat and drank. Headed that way, it was hard to contain his excitement. *My business here could get me killed, but it is good to be back in France.*

Gregory came to take the bell. Not just any bell, but an enormous bell, a melodic bell of the finest tin and copper alloy, a bell that would serenade the angels in heaven, and rebuke the demons in hell, with its glorious peal. Crafted by the fifth in a famous line of master founders, this bell would take a four-horse crane to lift, would swing on a yoke of the finest finished oak, and would bear the name of Great Walter. Struck by its balled clapper, this bell would speak louder than the rest, would herald the arrival of the great and, in time, mourn their death. From its hallowed place on high, above the land over which it laid claim, the harmonic thunder of this bell would become the trusted voice of generations. But the bell had yet to be made. And it would not hang in Abbeville but back in England. If it were to be properly purloined—a larceny, you see, by royal order—he would have to wait, only making his intentions known at just the right time. That meant he had to play the role, that of curious traveler, to mix and mingle with the local nobles, to approach and befriend the area merchants, all while oiling and polishing his half-truths and lies.

The bell, commissioned by a wealthy salt and woad merchant named Julien de la Vallée, was supposed to hang in the Abbeville belfry, the brutish square tower Gregory had eyed when he first arrived. The old bell had never been right—out of tune, not enough tin, and had finally been taken down, melted down, its metal put to other purposes. With merchant Julien leading a local coalition of sponsors and asserting himself as the chief financier of the project, a new bell was to be cast just off *la place,* and under the expert hand of a famous Parisian bell maker, Peter le Cloche. While the bourgeoisie of Abbeville might be easy to bamboozle, in at least a century it had never been said that a Parisian had been easy prey.

With a corner of crusted bread, Gregory sopped up the last of the onion sauce, that divine concoction of fat and spiced wine that had accompanied the canard. He wiped his mouth with the back of his hand, took a quaff of cider, and plucked the last bite of cheese from the trencher and gobbled it down. He spent extra so that the elders sitting all around him could enjoy a cup of wine they had not expected. They became boisterous with the new libation. In that din of jovial provincial banter, Gregory devoured a crêpe loaded with cinnamon and stewed apple. He held out the last bite toward the cook, just before eating it, to show his approval. Sitting among these northern men, Gregory felt at home. A different cut than he, him being a southern Bordelaise, and speaking in a different dialect. Still, deep down in them Gregory saw a bit of himself and took pleasure in the company of these old Frenchmen, their temples gray, crowfeet at their eyes, and much laughter between sips of wine.

He was about to become lost in them when he noticed what appeared to be an official city delegation heading his way—Julien and his entourage, Gregory presumed, so he stood from his stool to meet their arrival. Stopping a few feet short of him, this gaggle of town fathers, festooned as they were to the very brink of their status, were to Gregory a familiar sight—local burghers plump on their self-importance, made corpulent with their sycophancies, and nearly blind to how those outside their circle might see them. This giant bell in this little town. Gregory nearly laughed as he looked from one face to the next before settling his sights on Julien, who stood a step ahead of the others.

"Julien de la Vallée," he said. "Mayor of Abbeville."

"Gregory of London," he said. "After a stomach-churning voyage across the channel, it is nice to be in a town as beautiful as yours."

"And it will be yet more beautiful—when we have our new bell—to be cast next to where it will hang," he said, as the merchants behind him nodded and murmured in approval.

"Ah, what would our towns be without their bells," Gregory said.

"Indeed, and its maker arrives in Abbeville soon," he said. "You are here at a most joyous time. But tell me, what brings you here?"

"At least for now, the sauced canard and the stuffed crêpes," he said. "They are the best I have ever had."

Julien gave him a puzzled look.

"I noticed—your horse—when you came up from the quay. Excuse me for being intrusive, but an ordinary man in town for sauced canard and crêpes does not own a horse like that."

"She is not much more than a nag, I assure you," Gregory said. "She might have the coat and markings of a queen, but it is all for show."

"But your boots of Spanish cordwain and your spurs of worked steel," said one of the merchants. "From the knees down, you could be a knight."

"And your cloak," said another. "I was recently in Ghent and saw there no swath of wool that could compare."

"And your mail," said another. "Surely from the workshops of Cologne."

"And the hat you wear," said a fourth. "It could be from nowhere other than Flanders."

This time Gregory laughed at himself. The mud and dust of miles, and the salt spray of the sea, had yet to conceal his finery. Even if Julien and his associates did not know what he was, they certainly knew he was much more than what they usually saw. Dismissing them with talk of sauced canard and crêpes was not going to work. But Julien had given him enough information to begin weaving his ruse.

"I am on my way to Amiens," he said. "I have business there of which I cannot speak. But this bell—perhaps I will remain here until it hangs in the belfry and support you in your most noble endeavor. The making of a bell, they say, is the making of magic."

"Indeed," said Julien, restored by talk of his vanity project. He pointed past Gregory's shoulder, so Gregory turned. "The Egret Inn. For your stay in Abbeville."

"I will make my arrangements shortly," he said.

Satisfied with the exchange, Julien turned and walked away, his associates close on his heels. They turned out of view into the warehouse district along the quay, but before doing so, one of them stopped—the oldest, fattest, and to Gregory's mind, the wisest among them—and looked back, locking eyes with Gregory in a long stare of suspicion. Gregory feigned ignorance with a polite and deferential waiving of his hand, and then headed toward the Egret Inn.

Peter le Cloche arrived in a caravan of horse-drawn wagons. Accompanied by a dozen servants and a squalid tail of hangers-on, he sat tall and proud on the highest bench of the biggest wagon, himself holding the reins. Clean shaven and arrayed in his craftsman's finest—dyed Flemish wool, a tall, feathered hat, polished boots and a luxuriant green cloak with a shiny bronze brooch—he radiated success. The dark-haired gent had a cocksure air about him, too, completing the image of assertive competence. He pulled the wagon to a stop in the middle of *la place*, stood from the foot board, and with the waving of his hand, as if he were some sort of savior, said, *"J'arrive!"* At his utterance, Abbeville sounded an exalting cheer. Chief among the celebrants was Julien, standing front and center at the entrance to the town hall. Flanked to the left and right by his fellow merchants, Julien could not hide his satisfaction. With a big grin spread across his face, and with the assurance that he was about to make his lasting mark, he held out both arms in a fawning gesture of gratitude and said, "Peter, we are honored that you are here to bless us with your good works."

Peter jumped down from the wagon, greeted each merchant separately, and at last arrived at Julien, pulling him into his arms as if they were long lost brothers. Gregory stood just on the outside of this joyous circle, his thoughts going darker by the moment. The better things got for Julien and his supporters, the worse it would become when the truth finally emerged. But Gregory did nothing to dampen their spirits. Instead, he smiled and laughed with the rest of them, and clasped Peter's shoulder when the bell maker presented himself.

"Bonjour, Peter," he said. "May your bell sound the finest note in all of Ponthieu."

"Only Ponthieu? That is an insult. May this bell sound the finest note in all of Christendom."

It was only a simple boast, an utterance of conceit that a man of Peter's status was expected to make. But in that fleeting moment, when the two looked eye to eye, and when Peter one-upped him, Gregory detected something that he did not like. He didn't know quite what it was, but something lurked beneath the veneer, and Gregory was sure that whatever it was would emerge while Peter was here, expressing his full artisan's self. But Gregory did not betray his unease. Instead, he gave a smile and with a laugh said, "Yes, all of Christendom. And may the hearts in Paris and Venice rot on the vine of envy."

"Yes, envy," he said, his eyes widening at the word. "Let us make their black hearts ache with it."

If Peter was clean in his appearance and fastidious in his manner, the same could not be said of those who followed him. Prostitutes and vagabonds, outcasts and beggars, they commandeered the town tavern, and made of it a proper mess. Singing and dancing, and among the group a team of talented minstrels. It had all started out well. But perhaps buoyed by Peter's requested presence, and the unassailable status he held, they soon outlasted their welcome, demanding more wine when the cask had run dry, and pitching a small riot when the taverner did not fetch anymore. They broke the chairs and the tables, smashed the pottery, tore off the front door, and dragged the taverner into *la place* and beat him to within a breath of his life.

Peter, when asked about the ruckus, showed little concern, saying, "I cannot answer for the actions of others."

Gregory, seeing an opportunity ahead, decided to procure several pipes of wine. If needed, keep them drunk and happy, Gregory reasoned, and let them make buffoons of themselves. With his plan in place, Gregory sat and watched as Abbeville came under Peter's strange, toxic spell.

The first full day, at least part of it, went as expected. Peter's men dug a deep pit just off *la place,* and next to it they built a furnace of stones mortared with clay. As his men took care of the drudgery, Peter and a pair of his skilled helpers installed the great lathe, and next to that set up a table and laid out the turning tools he would need to shape the mold's core. Layer after layer of clay was applied to the lathe's spindle, but the going was slow as each layer of had to be dry before the next layer could be applied. The doing took all day, and at the end of it, the core was yet half made. As Peter and his men worked, the hangers-on built for themselves a ramshackle tent city. Drinking from the pipe of wine procured by Gregory, their celebration grew ever louder and rambunctious. As the day gave way to the night, a bond fire was lit, and from the window of his room at the Egret Inn, Gregory watched Peter's hoard dance around the flames. Alarm rang through the town the next morning when a local baker was found hanged from the signpost in front of his shop.

Julien, in a rage and backed by his fellow burgesses, confronted Peter at the worksite.

"Do you know anything about this?" he demanded. "Jean-Michel, our best baker, was murdered last night."

"I know nothing," Peter said, as he applied a handful of wet clay to the mold. "I am not their keeper, nor do I monitor what they do. But perhaps you should keep from making assumptions. As you know, every town has its secrets, and the baker may have died at the hands of someone who lives here in Abbeville."

Peter said nothing more, and casually scooped up another handful of clay and applied it to the mold, leaving Julien speechless and fuming. He turned to his cadre of merchants, the group of which Gregory had joined, and held out his hands in frustration. And in that moment of confusion, when Julien did not have an answer, the merchants indulged in a flurry of murmurs. Jean-Michel, after all, had had his fair share of tristes, bedding this wife and that, siring a bastard here and a bastard there. Despite his reputation as a master baker, he had a known list of enemy cuckolds in Abbeville. Aghast at how quickly the murder had been explained away, Gregory turned and looked at Peter's people. Just waking up from last night's revelry, they crowded around the glowing embers, refortifying themselves with more wine, and scrounging in their bags for morsels of food. A loutish lot, a bloody lot, and a lot that would have their way while Peter was there.

It took another long day, but Peter finally finished the mold's core. A beautiful hunk of turned clay suspended on the lathe, this would form the inside of the bell. Big enough for a man to stand inside it, this bell surpassed the size Gregory had imagined, and despite the growing menace of the caravan, he could not wait to see what would soon emerge from the pit in which the bell would be cast. But first he had to make it through another night.

Roused from his sleep, he went to the window, looked out across the town and, to his dread, saw the city gate open up and a new band of stragglers come in. They met with the others of their kind, and in little time, had taken residence at *la place.* Gregory refused to panic, but the realization was too obvious to ignore. These people, Peter's wretched host of castoffs, had invaded the town and were now holding it hostage. If Gregory wanted to leave, he would have to go through them, a losing proposition. Instead, he made the sign of the cross and said a prayer, not just for himself, but for the town and for his horse, sitting helpless in the stables.

Dawn broke with the hue and cry. At some point in the night, a group of Peter's dolts had broken into the workshops of the local draper, and now many of the stragglers, so recently dressed in rags, were now swathed in new, ill-fitting bolts of colorful cloth. The draper and his apprentices, a collective pustule of outrage, confronted the miscreants, many of them lounging about Peter's train of wagons and gear. One of them, a hook-nosed, toothless redhead with hanging shoulders and a limp, tilted back and laughed as they protested. But his face soon went wicked, and with the clicking of his tongue and the pointing of a finger, sent the dog at his side leaping forth. It bit into the draper's arm, drug him to the ground, and as the draper sounded a heartbreaking shriek of pain, the dog, its jaw locked and its head jerking, tore at him. A brown mastiff with a scarred hide and protruding ribs, this canine was an obvious leftover from some long-ago battlefield, and the proof of his lineage was in his viciousness. In but a few blinks of an eye, the draper was a leaking, twitching heap of misery, curled into a defensive ball and begging for mercy. His master called off his dog, but not until the message had been sent—do not protest, or you will be next.

But Julien had to do something. So, as he'd done the day before, he stormed across *la place* to the worksite, a group of merchants, town elders and Gregory behind him, and approached Peter. The bell maker, now applying the tallow mold to the clay core, paid them no heed as they made a semi-circle around him. With his legs aggressively planted and his hands on his hips, Julien said, "Peter! You must put a stop to this mayhem at once! If you do nothing, Abbeville will be in ruins by the time you are done!"

Peter finished laying more tallow across the core, smoothed it with his artist's hands, and then wiped them on his apron. He looked to Julien, showing no alarm or dismay by what was unfolding around him.

"If you want your bell, then this can't be stopped," he said. "They follow me wherever I go and make their own rules once they arrive. Surely you knew about this before you summoned me."

"No, I did not," Julien said. "Put a stop to this lawlessness or I will dismiss you at once—and without the pay you have been promised."

Peter returned to the bell. Piece by piece, he applied more tallow, joining them to the clay core with a hot iron. He took his time here, but soon enough the entire core was covered with tallow, which would determine the thickness of the bell. Julien and his people said not a word, as if they were transfixed by Peter's delicate work. As he put the last piece of tallow in place, and without taking his eyes off his task, he said, "Look around you, Julien, and tell me what you see."

Julien did as he was asked and saw what everyone else saw—the town was not in his hands anymore. Julien was no longer the master of this little realm. It belonged to Peter and his fiends. Their demands, not Julien's, were ascendant. Working the tallow with the iron, smoothing it to perfection as his assistant turned the mold on its lathe, Peter, again not looking up from his work, said, in a soft and sinister voice, "Please, ply these people with food and drink, and whatever luxury they so desire, or they will burn this town to the ground."

Julien did not quibble. He ordered the townspeople to bring what they could to *la place* where, a sack of deniers in his hand, he would pay market rate for their wares. Gregory knew this just might work, so to lessen Julien's burden, he himself paid for another pipe of wine and had the butcher slaughter the fattest hog available. And though the townspeople grumbled, they fell in behind Julien's plight, stacking the center of town with whatever they could afford—pots and pans, cloth and shoes, loaves of bread and hogsheads of cider. An old broken-down horse, a cage full of fowl, and an assortment of sundries wound up in a jumble in front of the town hall, an offering to keep the transgressors at bay, to keep them from digging deeper into the larders of their homes, from ransacking their precious winter stores, and from pillaging their modest heirlooms.

Though he may have been in the act of averting a catastrophe, Julien was still in the middle of a debacle, and as each good was delivered, and as each payment was made, the cloud of despair hanging over him grew ever darker. The deniers added up to sous, and the sous added up to livres, and in his face the story was told—Julien was approaching ruin. And that was not the worst of it. As Gregory had been told, Julien had arranged for the enormous sum of twenty livres for the bell, ten in advance and another ten upon completion. That the bell was yet to be finished meant Julien still owed on the deal, and Gregory was certain Peter had not forgotten that important little fact.

Gregory wanted to either console Julien, which he knew would be worthless, or to figure out a way to help him solve the problem. But as an outsider, he must first allow Julien's closest associates to provide their input.

"Julien, we owe Peter nothing if he does not finish what he started," one of them said. "Give him everything that you have gathered and ask him to leave. They will have a nice journey back to Paris, and we will have our town back. There is, after all, a fine set of bells hanging in the tower at the abbey, and Peter is not the only founder in Ponthieu."

"I have come too far to turn back now," Julien said. "By God's grace, my bell will ring from our beloved belfry."

Julien's associates did not take his side, and as residents of the town who also stood to lose everything, they begged him to reconsider. But he would not, and against their exhortations, he trudged back to the worksite, where Peter's men were fitting the furnace with two sets of bellows. Standing behind them and peering over the shoulders of the merchants, Gregory took a good look at Peter. He showed no signs of quitting his labor. To the contrary, he deftly carved an exquisite floral pattern along the entire rim of the mold, his men turning the lathe as he went, and when he was done with that, he added the finishing touch—Julien de la Vallée had me made—in Latin.

The artistry done, he then began covering the tallow with a layer of clay, which would form the outer shell of the mold. Julien and the merchants did not bother him with their concerns, and like Gregory, they marveled at the precision of his work, focused and steady while all about him the cacophony unfolded. And Gregory knew why. Peter had another ten livres coming his way. He was not about to let such a handsome windfall go unearned. Indeed, rather than try and convince Julien to ask Peter to leave, Gregory knew it would be best—for his own ends, and those of the king—if he instead helped Julien meet his obligation. He worked his way to the front of the crowd until he stood next to Julien, putting his arm over the shoulder of the downcast mayor.

"Julien, I know this has cost you more than you had expected, but if you have any difficulties meeting the deal's requirement, do not hesitate to ask of me my services."

Julien looked at him, a curl of optimism peaking in the corner of his eye, and said, "Master Gregory, it pleases me that you have made such an offer, and perhaps I will enquire into it further."

"Indeed," Gregory said, "for you are right. You have come too far to turn back now."

Gregory looked into the faces of Julien's supporters and, as expected, was greeted with long looks of disapproval. He had gone against their counsel, and a stranger at that. His business was not that of making friends, however, but of making the king happy. Gregory weathered the fury of their discontent and held himself with the cold confidence of a man in possession of a secret advantage. His demeanor disarmed those who had so recently looked upon him with suspicion, even scorn. The waning of their displeasure fortified Julien and, seizing upon the sudden upturn in mood, smiled and said, "What, Master Gregory, did you have in mind?"

"Oh, I have emeralds and pearls, enough to compensate for any shortfall you might have," he said.

The mention of jewels made the merchants giddy. But, as is oftentimes the case, a naysayer claimed the moment.

"What is your interest in this matter?" one of them said. "You are just a visitor, so why would you offer such a gift to those who you do not know?"

A good question, one that even aroused a doubt in Julien, who sanctioned the inquiry with a demonstrative nodding of his head.

"As you know, the County of Ponthieu is under the lordship of King Edward of England, and he would like nothing more than to see its capital, Abbeville, crowned with such a beautiful bell."

"So you are the king's man?" Julien said.

"Indeed, and I am here to ensure that your will is done."

He fished into the chest pocket of his robe and pulled out the Langley Credential. Just the sight of it, the king's seal and tassel dangling from the roll, was enough to quell the merchants. Julien bowed, as did the others, showering Gregory with the deference that a clerk of the wardrobe deserves. Now in control of this nervous clutch of merchants, and anxious to move beyond the concerns they no doubt continued to harbor, Gregory motioned his head in Peter's direction and said, "Now let the man do what he came here to do and let us focus on keeping his crowd under control."

Sating themselves on the bounty of Abbeville—gorging on a hog, guzzling wine, ripping chunks from the loaves, and slicing slabs from the wheels of cheese—Peter's rabble was, at this point, in good repair. But everyone knew that could change, and that it probably would. So, Gregory made sure another pipe of wine, among the last in a vaulted cellar not far from the quay, was procured and made ready for consumption. It could be no other way. The bell's outer mold had been applied, the furnace had been lit, and through the night, the bell mold would sit covered in its pit, where the tallow innards would melt and run out through the bottom of the mold, leaving a hollow space into which the molten copper and tin alloy would be poured.

The night went as expected, a dreadful celebration of the damned. With the residents of Abbeville barricaded in their homes, or in the stables, or in the town hall, or in the belfry, the visitors rioted amongst one another, fighting over the victuals and valuables so cleverly left to them earlier in the day. When dawn came, five people lay gutted and dead, and several more sat moaning and clutching at their wounds. But Abbeville, strewn with debris and stained with urine and excrement, still stood. When the townsfolk came out of hiding, they found Peter's people so flattened by the excesses of the night that they were suddenly vulnerable. As Gregory had seen before, back on some dark day years ago, the long knives appeared from nowhere. In a silent call for revenge, the townspeople set upon them, hacking down and swiping left and then right, choking necks and kicking heads, yanking hair and gouging eyes. Gregory just stood there, sickened as the ghastly heaps of massacre grew higher.

He glanced over at Julien who—shaken by the primitive act of reprisal committed by the otherwise orderly people he had known all his life—shook his head and put his hands to his face. Gregory then looked over at Peter. Willfully oblivious to the shrieking slaughter that was still underway, he counted the ingots—four parts copper and one part tin—that would at last be melted down to make the bell. His men hoisted the ingots, set in big crucibles, into the furnace, its fires fed by two huge bellows worked by a gang of boys. Once that step was done, Peter cleaned his hands on his apron, took a sip of watered wine, and wiped his lips with the back of his forearm. Thin faced and dark haired, alert and as ready as a crested finch, Peter seemed to enjoy the taste of his poison. The smile on his face was a frightening thing, and as he made eyes with Gregory and looked him up and down, it only grew more terrible.

"Judging by your accent, and if you are the king's man, you must have come over from England," he said to Gregory. "And judging further, you are no ordinary merchant. What is your obligation here in Abbeville? It is a question, I have heard, that has already been asked."

"The same as yours, the completion of a most beautiful bell."

"But there are many bells in England, so your presence here is curious. And from what I have gathered, Julien and his host are uneasy with you."

"With me? Look around you, Peter. Your followers wrecked the town, and now many of them lay dead. A foul spirit lives within you, and you have allowed it to escape and run free."

"If I have unleashed a spate of evil, it is equally true that you have enabled it to flourish. People tell me everything, and I know you have spent a fortune on wine and cider."

"To prevent an even worse riot."

"How could it have been any worse than what we see? If there is blood on my hands, there is also blood on yours. Once this bell is done and we have all gone our separate ways, you must take a piece of shame as your own. I do not know what your fascination is with my work, but I know the price you will pay. It is the guilt of fault, and it will linger with you—the massacre at Abbeville—for many years to come."

Gregory could not openly show his chagrin here at *la place*, but he certainly admitted to it within. This Peter, this artist of the devil's making, spoke with a certainty that could not be resisted. His voice, a hard tenor blessed with an effortless conviction, proved more than enough to convince everyone within earshot, and by extension those who would later hear of it second hand, that Gregory had been blamed for the crimes that had been committed. He wanted to respond, but nothing meaningful came to mind. Further still, a misplaced word would only deepen the chasm into which he peered, so he deemed it best to remain silent. Peter, sensing that he had beaten back the challenge to his primacy, nodded to his assistants.

"Bring me the alloy," he said.

His men, using a crossbeam, lifted the first crucible out of the furnace. Under Peter's direction, guiding them with a crooked finger or the open palm of his hand, they poured the molten, shimmering copper and tin into the mold. Crucible after crucible they went until Peter declared the job done. In light of all that had happened, Julien could not muster a mood of triumph, but standing next to the casting pit, he managed to open his arms in a gesture of resolve and said, "It is God's will that we will have our bell."

The alloy would need all night to cool, a detail that did not escape Gregory. As the winter sun began to fade into the horizon, he found an errant chair tipped over at *la place,* placed it near the founding pit and took a seat, one leg crossed over the knee, his hands clasped and resting in his lap. Peter's men sang Parisian work songs as they constructed the hoisting crane. At *la place,* the townspeople continued to make order of the chaos that had happened there, stacking the bodies of the slain, administering the *coup de grâce* to the injured deemed too far gone to save, and hogtying the rest. Shaking his head, Gregory noted to himself that he had not seen this much bloodshed since Scotland a decade ago. At least there one could make the excuse that the war was on, that the clans gave as good as they got, and that the English who braved the northern border were the authors of their own story, if it ended in death or in glory. But here? In Abbeville? Just the thought of it, and indeed the sight, sound and smell of it, was enough to nearly make Gregory vomit. But he held his composure, observed what took place around him, and otherwise maintained the detached air of a man in possession of royal authority, now a known factor among those who needed to know.

Perhaps it was the last of what Gregory had purchased, and well into the night another pipe of wine arrived as well as a cask of cider. This time, it was the townspeople who made merry. They sang their songs of sorrow and defiance and kicked out their feet during bawdy country dances. Once they had exhausted their need for music, they turned to more sinister entertainments. At the goading of one of the teens, one by one they hanged the remainder of Peter's followers, stringing them up, still hogtied, from makeshift gallows on the far side of *la place*. During this gruesome ordeal, the townhall somehow caught on fire, so the same people who had just been committing murder were suddenly formed in a bucket line, stretching from the River Somme, trying to keep the inferno at town hall from destroying everything. Julien and his merchants, rather than join in, walked up and down this line, urging the townsfolk to move yet faster. As the mayhem unfolded, and as the flames finally began to come under control, Peter cut a side glance at Gregory and said, "Do you think you will make it out of Abbeville alive?"

At this, Gregory did not stand up. Rather, he reached into the chest pocket of his robe, pulled out the Langley Credential, and said, "I do."

Peter, his men close behind him, put on a terrible frown.

"You do know your certificate carries no protection outside of Ponthieu."

"I am aware, but I have no plans to leave the king's realm, so that will not be an issue."

"Indeed, just a few lengths down that river and your king's word means less than the fart coming out of an old whore's ass."

"I will make sure I tell my king you said that. If ever you are in London, I am sure he would ask you to repeat yourself."

Peter laughed and turned away. He and his men equipped themselves with shovels, and just as they began digging into the founding pit, that glorious sun showed itself on the eastern horizon, a sash of glinting orange ripping across the river. At the sight of them digging, and as the stench and smoke of the fire hung over *la place*, the townspeople—covered in soot, streaked with perspiration, and heaving with the night's cataclysms—started gathering around. Shovel by shovel, the mold was revealed. Even Julien began to dig, as did all of his associates. At last, it came time to hoist it out of the hole. They latched the crane to the crossbeam, and with the power of four horses working the tackle, lifted the mighty bell from the womb. Peter and his men, trowels in hand, cracked the clay mold, removing it in chunks and pieces, and there it hung, swinging back and forth, the colossus of Abbeville. With a wool cloth and water, Peter wiped an area clean. From his apron he pulled a polished rod of steel, and ever so delicately, struck the rim. He leaned in with his hear, squinting his eyes in concentration. After a long moment, he struck it again. Finally, he turned to the crowd, a wolf's smile crouched in his face, and said, *"C'est formidable."*

The crowd erupted. Julien and his merchants collapsed into a group hug. Peter, beaming with his artist's pride, shook hands with one of the monks from the monastery. But this joy did not last long. As Gregory surveyed the scene, he noticed something more terrifying than what had already transpired—everyone was looking at him. One by one, and then in groups, Gregory, the stranger whose business here had never been fully explained, became the focus of their consternation, the answer to their question. The events of the last few days dictated that there be a price. Someone, someone other than a nameless wretch from the slums of Paris, or a beloved resident of the town, had to pay. He struggled for something witty to say. No quip or bribe would do. Too many people had perished. Too many sins committed. And from Gregory's guess, too many records lost in the townhall fire. Peter and Julien, now standing next to one another, bore into him with accusatory stares. Seeing the dire circumstance in full, that he could be next on the gibbet, Gregory knew the time had come to level these locals with a truth he had known all along. He fished into his satchel and pulled out the writ.

By order of the most glorious and benevolent King Edward, Count of Ponthieu, the new bell at Abbeville is to be taken to the port at Sandwich forthwith. It is Edward's solemn wish that the residents of the town gladly assist in this endeavor. Failure to embrace the king's will shall result in an assortment of punishments which will be administered within the year. All rights of trade and franchise will be suspended, the warehouses will be razed, the quay dismantled, the orchards salted, the wells poisoned, and any individual found to have flouted King Edward's desires will be taken to London and hanged, without trial or rite, at Smithfield.

Gregory, looking up from the writ, saw a multitude of dumbfounded expressions. This bell, the bringer of so much havoc, would not surrender any joy. As the weight of the command settled in, the eyes of many turned to Julien who, as the mayor and the instigator of the entire enterprise, had to respond. Failure to do so would only hasten his demise. If there was one person in all of Ponthieu who must save face, it was Julien. Cornered in this way, you see, he only had one response available to him.

"I defy the king's order," he said, and spit. "Edward must pay us thrice the expense, and only then can he have his bell!"

The crowd bellowed in support. Julien, animated by the rush of defiance, continued.

"We will not lift one finger to remove this bell. In fact, we will draft a plea of protest and set sail for Westminster on the morrow!"

"Or," Peter said, "we can take Gregory up the river a way, where this writ—and the person who served it—will be moot."

And it was then that Julien began to think about it. Gregory watched him weigh the options, knowing that the verdict and penalty would be quick if indeed he sanctioned yet another murder. The expression on Julien's face slowly transformed from one of confusion to certainty, and upon arriving at his destination, standing in the shadow of the bell, a dark day dawned in his eyes. He raised an index finger, the preamble to an important statement. But he was cut short by a new disturbance. A group of riders, all of them glinting in war gear, came charging into town, up from the barge that had brought them to the quay.

Dismayed by the sudden appearance of many armed men, Julien, Peter and the townspeople looked around, searching in vain for an explanation. But Gregory knew what was taking place. This was Henry de Thornhill and his retinue, down from Brabant—in accordance with the Christmas ale oath de Thornhill had made in Sandwich. Though Gregory detested these men, for now he was one of them, and he was more than pleased with their arrival.

"We have come to claim the king's bell!" de Thornhill said. "Load it up—now—or with God's grace we will start killing people, and we will make of Abbeville a stain!"

Julien and Peter, so recently in control, seemed lost. But not the townspeople. They went to work, gathering what they would need to take this gigantic bell down to the quay. Still reeling with defeat, knowing that he had lost just about everything, Julien looked long and damningly at Gregory.

"When you said you were on your way to Amiens, you lied!" he said.

"Indeed, I did. But when I told you the sauced canard and stuffed crêpes were the best I have ever had, I spoke the truth."

A Channel Crossing aboard *Hastings Whale*

They took Julien's bell by barge down the River Somme, past the tributaries and the fens, to the estuary and its twinkling marsh waters, where wading birds feasted on fish and where lazy seals idled away the day. At anchor out in the bay bobbed the great ship *Hastings Whale*, castles affixed fore and aft, a mighty mast rising high from the deck. A royal warship, the one on which Gregory and the others had made the crossing, and Gregory could not wait to climb aboard and leave Abbeville behind.

"Row, you dogs, row," said de Thornhill, as his servants and fellow knights tugged at the oars.

As the barge glided into roiling heavy water, the work became more arduous, the tide having its way. De Thornhill looked askance at Gregory and said, "Do not think of yourself as better than those who got you out of Abbeville. Grab an oar, boy, or we will toss your overboard!"

Gregory scooted in on a bench next to one of the grunting knights and did his best, pushing and pulling in time, finding the rhythm of toil, and choking back the invective that so wanted to spill from his mouth in a black cascade. De Thornhill, leaning against the canvass-covered bell, made a mocking face, and to his men said, "Look at the poor merchant. He will soon break his back!"

As the men laughed, and as Gregory swallowed his allotment of humiliation, he also had to admit that de Thornhill was right. Though he had only pulled at the oars a dozen times, he was already exhausted, sweating in the January chill, his arms and shoulders burning with exertion. When at last they arrived at the ship, Gregory collapsed across the oar, gasping for air. To add insult, de Thornhill made sure that Gregory and his horse were the last to board the ship.

"You have made us late," de Thornhill said, as the deckhands removed Lady Tatenhill from the crane and harness. "Were it not for you, we would be halfway to England by now."

"Yes, but I delivered your ale, and I delivered your bell," Gregory said. "Somethings take a bit more time than we'd like."

De Thornhill, incensed by the retort, cocked his head and stared. Everyone else stopped what they were doing to witness what would happen next.

"Bordeaux, I will give you that one reply, due to my benevolence, but if there is a second one, I will beat you stupid with my gauntlet."

Without moving his head, Gregory searched the crowd, darting his eyes from face to face, reading the expressions of those who knew de Thornhill. They all conveyed the same thing—if he wanted to keep his teeth, and if he wanted his nose to sit proper on his face, and if he wanted to see out of his eyes, then he needed to keep quiet.

"My apologies, Sir Henry," Gregory ventured. "It has been a long week, and perhaps my wits are frayed."

"That must be the case," he said, with a facetious note of charity. "Still, as it relates to you, I have already counted to one but would be ill pleased to count to two. Enjoy the voyage back to England—and enjoy it in silence you foul commoner!"

Gregory shrunk into a corner of the deck, sitting with his back against the gunwale and his arms across his knees, looking into the nothingness of the sky. His thoughts turned to Abbeville and all that had seen there. He would surely ask about the town in the future, curious to find out whatever would have happened to all of them. Julien and his pointless vanity, a town burdened by its conscience, and Peter, indifferent Peter and the license his artistry bequeathed. Had Peter been right about me? Was I to blame? Gregory asked the question a few times knowing the answers, and the justifications that would go along with them, would come in the small hours, those lonely hours when one looks in on himself for validation or scorn. He looked over at the bell. It hadn't been worth it. But the king would think otherwise, and for now it was enough to know that thus far, he had finished all the tasks forced upon him.

A sharp whirl of wind whipped across the deck, ripping a side of canvas away from the bell, revealing the dazzling curvature of the piece, dust and chunks of clay yet to be polished from its surface. Still, the splendor of it was apparent, even in its placenta. And having watched it being created, Gregory still couldn't believe that Peter had been able to craft such a thing even as the world around him unraveled. And it was then, when the majesty of the bell began to capture him, that he heard a haunting sound. He sat up a bit straighter, strained his face and raised his ear. Indeed, an angelic tremor cascaded through the tumult of a sea crossing. He hadn't heard it in Abbeville, but this was surely the sound the bell had made when Peter first plucked it with the rod. He heard it once again, Peter's second test. *C'est formidable.* Though the sound delighted him, Gregory was unsettled. He turned away, breaking the spell before it could capture him.

The conversation next to him was coarse, aided by an abundance of ale. The back and forth among knights only grew more outlandish. Gregory did not join the banter. The last thing Gregory needed was to discover what would happen if de Thornhill were to arrive at his second count. So, stayed by the steady hand of his merchant's restraint, he was content to no longer be rowing the barge, to be headed back to England, and to find sullen pleasure, over and again, in the bottom of a cup of big ale. But the urgency of the raucous talk around him climbed higher, to the point where Gregory could no longer tune it out. Sensing that something important was at hand, he stood, steadied himself with one hand on the gunwale, and looked in the same direction as the others. Heading south was a single merchant vessel, an old cog, and due to its deep draft, it appeared laden with heavy cargo. The ship was too far away for Gregory to make out any details, but of one thing he was most certain—merchant vessels were not supposed to sail alone.

De Thornhill, standing tall in the after castle, traded looks with the ship's captain, and then nodded resolutely. And all at once, the sleek warship veered southward, its sail bulging with a fortuitous wall of wind, and cut down the channel. To Gregory's horror, he watched as deckhands unfurled and then raised a billowing blue, false flag emblazed with the golden *Fleur-de-lis*—the royal arms of France. Those on board pumped their fists and then readied their bows and axes, their rope ladders and grappling hooks. Gregory looked out at the little ship ahead, and even though its crew worked urgently to turn it and try for an escape, it seemed as if it sat still, a piece of flotsam swirling at the mercy of the sea. De Thornhill drew his sword, pointed it toward the vessel, and called, "Make yourselves rich, lads, and leave no survivors!"

His men, strapping on their helms and shields, crowded along the starboard side, taunting and threatening as they drew closer. A volley of arrows arced from the merchant ship, and a large stone tumbled through the air. But the arrows weren't true, the stone splashed into the channel, and as they readied to launch another round, de Thornhills's men responded. They let loose a whistling salvo of missiles—arrows and bolts, sling stones and spears—that pierced mail and cracked bones, that blinded eyes and stopped hearts. From just that one rejoinder, the deck was strewn with victims. Soon in reach, de Thornhill's men lofted their grappling hooks, and with the gunwale firmly in their grip, pulled the ship toward them. A few valiant survivors attempted to cut the ropes and release the hooks, but they were repulsed by yet another barrage. De Thornhill's men continued to grunt and pull, and in short order the creaking cog was ready to board.

They leapt from their ship to the one they had captured and readied themselves for plunder. But the door to the cargo hold flew open. A phalanx of men charged up the ladder and out onto the deck. From where he stood, Gregory watched the terrible *mêlée* unfold, with the merchant men pressing against de Thornhill's retinue with their own arsenal of swords and axes, hacking and stabbing with the desperation of men who could not afford to lose. One man and then two, a severed hand and a gashed foot—de Thornhill's men buckled under the weight the merchants had brought to bear, and for a moment it looked as if they would push them back to their ship, or perhaps into the sea, or even claim *Hastings Whale* as their own. And that's when de Thornhill himself, his green cape rippling in the wind, his armor glinting in the afternoon sun, joined the battle.

Pouncing onto the deck, his great sword held aloft, he charged the flank, running one man through. He yanked his blade from the man's gut, and then cleaved down, splitting another from neck to chest. A foul explosion of entrails and the gaseous goop within. The sight of it shook the merchants, giving de Thornhill's unit the moment it needed to regroup and renew the assault. And they made good work of it the second time around.

Aghast, dumbfounded, shocked, sickened, angry, traumatized, terrified, and in denial of the goodness of God, Gregory watched the second massacre in a week, and this time it was just too much. He leaned overboard and wretched. Regaining himself, he turned back to the slaughter, and to his sorrow, saw a face he recognized in the pile of the doomed. He did not remember his name, or what trade he plied, but he was one of the newcomers to the London waterfront, a jolly fellow who, like all the rest, was trying to make his name in this abhorrent world. And when their eyes met, he knew that the dying man recognized him. He lips moved, and in that last gasp of life, Gregory knew that the man said his name.

De Thornhill, wicked and triumphant, wiped his blade clean using the cloak of one of the men he had killed. His retinue, jubilant with victory, took to the looting, singing, and laughing as they did. It took them the rest of the day, but in that time they managed to load their ship with sacks, casks, and trunks, had stripped the slain naked, and had stripped the ship of its sail, rigging, and tackle. When the dirty work had been done, they doused the deck with pitch and set the ship on fire. As they sailed away, the burning wreckage aglow in the twilight, Gregory glanced up at the after castle. There stood de Thornhill, guzzling ale and gloating with his lieutenants. Holding up an index finger, de Thornhill stared at Gregory and smiled. He made as if to raise a second finger—the count of two, the signal for Gregory's demise. Instead, he took just that one finger and put it to his lips, his demand for silence unyielding. His gesture made, his oath signaled, de Thornhill turned to the merriment of his men.

Gregory turned his attention to the bell, now surrounded by a towering trove of plunder. One day this Great Walter would hang in a beautiful belfry, a gift from King Edward to one of his cronies. They would hear the splendid peal and think to themselves how wonderful it was. If time worked as it always did, it would be this way for generations. Babies are born as those before them grow old and die. The voice of God, the sound of home, crops in the field, and a fire in the hearth. The clattering of a horse's hooves, the mooing of the cow, and the rooster's crow. The war would be on, and then would come the accord. Holy water and the cask of ale. The bounty of harvest and the rigors of Lent. Looking into the vast gray expanse of the channel, Gregory knew that's all they would ever know.

A Third Child and a Rebellion

Gregory landed at Gravesend. After Lady Tatenhill was lowered to the pier and unhooked from the loading tackle, Gregory climbed into the saddle, snapped the reins, and sent her sprinting down the waterfront and into the town. He wheeled her to a halt and took one last look at *Hastings Whale*, sagging with the weight of loot and that cursed bell, gliding up the River Thames to London. He was not sad to see it go.

"Let us get you some oats," he said to Tatenhill, and steered her toward the market.

He could have sailed all the way to London with the rest of them, but their company, chiefly that of de Thornhill, was unbearable. Gregory could not in good mind spend time with a person who had committed such atrocities against innocent men. He knew he'd see de Thornhill again. As long as both of them worked for the king, they were bound to cross paths, and probably not in the too distant future. But for now, Gregory was done with him and his retinue of remorseless knights and squires. Of course, he took with him the secret of the debt of silence, the implied promise never to tell of what he'd seen out in the breaks just beyond the Bay of Somme. If the story were ever told, even if by another, Gregory was convinced he would be the one to bear the blame. The price for betrayal was obvious, and the prospect of death at the hands of de Thornhill was enough to make many a man hold his tongue. But, as Gregory knew as well as any, a secret could be a prized commodity on the black market of truth and hearsay.

He trotted Tatenhill into the market, shoppers and stall hawkers urgently stepping aside as the great silvery horse strutted down the high street. Gregory pulled her to a stop in front of a soaring barn, the merchants there selling all manner of grain—wheat, oats, barley and rye. But something else caught Gregory's eye, heavy loaves of horse bread made of beans, peas, and bran. Tatenhill's favorite. As she ate right then and there, Gregory dismounted and made small talk with the merchants.

"Traveler, from whence did you come," one of them said.

"From Abbeville in beautiful Ponthieu," he said. "And it is good to be back in England."

The next morning, he took the Dover Road to London. But instead of heading into town as he would in normal times, he dismounted in Southwark, London's stinking den of venereal sin. On the south bank of the River Thames, Southwark had a precinct that was under the authority of neither the city nor the sheriff. What was verboten just north of the bridge was allowed on the other side. Under such a jurisdiction, Southwark bloomed as the capital's pleasure district, its squalid streets lined with taverns and inns, boisterous with men making themselves happy in the brothels and at the blood sports on which they wagered. A cesspool of sorts, but as man must endure his toil, so too must he have his entertainments.

Gregory knew he could see a familiar face at any moment. Plenty of Londoners crossed the bridge each day for legitimate business or for darker delights. Still, he never did commerce here, was not part of Southwark's burgeoning markets and hierarchy, and had a good expectation that he could be anonymous here. And anonymity was what he wanted. Since the channel crossing, Gregory was troubled by the thought that his work for the king had deeper meaning than he had first considered. What, he still did not know. But now de Thornhill was part of his life, and with that being the case, Gregory knew that something big, and something terrible, was to happen within the year. With that in mind, the last thing he wanted was to make a big splash in London. And his arrival there, after such an abrupt departure, would certainly unleash the black flood of gossip, gossip that would certainly reach the ears of de Thornhill and the king.

He took Lady Tatenhill to the finest stable in Southwark, paid the premium, and then found an inn, its rooms and tavern jammed with happy pilgrims making ready for their journey to St. Thomas Beckett's shrine in Canterbury. He felt lucky to find lodging, and once situated, went to the market, where he bought a robe and breaches of coarse common wool, and a tall hat with a considerable brim. Back at the inn, he went to his room with cheese, bread, and a tankard of wine. He ate, and with his cup on the windowsill, watched the comings and goings of gritty old Southwark. For January, a warm evening, so the streets were busy even as day turned to night. Out in the alleyways and along the main thoroughfare, the laughter and the fights, the false starts and the unfortunate ends. All of them, Gregory thought, in search of something they would never find. But he could not say the same of himself. On the morrow in London, he would see his wife and kids. He knew the way and would not get lost.

Dressed in his coarse woolens, Gregory crossed London Bridge with a group of tired pilgrims returning from Santiago de Compostela. Filled with Christian joy, and bedecked with their souvenirs, the pilgrims frolicked into the city and went their separate ways. Gregory stayed close to a few that were headed in his direction, tucking in behind them but otherwise minding his own. As he got closer to his home ward, the Vintry, he began to recognize people, merchants and porters, shopkeepers and roustabouts. As much as he wanted to stop and chat, he allowed himself no such indulgence. He ducked into an alley, rounded a corner and re-emerged in shadows along Royal Street, in front of his stone and timber hall.

Looking left and right, he noticed no prying eyes. He rapped on the door, and to keep from showing his face, looked at his feet. The door finally opened. At the threshold stood his manservant, good Thomas. No disguise could fool him, nor could he mistake the look of urgency in Gregory's eyes. Without a word, Thomas held the door open, and Gregory quickly stepped inside. The crossbar firmly in place, Gregory and Thomas hugged, exchanged quick pleasantries, and soon a cup of watered wine was ready and setting on the table. Gregory took a gulp, sighed, and looked around the hall.

"It is quiet this morning," he said. "Where is Lady Joan?"

"At guildhall, Master Gregory," he said. "Shall I fetch her?"

"Indeed, but do not tell her I am here, lest someone hear you speak my name."

"I shall use all discretion, Master Gregory," he said, and donned his hat and cloak.

Before leaving, he called out to the nursemaid, Joan's niece, Agnes. She appeared from behind a screen, where she kept her lodging, and was soon joined by Gregory and Herlève. At the sight of their father, they both said, "Papa," and ran to him. Gregory bent down on one knee and corralled them into his arms when they arrived. Oh, the love of them, enough to chase away the clouds, to beckon the sun, and to bring warmth against the chill. He kissed them and held them, drinking in their innocence with deep and thirsty swallows. He simply fell to the floor, and they crawled on top of him, wrapping their little arms around his neck and burrowing in with their smooth rosy cheeks. So overcome was he that a tear came to his eye, and when he looked up at Agnes, crouched on her knees and smiling, he began to laugh for the first time since he left home nearly two months ago.

Lost in the euphoric reunion with his twins, he also felt a touch of sadness. He would have to leave them again, and soon. Further into the future, when they were older, they would be fostered in another household to learn the ways of the world and solidify the family alliances that society demanded of married couples like Gregory and Joan. He managed to stave off those serious thoughts, and found himself sitting in front of the fire, Gregory on one knee, Herlève on the other, the three of them chirping like a trio of goldfinches.

The only person he could possibly love more than his children was the woman who birthed them. And after what seemed like an eternity, albeit a joyful one of fatherly love, she entered the hall. Gregory, looking over his shoulder, watched her, with Thomas on her heels, sweep into the room, her staid tranquility frayed at the edges with concern. The kids ran to her. Gregory allowed them their time with their mother. But even as she hugged and kissed them, her eyes remained on Gregory. Now came his turn to enjoy the attentions of the matriarch. He pulled her into his arms, kissed her forehead, and breathed in the rose and jasmine of her perfume.

"Dear husband, we would have come earlier, but we did not want to cause a scene," she said, looking up at him. "Everyone is asking about you, and even the slightest hint that you are here could cause a disturbance. We took the long way home and stopped off at the haberdashery, as if everything was normal."

"Dear wife, the longer I wait, the sweeter it is when we meet," he said, and embraced her anew.

"You look well," she said, "but there is worry in your eyes."

"I fear there is too much to tell and too much to know," he said. "I cannot stay long and do not want to waste this time speaking of matters that do not please me, and that will not please you."

They exchanged a furtive glance, one that Thomas, to his embarrassment, recognized. He cleared his throat and looked away. Joan's niece, Agnes, awkwardly returned to her knitting spool and needles. Seizing the moment, Joan pulled rank.

"Agnes, watch the children. Good Thomas, cancel my appointments and tell them I have eaten a bad bowl of pudding."

Gregory liked what he heard. As Thomas made to leave, and as Agnes bent over her distaff, the kids at her side, Gregory and Joan went upstairs to their bedroom in the solar. It did not take Gregory long to be overcome with lust for his beautiful wife, and for her to reciprocate with commensurate fervor. Soon enough they were in bed, with the canopy closed, naked as newborns and mating as do the dogs. And oh, how the bed shook and squeaked that morning, and when the groaning and shrieking met the height of its crescendo, oh, how Agnes, downstairs dutifully knitting a cap, must have heard and blushed.

While the eruption of delight did not last long, perhaps it would last forever. Joan, stripped of the rigid formality that marked her presence in the public world, was again the secret woman that only Gregory knew, his sweet Somerset Rose. She reached out from the canopy, and from the bedside table grabbed the silver, pearl-studded circlet she had so recently worn. She slid it on, without the veil, her auburn hair bouncing over her shoulders and across her bosom. She straddled Gregory, rubbing him in slow circles with her wet center. She put her hands on his shoulders and leaned in. With a pixie's grin, she said, "You have already given me two children, dear husband, and now it seems you have given me a third."

"Then I should say it is good that I arrived this day."

"And before you leave, we will try for that third yet again—just in case."

"Indeed, dear wife," he said.

They fell fast asleep, only to rise again later. Equals in effort and equals in joy.

Gregory veered Lady Tatenhill around a swollen pothole in the road and worked his way alongside a small caravan of country folk heading to Southampton with their homespun winter wares. A little starry-eyed girl sitting in the back of a wagon, a basket in her lap, looked up at the curious stranger who had suddenly joined their train. The innocence in her eyes, and the sheer wonder in her face, coaxed from Gregory a faint smile. She must have noticed the gold and sapphire brooch, the silver ring, the chain and pendant, as well as the worsted wool and beaver—all the touches that marked him as a man of means. Warmed with conceit, he dug into his quick pouch, pulled out a penny, and set it on the basket. She grabbed it, held it up to the sun and marveled at the shiny coin. She looked back to Gregory and grinned.

He had no use for the town, and as soon as they arrived, and with a wink to the little girl, he cut off from the caravan and sent Tatenhill galloping toward the castle. The gates were closed, and the walls and towers were crowned with timber *hourding*—battlements on top of the battlements that gave those inside the walls an enhanced ability to defend. Southampton was on a war footing. For a castle that guarded the south coast against the French and other belligerents, not too surprising. But Gregory guessed it had more to do with King Edward and the malignancy now taking root within the realm. Looking up to the top of the gatehouse, Gregory saw armed men looking down at him. In his finest Gascon accent, he bellowed, "I am Hugo of La Réole, and I have urgent business with the earl!"

Not much of an alias, the name of his great uncle. But he could say it on the spot without stuttering, and if someone were to address him as such, even by surprise, he could respond without hesitation. Southampton new this little trick of appellation, and in these times, one must always have a trick or two to play. Soon enough the gate opened up, and Gregory rode his horse across the bridge and into the sprawling bailey. A groom fetched Lady Tatenhill and took her to the stables, while a valet led Gregory to the great tower, where a lord, in a time of war, chose to spend his time.

In between two armed men and heading into a stronghold from which it would be all but impossible to escape, Gregory hoped that things had not changed. The letter he had written to Southampton could very well damn him, and if the earl had switched sides, and was now one of the king's men, then Gregory could very well be headed toward trouble. Even with his doubts, he knew it was too late to turn back now. He ascended the spiral stairwell, the attendants in front and back of him, and with each step, grew ever more curious as to how he would be received.

He stepped into the hall on the third floor of the tower. Smoke hung in the air, fragrant with the mingled scents of burning wood and frankincense. Gloomy, this room, with its faded tapestries and timeworn furniture, its peeling opulence and accents of decay. Seeing it firsthand, Gregory knew the talking was true. Though Southampton was still an earl, and though he still wielded immense power, he stood at the bottom rung of the peerage, looking up at a dozen men who could tell him what to do. He had lost a court case brought against him by the very wine merchants his castle protected and had yielded a vast sum of annual profit made along the city's busy quay. The only heir he had sired had drowned in the River Test, leaving Southampton denuded of legacy, and in the eyes of many, leaving him as but half a man. A leg broken a year ago in a riding accident had never quite healed, impeding his ability to do what every lord must—charge into the thick of it and deliver hell to those who opposed him. Indeed, old Southampton was not the man he used to be. And when he peered through the haze, Gregory glimpsed the shadow of the young, virile man he had met all those years ago in London. The sight of it saddened him. But there he sat at his long table, still in possession of his title, still clinging to the dignity of a high noble.

Gregory and Southampton shared a moment of melancholy—an implicit and mutual acknowledgement that times had changed, and not to the old lord's benefit—but the sprouting shoot of friendship soon burst through the dark soil of time, and in that green instant that took them back to the beginning, they managed to chuckle and grin.

"My lord," Gregory said, and bowed.

"Bordeaux," he replied. "It is good to see you again."

He gestured toward a chair, and as Gregory took his seat, the earl poured two glass chalices of wine. Gregory took a sip. Oh, the plump *Saint-Sulpice*, and what a pleasure it was after the swill Gregory had consumed since November. He savored the luxury of it, and soon took another sip. The earl did the same, and in a pure moment of brotherhood, they sat and drank in contented silence. But Gregory had not come here for the wine, and the earl had not taken this meeting for the sake of simple joys.

"Tell me of your adventures, Bordeaux."

Gregory shook his head and rolled his eyes.

"The king has sent me on a series of errands, and while they have caused me much distress, they are, at least in regard to royal business, rather mundane. I levied a fine in Norwich, procured a batch of ale in Kent, and commandeered a church bell in Ponthieu. And from here I go to the tin mines in Devon to settle a dispute. If God is willing, my travails in Ireland will not be the best of me, and I can go back to London where I belong."

"And you have come here for gossip, rumors, and tales," the earl said. "Perhaps even the truth. I am sure you want to know why you are cavorting through the realm representing the king as a clerk of the wardrobe."

"Yes, it would be nice to know. Tell me, what have you heard?"

Southampton did not immediately respond. Instead, he refilled both chalices, stood from the table—wincing as he did—took his cup with him and leaned an elbow against the high corner of the fireplace. The light illuminated him in an orange wash and cast the earl's lanky shadow across the timber floor. He crossed one foot over the other, so that the left was on the right and vice versa. So situated in repose, he held out his chalice in a gesture of condolence and said, "King Edward wants to appoint you as royal warden of London—for as long as it pleases him."

Just the sound of it was so preposterous that Gregory paid it little mind. He grinned, took a sip of wine, and set his chalice back down.

"That is almost funny, my lord, but we both know that now is not the time for jest. Tell me, what does the king have in mind?"

The earl's expression turned from one of condolence to one of grave sincerity.

"As I said, he wants to make you warden of London. This journey you are on? He is making sure you have the mettle for the job."

Gregory searched every inch of Southampton's posture, every wrinkle in his face and the expanse of his brow. He arrived at the eyes, those old noble orbs of wisdom won and lost, of innocence and depravity, and of black lies and darker verity. When Southampton did not flinch, even under Gregory's bewitching, grave-digging gaze, Gregory knew that the time had come to panic. As royal warden, Gregory would lose all he had worked to achieve. Not his riches. They, perhaps, would remain and even multiply. But his friends and associates and, indeed, the roiling pride he nurtured in being an upstart member of the London franchise, would wilt beneath the royal banner. From trusted merchant and community beacon to villain overnight. An opportunist of the most reviled kind, put in place by an act of caprice, not of consensus. Had he been a bigger man—better connected to the halls of power and with a suitably English pedigree—it just might work. But as it stood, he was just a wealthy merchant, a lucky vintner from Gascony. As royal warden he would be considered a pretender, the clueless face of one of King Edward's silly stunts. They would drag him from his home, feast on his flesh, and leave his bloody bones for the rats and dogs. Indeed, being appointed royal warden would be his undoing, and a humiliating one at that.

"This cannot be allowed to happen," Gregory said.

"And we will not let it become so," Southampton replied. "But we must not let the king know that we will resist his plan."

"Before we go farther, might I ask you why he wants to do this?"

"I do not know all the details, but my informants tell me he wants to enact reforms."

"Reforms?"

"Yes, with your connections in the city, it is believed that you can garner support for the king's designs on the city charter."

"Even if that were my wish, there are surely better men for the job, like Sir John le Blund, who even now occupies the mayoralty."

"But he is one of the old king's men, and as you know, our new king likes his own people."

Gregory drained his chalice. The gulp of wine brought a rush of inebriation, but it did not offer the comfort he had hoped it would.

"You say we will not let this happen. My lord, what do you propose?"

"The nobles are not pleased with the king. He recalled his favorite, Piers Gaveston, from exile and named him Earl of Cornwall. As you can guess, that did not sit well with the peerage, me included. This spring, we are meeting at a tournament in Dunstable to discuss our options. I would like you to be there."

"Dunstable? How does this relate to me?"

"For now, you are the king's man—and we want you to continue to serve him. When the time comes, at Parliament, we will put forth a petition opposing your appointment as warden, and instead make a motion that you be installed at a vacant estate in Cambridgeshire, where one of the king's cousins, a knight named Sir Henry de Thornhill, is rumored to be the designee."

Sir Henry de Thornhill. The knight who served the original summons, who tested the ale at Sandwich, who confiscated the bell at Ponthieu—and who looted and sunk an English merchant vessel during the channel crossing just a fortnight ago.

"What is wrong, Bordeaux? Something disturbs you."

Gregory filled his chalice, the wine splashing in the bowl, a dark bead trailing down the outside and onto the table. He narrowed his eyes and glared at Southampton from beneath the deep brim of his beaver and peacock hat.

"I know Sir Henry de Thornhill. He is my liaison with the king—and I was witness to a terrible crime he committed not too long ago."

The earl nearly choked on a gulp of surprise. His eyes brightened, he returned to the table and took a seat, settling in for what he was about to hear.

"You have come to listen to my gossip, but it seems you have your own story to tell," Southampton said.

Gregory wasted no time in the recounting, elevating his every word to match de Thornhill's every deed. Though it unsettled him, he did not protest when the earl, bathed in the candlelight flickering from the candelabrum, eased a piece of parchment from a pile of documents, dipped a quill into the ink well, and recorded what he said. After all, Gregory reasoned, de Thornhill had committed numerous murders while in direct service to the king. In normal times, such an act might conveniently go overlooked, but these were not normal times. What happened out on the channel—the ship, the goods it carried, the merchants on both sides of the transaction, the families, the debt and profit—affected ten times the number of people who were actually killed. It may have been pure adventurism on de Thornhill's part, but it meant much more than that to those in opposition to his royal employer. And for his own selfish ends, Gregory knew he must tell his side of the story lest he be wrongfully implicated by one of the other witnesses. When Gregory finished, the earl applied two dollops of sealing wax to the bottom of the parchment, the earl affixing his seal to one, and Gregory's to the other.

"We now have our cudgel," the earl said.

"And may you wield it wisely and to great effect."

The official testimony done, Gregory and the earl went back over the story, casually, commenting about this and that, trading jabs at the king, speculating about the fault lines and tremors in the greater realm, and otherwise enjoying a private, and exceedingly dangerous, discussion. Looking out for his own interests, Gregory at last circled back to his place in this unfolding drama.

"An estate in Cambridgeshire sounds good, my lord, but this still does not make sense to me. If I am to be used as a pawn, you must know that I am but a little piece, hardly of consequence to the king and to magnates like yourself."

"You will be part of a much bigger set of petitions, Gregory. Just one bit of a complete rebuke of our dear king. He will have you, and then we will take you away from him—"

"—As you take many other things. And as an insult, you will promote me to the estate rather than Henry de Thornhill."

"That is the thinking."

"So, I understand the part about London. But still, the estate? How does that fit into your plot?"

"Out of chaos comes opportunity, Gregory. You, more than any man, should know that. An estate and a title, agreed to by the king and authorized by Parliament. You could not ask for anything more."

"No, I could not."

"You already have a wife and an heir, and with an estate you would be a lord with a seat at Westminster."

"And from there, able to reliably support the Earl of Southampton and his affinity when it comes time to vote?"

"Yes, all of us must have friends and allies. But you must be bold in your duty to the king, so when your name is uttered in the petitions it means something to everyone there—that you will be a worthy candidate."

Gregory filled both chalices.

"Being bold has never been a problem, my lord," he said.

"I know, and it is why you have been conscripted into the rebellion, which begins in Dunstable."

THE TRIPLE FISH AT EXETER

Back out to sea, heading west to Devon. The Dorset southlands stretched out beyond the starboard side, the southerly drifting littoral, its inlets and coves, its beaches and sprawling heaths. Past the beacon at Portland, tacking northward across the bay lined with fish towns and port shanties, its shallows busy with wading birds, its rocks topped with laughing seals. From where Gregory stood, with his elbows resting on the gunwale, it all seemed so peaceful. And for now, it was. But this ship would sail into port soon enough, and the idylls of the wild would give way to the constructed discord of man. Gregory's world, this place of striving and competition, of winners and losers and the helpless in between. He took a longing look at the orange beginning of the western twilight, the end of another day in this life of his. The muffled roar of the hull cutting through the waves, the scent of salt spray, and the call of gulls circling off the stern. The rustling of the sail, the creaking of the beams, and the steel eye of the captain working the rudder. The cargo, Gregory himself, a rare and terrible commodity of uncertain value.

They sailed up the River Exe to the weir at Topsham. From there Gregory took the road to the cathedral city of Exeter. He had grim business there. A condemned man, a noted and beloved miner of silver and tin, sat awaiting his execution at the gallows. Gregory, as the king's man, was there to witness the event and to enter the miner's death into the official record. His name, Richard Strode. His crimes, theft and murder. Already found guilty by a jury of his peers and sentenced to death, he was allowed to sit in the goal and think about his crime and how he had wasted his life. A nice little cruelty, to allow a man to ponder his self-inflicted demise, and to allow him fanciful notions of perhaps cheating his fate and going free.

But the gaol at Exeter was known to be a strong house, a coffin of iron and stone, a dank place where dreams dripped away into the dark crevices of despair. Indeed, Richard Strode was in a bad place, and Gregory was there to make matters even worse for him. Death dealing, of course, was nothing new for Gregory. So, as the wind and rain whipped at him, and as the spit and spatter of sleet stung his cheeks and clung to the brim of his hat, he kept his head down, drove Tatenhill at a trot, riding into Exeter with the dark confidence of a man who knows how to do the job.

What worried Gregory was that Richard Strode was no ordinary miner. A man of mystery who arrived in Devon at some foggy time in the past, he had somehow risen to prominence out on the moors, and at the time of his arrest, oversaw as many as two hundred men, all of them working claims tied to his patronage. A lord in all but title, flush with tin and silver and lead, all of it sold to the merchants who took it all across the realm, and, indeed, across the world. And there sat Richard Strode, the wellspring of this far-reaching trade, fat and happy and with many men at his command. Until, that is, he murdered the royal Warden. Strode had been smuggling, and when the Warden had confronted him, he took a big, round stone and smashed it against his head. According to the record Gregory had read, it had taken a dozen men to subdue him, and a dozen more to stuff him in the gaol. It had been a riot, in fact, with several men dying in the upheaval that ensued when the great Richard Strode, supported by scores, was bludgeoned and drug from his home. Gregory figured there was someone else who could do this job. Witnessing an execution was not too terribly difficult. But he guessed that this was another test, the king's way of seeing if he could handle himself out on the moors and out in the mines, where the men were as hard as the stone they worked with pick and shovel. Gregory wasn't so sure he was up for all this, but he was not going to let anyone see his doubt.

He stabled his horse and went to the town hall. There he met with the Vice Warden, a low-level official in the mine hierarchy. A static man with no hint of ambition or wit, but perhaps comfortable enough in his cloak and mantle of middling authority. Gregory asked for wine and was surprised when the Vice Warden had his servant fetch a tankard of good Spanish red. He took a few deep sips to chase away the cold, removed his soaked cloak and hat, and nestled down in a chair at the end of a long table. He crooked his lip into a terse smile, gave a nod of approval, and said, "The wine is good."

"Indeed, we have a merchant here with great connections in Cadiz," the Vice Steward said. "His ships always leave, and by God's grace, they always return."

Gregory and the Vice Warden fell into the easy chatter of the beginning. The latest news from here and there, small talk about the weather, and a cursory mention of the bigger troubles out in the realm, of the king and the complications he was having with his nobles. Nothing incriminating, nothing that could cause either of them problems, but enough to glimpse what lurked just beneath the surface. A faint expression of disapproval, a wilting tone in the voice, a sigh of pregnant indifference, or a dismissive shrug. Gregory was an expert with such things, unearthing the hidden ironies, decoding the innuendo, and teasing out the tangles of insinuation—without such clues to his counterpart. When the Vice Warden lowered his chin, glanced sideways over both shoulders and said, "Our dear king enjoys the sun—but has spent more time in the rain," Gregory heard all he needed to hear. The Vice Warden did not much care for the man who now sat on the throne.

"Tell me about this Richard Strode," Gregory said, and took a sip of wine.

The Vice Warden laughed the grim laugh of a man who knows too well of what he is about to say.

"The devil of the mines," he began. "A merciless driver of men, his blood the ore of the land, his arms the limbs of the oak, and his will the tide that does not ebb. He can split a boulder with one swing of his pick and lay open a vein of silver with one thrust of his shovel."

Mindful of the hyperbole, Gregory was still terrified by everything he had heard. He took another sip of that sweet Spanish red, licked his lips and said, "In the morning I should like to go and see this devil of Devonshire."

At that moment a tremendous gust of wind pushed against the town hall and a bank of sleet lashed against the shingles. The shutters creaked, the candles guttered, and the hound sitting next to the fire raised his head and pricked his ears.

"What you want is impossible," the Vice Warden said.

"And why is that?"

"Richard Strode is not in Exeter. He is in the prison at Lydford Castle, a two-day ride to the stanneries out in moors."

"But I was told he would be here."

A grin, one part sinister and one part gloating, came to the Vice Warden's face, and he suddenly seemed older, and much more jaded and capable, than Gregory had at first suspected.

"If that is what you have been told," he said, "then you have been misled."

ydford Castle. Gregory did not like the sound of it. The thought of heading into the moors and the mines brought on a bout of anxiety. It had not been part of the plan. And even if Gregory prided himself on his ability to change direction when circumstances demanded it, it's not what he had wanted to do here in Devon. Arrive in Exeter, witness the hanging of an outlaw, give signature to the record, and leave. Easy enough and, in watching a man dangle from the gallows, routine. But now he must consider the prospect of either fetching Richard Strode and bringing him back to town, or having him executed right there at Lydford, where he was sure to have many loyal supporters. Whichever way Gregory approached the situation, he always arrived at the same conclusion—if he went to Lydford Castle, he would never return. These troubling thoughts simmered in his pot as he sat at the tavern with the Vice Warden and his friends, turning fine French playing cards with wagered farthings and half farthings in the balance.

"Vice Warden," Gregory said, as he played the triple fish, "I should like to send word to Lydford and request that Richard Strode be brought here."

The Vice Warden looked up from his cards, held tight to his chest and splayed in his left hand. He frowned, before laying the queen and heart, and said, "And who should go to make such a request?"

In the silence before the answer, the next player pulled the triple fish Gregory had played, inserted into his eight-carded hand, and then himself played the double swan. The next player laid two double swans of his own, forming a triple set, and with an index finger, slid a half farthing back into his pile.

"As the Vice Warden, that would be you," Gregory said, not looking up from his cards.

The Vice Warden flicked his cards face-down on the table, looking for support in the faces of his friends and associates. Not finding as much as he had hoped, and thereby deprived of the backing he needed to protest, returned to Gregory, and with a pinch of bitters, said, "I would be honored to do as you request."

Gregory knew a bit about the mines. But he knew much more about the world. Anything that is good is worth keeping, or, if it was one's way, worth taking from someone else. If envy was one of the seven deadly sins, it was also certainly the most common. As it pertained to these mines out in the wastelands of Devon, it meant that someone wanted what Richard Strode had. And Gregory knew that the official forfeiture of his holdings would not be complete until he had been executed and buried. In all of Devon, there must have been at least someone, or some group, with designs on Richard Strode's wealth and influence. All Gregory had to do was figure it out. Though he had never been here before, he did not fashion it too difficult a thing to do.

It was with a touch of excitement that Gregory watched the Vice Warden and his men ride out of town early the next morning, their mission to fetch the outlaw and bring him bound in shackles to Exeter. The Vice Warden, of course, had begged Gregory to ride with them. Instead, he produced his Langley Credential, told him Lydford Castle was not part of his itinerary, and remained adamant that the deal would be done to the letter of the king's command. Yet Gregory had no such intention of staying put. He, too, would ride into the moors, but before going to Lydford, he would make a stop or two of his choosing. After all, there were German mining camps out there, and while Gregory was sure they knew what had happened to Richard Strode, he also knew they would be keen to learn of what would become of his chattels and claims once his ordeal had been settled.

The Vice Warden and his men finally disappeared from view, cresting a ridge and heading down the other side. Gregory took his time heading to the market. He purchased a sack of unleavened bread, a hunk of cow cheese, a side of smoked pork, and a large skin of ale. So encumbered, he walked to the stables, caught the attention of a groom, and said, "My horse, the silver mare with the chestnut points. Bring her to me and do not dally."

his land of granite, with its sweeping flatlands and jagged hills topped with tors—outcrops of bedrock—the jumbled staircases that had collapsed well before they reached heaven. Windswept,

hostile to crops and opposed to the hearth, these moors delighted in the scorching heat and the damp cold. But this unforgiving land was also the bosom of freedom. Once a claim had been made and authorized, the miner no longer owed allegiance to his old lord of the soil, released from his taxes, toils, and the caprice of his rule. Freedom, enough to entice men in droves to lay down their plows and run to the riverbanks and bogs, to its hills and valleys, to look over their shoulder one last time, to make a rotten face and a vulgar show of the hand and say, "Farewell, my lord, and may we never meet again." From across the realm they came, to work the king's mines, to satisfy his expectations and to incur his good will, to live under his laws and not those of the petty shire tyrants they'd left behind.

It was to this moor that Gregory came, and with trouble on his mind. Lady Tatenhill finding the worn trails, traversing the cuts and drops, enduring the climbs and trotting over the flats. He looked for Germans, a gambit he was not sure would work, but one he would try nonetheless. Asking directions, a sheep herder pointed west, and another pointed east. A wanderer told him to go past the ancient stone circle and turn south, and from there, head to the stand of alder and the slope of birch. There, the wanderer said, he would find Germans in abundance, working an open vein in the crook of a gorge. Gregory nodded and went about his way.

As fantastical beasts bayed from the wild, he spent a long night by a meager fire, welcoming the dawn as he always did. He resumed his journey, stopping at length to ponder that ancient stone circle of which the wanderer had spoken. Upturned rocks, some the size of a child and some many times the size of a man, a crude and beautiful monument to the pagans of old. Gregory tried to ride up and touch one of the stones, but Lady Tatenhill refused to go within a length of the mossy henge. Gregory worked the reins and went on, now searching for that stand of Alder that at some point would surely show itself on the horizon.

Up ahead he saw what appeared to be it, that hedge of old bark reaching up from the barren plain, grabbing at the dark sky but clutching nothing but the fleeting February wind. Gregory pulled Lady Tatenhill to a stop.

He did not have to go farther, he told himself. Back to Exeter he could ride, wait for the Vice Warden and Richard Strode, and congratulate himself on playing it safe. Head out of town after the king's errand was done, and head to the next task. Giving credence to his doubts, he turned Lady Tatenhill in a half circle, looking long upon the winding path over which he had come. He just couldn't shake the thought that an ambush had been set in Lydford. Why and by whom he did not know. And perhaps he was wrong. But as Southampton said, in order to betray the king, he must serve the king. He eschewed a retreat and continued on.

On the other side of the forest, he drew Tatenhill to a halt, looked all about, and to his right, spied an army of gray-trunked birch trees climbing a hill. As he rode in that direction, he reminded himself that he did not speak good German. That nagging thought was not enough to make him lose faith. In no time he had ascended the hill and found himself looking out upon a wide valley, its floor lined with a sprawling camp of stone huts and timber shanties, tails of smoke rising from the many fires, and men picking at a curving granite shelf.

I've finally arrived, he said to himself, and made the sign of the cross.

He guided his horse down the switchbacks. As he did, he made himself look important in the usual way, that all the tips and points shone bright and that his face was long and mean. They needed to see him as he was, a stranger of consequence, a traveler with more than a bit of gossip to tell, and more than a trifle to give. He clicked his tongue against the back of his teeth several times, making the three-beat signal for Lady Tatenhill to prance, to flaunt her pedigree, and to otherwise announce herself as a horse who would kick, trample, and maim. The theatrics apparently worked. As the duo passed, the miners stopped their work, or looked up from their gruel and ale, or otherwise recognized this intrusion into their hitherto regular day.

Gregory looked for the largest shanty, the one surrounded by the most windlasses, near the largest smelting house, and with the most obvious markers of dominance. As Gregory moved farther into this soot-stained camp, a train of miners formed behind him. Ahead stood even more of them, alerted to his presence by a series of calls, belched out in that foul German tongue that Gregory despised. Indeed, they had surrounded him. And by the time he arrived at the hub of things, it was him and them, and them by an unsettling majority. Gregory, as he had done many times before, swallowed his fair portion of dread, hid his emotions behind an imperious glower, and braced himself for the unknown. But he had to admit to himself that so far, he had gotten what he had come for, an audience of hardened men, from places like Bautzen and Freiburg and Görlitz and Meissen, who just might want what Richard Strode was about to lose. Or so Gregory hoped.

"*Grüß gott jungen,*" he said. "*Ich heiße Gregory von Bordeaux.*"

The miners liked the sprinkling of their language, a little trick Gregory had learned while doing business on the London waterfront. Give them at least something that they wanted to hear so when the going got difficult, at least a touch of good will would remain. But he did know enough in their tongue to explain the deal he wanted to propose, but then again, that was the point of his salutation, to let them know that he had tried, but that he would need a bit of help if the full meaning of his visit was to become known. It arrived in the form of an Assayer, one of the people who judged the quality of the tin, who made sure the taxes were paid, and who helped broker the tense transactions that oftentimes took place when a merchant arrived and wanted his payload right then and there. An Assayer, a royal man, and Gregory acknowledged him with a stern yet welcoming nod.

"What brings you to the mines," the Assayer said, his eyes a skeptical jury of two.

Gregory produced his Langley Credential, held it up next to his face, and said, "I am here to make sure that Richard Strode is executed for the murder of the Warden."

With an acid little laugh, the Assayer said, "If you have come for Richard Strode, you have come to the wrong camp. He is many miles west at Lydford Castle."

"Yes, but is he in the goal, or is he yet free?"

"Whatever do you mean?"

"My understanding is that he was supposed to be at Exeter. It is cause for concern that he is not."

"Again, you should go to Lydford," the Assayer said. "With a horse as nice as yours, I'm sure it would be little work for you."

"I will, but I do not want to go alone."

Gregory, peering down at the Assayer with all the royal certitude he could muster, could tell that this man had not quite deciphered the message that he was trying to deliver. Gregory came at it again.

"Tell me, Assayer, who commands this *German* camp?"

The Assayer half turned, and pointing behind him said, in a voice of reverential fear, "Jörgl of Halberstadt."

"Take me to him, and make sure that the three of us speak the same language."

Gregory, leading his horse by a tether, followed the Assayer. As they made their way to the meeting with Jörgl, Gregory marveled at what was all around him. The stepped cuts in the stone, the exhausted veins and those still pulsing with life, a watermill along a meandering creek, scaffolding climbing up a cliff, the clink and ping of the picks and hammers, the scraping of the shovels, and the deep-chested singing of the men. All of it echoing down the long gray valley, this haven for the brawny flotsam from far away Saxony.

They arrived at the largest shanty of them all, a leaning, steep-roofed hall tacked together with an assortment of timbers and hides and resting on a granite wainscot. The yard around it barren and strewn with the detritus of life, the hovel of a man who did not care much for the niceties of the world. Gregory looked at the Assayer, and with a subtle nod suggested that he should be the one to darken Jörgl of Halberstadt's door. The Assayer did not look too pleased with the duty, but he did it nonetheless. Moments after he had knocked, a crude woman of bosom and girth appeared at the door. Gregory could not discern what was said, but the woman was soon staring at him, sizing him up, decidedly unimpressed by his arrival. He nodded, maintaining his composure, reminding himself that the gifts he had come to give could melt even the coldest of hearts.

And then he waited, trading perplexed looks with the Assayer until he figured it out—he had come at an inopportune time, and nothing, not even a visit from a clerk of the royal wardrobe, would come between Jörgl and the aftermath of his carnal delights. When he emerged from his sprawling hovel, ostentatiously fastening his belt as he did, he emerged as a triumphant and satisfied man, standing there as a hulking testament to liberty. A wave of blond hair crashed over his head, his eyes a deep Baltic blue. Across his wide shoulders a mantle of fur, and crossed beneath it a pair of arms, that of iron and anvil. His booted feet set wide and sturdy, the totality of him the arch and pillar.

"*Grüß gott, Herr Halberstadt,*" Gregory said, and doffed his hat.

"*Grüß gott,*" he said.

He motioned to a table and stools in front of the house as the place where they would collude. The Assayer made haste with the introductions, with Gregory parsing out a word here and a word there, convinced the Assayer was saying what he was supposed to say. With the opening done, Gregory went to the meat of the matter.

"Tell Jörgl, if he doesn't already know, that Richard Strode has been sentenced to death for the crimes of theft and murder, and that after his execution, his claims will be forfeited to the crown," he said to the Assayer, and turned an ear inward as the translation was made. Jörgl smiled when the Assayer was done, and emphatically nodded his head.

"Tell Jörgl that Richard Strode is now kept at Lydford Castle, and that I should need help bringing him back to the gallows at Exeter."

From the expression on Jörgl's face, he no doubt had a good understanding of what was being proffered. He spoke at length to the Assayer, who, looking surprised and increasingly uncomfortable with the direction this conversation was taking, turned to Gregory and said, "Jörgl would be eager to help bring Richard Strode to justice, but he must first know what is in it for him."

Gregory looked long and hard at Jörgl. Peering into his eyes without looking at the Assayer, Gregory said, "Tell Jörgl I will give him Richard Strode's claims and have them authorized by the stannery court at Tavistock."

The Assayer's mouth dropped with incredulity, and then his face soured. "You do not have the authority to do such a thing!"

"But I do," he said, pointing to the Langley Credential sitting open on the table. "I am a clerk of the wardrobe and have the authority to do as I must in the service of our dear lord, the blessed King Edward of Carnarvon, Lord of Ireland and Prince of Wales."

"And what of the Vice Warden?" the Assayer said. "Have you made your intentions known to him?"

"The Vice Warden, unfortunately, is ignorant of my arrangements, and shall remain so. Now, tell Herr Halberstadt what I have offered, or I shall exercise my authority in ways that will not please you."

The Assayer did as he was told, not so much, Gregory guessed, due to his prodding, but for the fact that Jörgl wanted an answer as to what his reward would be for agreeing to Gregory's terms. Upon hearing them, Jörgl gave a terse nod, curled his lip with satisfaction, and said, "*Es ist gut!*"

The Assayer stood from the table, stretched, and meandered through the yard. The woman who had just recently scowled at Gregory now came to the table serving two large leather steins of frothy ale.

"*Prost!*" Jörgl said and clanked his stein against Gregory's. They both took a big drink, and Gregory, pleased that he had his deal, swallowed the first swig and took another. As he savored the deep joy of a German ale, there came a commotion, the disruptive sound of alarm. Gregory and Jörgl looked at one another, and then turned in the direction of all the others. Gregory saw the Assayer speeding west on his horse. He stood, took a long draught of ale, and placed the stein on the table. He dashed over to where Lady Tatenhill was tethered and leapt into the saddle. He dug at her with the spurs, snapped the reins, and with a burst of expletives, implored her to charge forth. And as she'd always done, Lady Tatenhill lurched into the challenge with glee, and in a few strides was at full tilt, bursting through the valley as the miners raised their picks and cheered.

Racing over the sunken path that snaked its way through the moor, the panicked Assayer kept looking over his shoulder, always seeing the same thing—Gregory gnashing his teeth in a snarl and Lady Tatenhill gaining on him. The chase did not last long. Banking through a tight turn between outcrops of boulders, the Assayer's horse lost its footing and crashed across the path. The Assayer, thrown from his saddle and stirrups, fell headlong into a jutting rock, arriving sooner than expected at his inglorious end. Gregory trotted his horse up to the spot and, looking down at the crumpled man, shook his head and made the sign of the cross. He dismounted, leaned against one of the cold, wet rocks, and for a short while gazed into the horizon. A distant rain shower, a dark cascade in the slate sky. The boulder-strewn tors rippling out in all directions. The famous whistling Dartmoor winds, and a kestrel, its wings spread and on the hunt, suspended in the current above. He looked back to the Assayer, his young face frozen in the tumult of death.

"It does not please me that you have perished, but you should not have tried to betray me—and you should not have tried to outrun Lady Tatenhill."

He loaded the Assayer back on his horse, returned to the mining camp, and laid the dead body near a group of men taking their afternoon ladle of gruel. He returned to Jörgl's hovel, the grand man standing there, hands on his hips, and with a look of respect on his handsome, pitted face.

"Tonight," Gregory said.

Jörgl grunted with understanding and took a drink of ale.

While Gregory rode his horse, the miners were on foot, picks over their shoulders, knives at their belts, jogging indefatigably down the path. In single file, Jörgl bringing up the rear, they sped west through that moonless night on the moors. Two dozen of them, half the camp, and by the winding route they took, it was evident they knew this area well. Not a single soul did they encounter and not a single camp did they disturb as they rounded the marsh and cut through the bog, crossed the chasms and climbed the hills, skirted the alder and birch, and trotted past the tumbled rocks. Neither did they hesitate nor falter when came the fog. And it was in that moment of wrenching fear, when Gregory was blind and felt all would be lost, that he fell in love with Lady Tatenhill all over again. She had pulled in behind the last miner in that ragged little line, her head down low, and did as they had done before her, ambling through the terrain with courage and without miscue. Finally, Lydford Castle, a low-slung heap of stone, its tower a silhouette in the darkness.

A yellow eye of firelight shown through the shutters of the top window. When Gregory and the miners stopped to collect themselves, they heard the feint drift of laughter and music coming from within. In a broken slog of words, the plan had already been discussed, so they wasted no time discussing it again. The miners crept up to the wall, and six of them, including Jörgl, formed a base. The rest of them, climbing atop in twos, formed a human ladder that scaled the height of the wall. When it came time for Gregory to climb, he swallowed his second thoughts, and made quick if clumsy work up the scaffolding of thighs, arms and shoulders, until he reached the top of the wall. A rope affixed with a grappling hook was secured and dropped on the outside, while the same was done with a rope on the inside. In that way, the remaining miners climbed the wall while others descended it. Breathtaking it was, this flash of banditry, and before Gregory could talk himself out of going through with it, he and the miners were racing across the bailey to the tower.

And they did it again, crawling atop one another, forming a human trellis, as those inside enjoyed their libations and a spirited piece with lute, pipe, and drum. They climbed over the battlement and came down softly on the timber roof, one, two, four, six of them. They lowered a rope, and with the work of many hands, pulled Gregory to the top. Once on the roof, he pulled his knife, *La Bonne Vie*. He looked each of the miners in the eye, and at the agreed upon signal, a downward cut of his hand, they began their assault.

One of them crouched down and held an iron wedge at the seam of the roof hatch. Jörgl, cocking the hammer over his shoulder, squared his feet and made ready to strike. After a spell of calm, he brought the hammer swinging downward in a wheeling motion so that it struck the wedge inward, and in one cacophonous moment of impact—splitting wood, the ringing of iron and the squeal of hinges torn asunder—the hatch was borne away. The golden light from inside the room below burst into the night, and in that moment of calamity, Gregory peered inward and saw the awed faces of those inside, their mouths agape, their eyes wide with shock, and the shadow of apocalypse rolling over them.

The miners leapt through the breach, Jörgl leading them. As they reached the floor they pushed forward, the hammerheads falling, the pointed picks dipping, the booted feet and the gloved hands kicking and striking. Jörgl split the oaken table with one stroke of his maul, sending the wine and ale splashing across the room. For a moment it appeared that this would be a slaughter, but the minstrel, at first shrinking in a corner, stepped up and cracked his lute over Jörgl's head. The English collected themselves and began fighting back. Richard Strode, pressing forward, balled his fist and laid out a miner with a fantastic hook. As the man fell, the eye-patched giant yanked the pick from his limp hand and began hacking. Through the mayhem, Gregory managed to grab hold of a torch. He dodged a stool thrown at him, sidestepped a knife thrust at him, and ducked so that one of Jörgl's wild hammer swipes went just over his head.

He found the door. The torch held in front of him, he scampered down the spiral stairwell. Just as he expected, he heard the feet of many men coming up from the ground floor. He stopped, leaned forward so that his voice was strong, and yelled, "Come now, men, and come you all!"

From around the corner appeared a clutch of tower guards, all of them in helm and mail, weapons drawn, and ready to join the fray.

"What in the devil's name is going on up there?" one of them said.

"Marauders have come through the roof and they have come for Richard Strode!"

The guards raced past Gregory, who continued down the stairwell to the landing. In the torchlight, he found the front door, which, as he had been told by one of the miners who had spent time in this very goal, was locked only with a crossbar. Before the tower guards realized who he was and what he was up to, Gregory gave a grunt and lifted it. As soon as the door opened, the rest of the miners, sounding their cries of battle, poured through the door and ascended the stairwell. Gregory waited, alone in the torchlight, and listened to the terrible brawl ongoing upstairs. He shook his head at the tragedy of it all. He also knew he had made all of it happen, and that he had to be a part of this moment or he would lose what he had come for. He raced back up the stairs to find that the miners had claimed the advantage. Their numbers, aided by Gregory's treachery, had ensured that it could be no other way. The carnage, confined to such a small space, was sickening. Shattered heads, crushed arms and legs, gutted stomachs, and one unfortunate Englishman burning in the fireplace. Among the dead was the Vice Warden, his ruined corpse strewn across the wreckage of the table. Along with the Assayer's, his demise would be easy to blame on Gregory—should the king, in an easy act of fiat, deem it advantageous to do so. Yet Richard Strode still lived. Indeed, he seethed as no less than five miners held him on the ground as a sixth one attempted to bind his hands behind his back. And then there was Jörgl of Halberstadt, in the middle of the waste, standing victorious, the hammerhead on the floor, his hands crossed and resting on the handle.

With a crook of his head, he beckoned Gregory forth. When he was within Jörgl's reach, the German took him by the hem of his robe, jerked him off the floor, and pulled him in until the two were almost nose to nose. Jörgl snarled, and in perfect English, English Gregory did not know Jörgl could speak, he said, "Where are my claims, boy! Give them to me, or I will stuff you in a mine and watch you starve!"

Dangling in the air, locked in Jörgl's grasp, Gregory darted his eyes left and then right. He saw nothing of note. He looked again, knowing full well that this second search was likely his last. Instead of just using his eyes, he craned his neck. Seeing nothing, he craned it even harder in the other direction, feeling a stretch of his sinew and a crack in his back. And there it was, partially covered by one of the slain. Up against the wall sat an ornate wooden chest adorned with polished brass works and a gilt silver lock. He had seen it before, back in Exeter, when the Vice Warden and his men had prepared to ride out a week earlier. Gregory looked back at Jörgl, and in a voice that conveyed his relief, said, "Herr Halberstadt, let me down and you shall have your bloody claims."

Bound, gagged and hooded, Richard Strode was hanged at the town square in Exeter. Gregory rushed to Tavistock where, in front of a hastily convened stannery parliament, he verified the forfeited claims and had them authorized for Jörgl of Halberstadt instead of deeding them back to the king. His Majesty would be furious when he found out, but Gregory cared not. Service with betrayal was now his way, and he had done both on the moors.

Delivering justice in an unjust world is difficult. When there is no hard distinction between right and wrong, the truth—what we know in our hearts to be the proper thing, even beyond what we hear and see—must be as we make it. Our debts do not die. If there is anything that lives beyond us, it is the good, or the bad, that we have done for our friends, our families and those we do not even know. When the table is broken, it is hard to eat. When the rooster crows at the wrong time, it is hard to sleep. If you are in doubt, play the triple fish, a winning hand.

Dried Cherries and New Shoes at Neath Abbey

Lady Tatenhill pranced down the gangplank, up the pier, and onto the muddy embankment at Swansea. Gregory turned and looked back at the body of water they had just crossed, the Severn, a big blue swirl rolling up into the heart of western England. The voyage had been routine, under heavy skies but no storms, and though many boats and ships plied the bay, no degenerate act of piracy. Just jolly old fishermen working the sail and rudder, happy to dream of Gregory's coins once they reached land.

Gregory dismounted. As his horse drank at a public trough, he stretched and yawned, still drowsy from the tedious crossing. His horse finished drinking, Gregory remounted, gave a cutting glare at the few townspeople who gawked at him, and then drove Lady Tatenhill up the winding High Street and out into the emerald vale beyond. The country opened up, the scent of salt spray giving way to the humid breath of grass and hedge, the resident gulls replaced by the visiting woodcocks.

He still had enough daylight to make his destination. He drove Tatenhill with the urgency of a man who wishes to arrive and make proper arrangements before the sun goes down. Though hidden behind a thick band of leaden clouds, it yet shone, a silver tiara bending through the sky. Later, a misting rain. The sun that had so invigorated Gregory was now dying in a crimson bath behind him. But the empty horizon soon offered a reason for joy—the austere peaks and noble arches of Neath Abbey emerging in the wilderness. The vast, neatly kept grain fields and grazing lands swept out in all directions. A swath of glowing twilight gathered in the highest reaches of this sprawling assemblage of monastic stonework. At last, the Cistercian abbey of Glamorgan in Wales.

"Good Lady," Gregory said, as he slowed his horse to a canter.

He pulled to a halt at the gatehouse, looked up at the pair of monks looking down at him. He removed his hat, bowed his head, and then put his hat back on.

"I am the king's man," he said, "and I am here to see the abbot."

"And what business would the king's man have," one of them said.

"The *king's* business," he said, producing the Langley Credential and holding it out in front of him.

"The abbot is a very busy man and does not take visitors unannounced."

"Then go ahead and announce me," Gregory said. "It would be in his interests to perhaps break one of his rules this day."

The monks, surprised by the brash words they had just heard, exchanged puzzled expressions. And then their faces went sour, but Gregory remained steadfast.

"Go, novice, and do your duty," he said. "Go tell your abbot that a royal man is waiting at the gatehouse."

One of the monks, protesting as he went, descended and was soon out of view as he melted into the abbey precincts. Gregory waited, and haughtily so, not deigning to make small talk with the one monk who remained. He began to regret his rude demeanor as they sky grew darker. All about him a beautiful land, but he did not want to spend the night out in it. Indeed, after the moors, he longed for a clean bed, a fresh loaf of bread, and even a thin cut of meat for his growling stomach. For a royal man, all could be had at the abbey. That is, if he had not spoiled his arrival with a spate of bad manners.

He rejoiced when he heard the gate open. On the other side stood three monks, all of them much older than the two who had first greeted him. Gregory could tell that one of them was the dean, the man who did all the abbot's dirty work. Though this man would be tough, Gregory was pleased. The abbey's second most powerful person had come to meet with him, which meant they took him seriously. Now, Gregory reminded himself, was the time to be a bit more cordial. He gave a curt bow, effected a subservient smile, and, in his finest French, said, "*Bonjour, mon Frère. J'espère que cette journée vous a été bénéfique.*"

"*Bonjour, bon homme,*" the dean said. "*C'est toujours un bon jour quand on œuvre pour Dieu.*"

Leading Lady Tatenhill by a tether, Gregory entered the abbey's grounds. The gate shut behind him.

"What brings you to our humble abbey?" the dean said.

"A weary traveler, looking for food and rest, and oats for my horse."

"We will see to your needs," the dean said.

He gestured to one of the lay brothers, who scurried to his detail, leading Tatenhill off to the stables. The dean gave Gregory an empty look that betrayed neither welcome nor hostility.

"Follow me," he said.

The Cistercians had started out as hard ascetics, fanatical adherents to the old rule of St. Benedict. Isolation, backbreaking labor, poverty, and utter devotion to God. And so it was, with the Cistercians heading out into inhospitable lands, establishing their abbeys and clearing the rugged areas surrounding them. Leveling fields, draining swamps, planting crops, brewing ale, erecting unadorned stone monuments to their faith, and breeding all manner of sheep, cow, and fowl. They used armies of lay brothers—poor fellows fleeing from the manors and the cities—to power their pious push into the wilderness. Capturing the water and harnessing the wind, and bending timber to their immovable will, they burnished their brute labor with technology and commerce. And they grew fat and happy, and in time turned away from the stern face of St. Benedict and looked instead into the eyes of those buying their goods.

From the looks of things, Neath Abbey was no different. Indeed, it still bore the scars from a Welsh rebellion not that long ago, and the grounds were not yet complete in their construction. But the place was sumptuous, planned and built by astute engineers, betraying the subtle conceits of an operation that had plenty of silver in its coffers.

This is as Gregory had hoped, for it would be easier to work with people who thought of pennies as much as they thought of penance.

The dean led him to the chapter house, down the cathedral nave, through the cloister, and past the book room. He waited in the parlor for a long while. He heard voices coming from inside the chapter house but could not discern what was being said. The conversation must have gotten hot because a voice, then another, sounded the octave of alarm. A royal visitor in these times, when no one really trusted the king, was certainly cause for concern. But what Gregory would tell them when he had the chance is that he only wanted a place to stay, a secluded spot to remain for the last dying days of winter, a place that he could call his own for a time, to write the letters, or even a poem, song or romance, that ached to come out of him.

The chapter house door creaked open. The dean stood at the threshold.

"Abbot Carmarthen will see you now," he said, and gestured inward with his right arm.

Through the smoke and gloom in the dark chamber, Gregory saw several men waiting on him. All of them standing, all of them draped in their billowing white robes. If this was meant to intimidate, it had been successful. Regardless of Gregory's flippant thought of the Cistercians as being enamored of the coin, he did not fail to see their dour sense of duty, their windswept, rain-soaked devotion to their task, and the graying maturity of their intellect. The Cistercians, a match for any man, so Gregory reminded himself to watch what he said.

"Greetings, Abbot Carmarthen," he said, and bowed. "I am Gregory of Bordeaux, a tired and hungry, but loyal, servant of our dear king."

"And what brings you to Neath so late in the day?" he said. "You could have been poached by a wild Welshman?"

"I have come from the mines in Dartmoor, so the least of my worries is a Welshman and his bow."

"You must know that Neath has estates in Devon."

"Oh, I know, but I did not have the honor of visiting the lands worked by your brethren."

"But you are here now, and if you are the king's man, then I would suppose you come with a message?"

"I do not, just looking for respite. Winter is not a time to be out in Wales, and I should like to wait for the spring before heading west."

Even a seasoned Cistercian like Abbot Carmarthen could not hide his thoughts from Gregory. He had peered into too many eyes, seen too many moments of anguish and delight to be off put by anyone. Even in the inviting, yet stern expression of the abbot, Gregory could tell that he wanted more. To give a traveler respite from the road? Neath did that every day of the year and had a substantial guest house for that very purpose. No, the abbot wanted more. Information, gossip, coins, or all of it together in one feast of an evening with a worldly man of the court.

"Perhaps you have wine and fowl," Gregory said. "Perhaps we can eat and drink and I will tell you about what is happening back in London and thereabouts. If you are interested."

"Indeed," said the Abbot. "Eat and drink as you please and tell me of what you know."

They boarded him out on the grange in a whitewashed, thatched cottage beneath an ancient oak tree. A fence and a barn, a door that opened up onto a rolling field of winter wheat, and on the northern horizon, a glade of beech. Inside, a fireplace with coal, a long table, a beaten earthen floor, and a goose-feather bed snugged up against the wall. The lone window offered a view of the southern fields, where sheep grazed. Altogether a nice place to rest and to collect one's thoughts. It had been since November. Sated by the feast back at the abbey, and a bit drowsy from the ale and wine, Gregory fell into the bed without a thought given to removing his cloak and robe. All he did was slide off his boots, drop them to the floor and fall into a deep sleep. What he'd heard, and what he'd told, should have bothered him. But his concerns would have to wait until the morrow.

The ship that Henry de Thornhill had sunk out in the channel was not just any ship. It was owned by Edmund Fitz Alan, the Earl of Arundel, a leading magnate and a known opponent of the king. Gregory was not necessarily surprised that Abbot Carmarthen knew of the incident. Messengers crisscrossed the realm, from abbey to abbey, castle to castle, and city to city. They always delivered their official news and dispatches—and then told of what they had been forbidden to say, the dark whispers and the bright protestations, the unhinged speculation and the reasoned surmises. Nothing new. If it weren't for chatter, business would never get done.

But what astounded Gregory is that it was his account of the event—at this point it could have come from no one else but him—that Abbot Carmarthen spoke of. Julien's bell, the name of the ship, *Hastings Whale*, the false flag of France, Brabant, the casks of ale, the name of the bellmaker, Peter Le Cloche, and the riot at Abbeville. At that level of detail, it was without doubt straight from the testimony he had given to the Earl of Southampton. Through the Earl of Arundel's attachment to the episode, an otherwise cruel and ill-advised act of piracy had been elevated to a crisis of state. Arundel had demanded that he be heard at the king's spring parliament at Westminster, and his demand had been supported by an assortment of earls, barons and second-tier nobles from across the realm. Gregory's testimony had been the bucket of pitch poured on the fire already burning amongst the king and his wary vassals.

What bothered Gregory is that during the abbot's telling of the tale, he had made a mistake. Instead of playing dumb and acting as if he was hearing the story for the first time, he admitted to the Abbot that he knew of the de Thornhill incident. He lied, of course, and said he had heard small talk of it while at an inn in Exeter. But as the conversation unfolded, and as new topics were discussed, Gregory unwittingly revealed that he knew plenty of what went on in the realm and that he was conversant well beyond the normal claptrap that a royal messenger would be expected to know. With each word, with each sentence, he gave weight to his title, Gregory of Bordeaux—not an unknown appellation—betraying himself as much more important than a lowly clerk running random errands for the king.

The dean, with a languid yet frightening smile of discovery, looked at Gregory and said, "You work for the Earl of Southampton, do you not?"

"Not presently, but I have in the past," he said.

"Well, your *former* employer is no friend of the king, and if you have yet to renounce Southampton, then you would be serving two masters."

"It has been years, and times change," Gregory said.

"Perhaps," the dean said. "But sometimes things remain the same."

"That will be all," Abbot Carmarthen had said. "Our guest is tired and the hour has grown late. Show him to his lodging and let him rest."

hen he awoke, it was with a start. *What did I say last night?* He took stock of the situation. These were the Cistercians out in the wilds of south Wales. Not a place that was easy to get into or out of. And it was well known that King Edward preferred his Dominicans, and it was with them, not the Cistercians, that the conniving took place. If anyone were interested in finding him here, de Thornhill chief among them, Gregory would not expect them for at least another fortnight. Plenty of time, he reasoned, to take care of his letters, fatten himself on whatever the abbey had to offer, and then head to Gloucester in good repair. He tucked away his worries and showed himself to the door. When he opened it, the wet, emerald field greeted him, as did the swath of winter wheat. He rounded the cottage's corner and went to the lean-to barn, where good Lady Tatenhill, in a stall, neighed when he arrived. He scratched her on the forehead, and in a gentle voice, said, "The brothers here at Neath will feed us well."

He visited the outhouse, neatly situated over a babbling brook, and returned to the cottage a new man. He washed his hands in the basin, dabbed them dry with a linen cloth, and dug into the round of bread, the hunk of hard cheese, and the watered ale the lay brothers had set out for him the night before. He went to the threshold of the door, stretched his shoulders and yawned, and once again surveyed his surroundings. The sheep bleated. The woodcocks sang their chorus. Out somewhere on the grange a dog barked, and when the wind came, the clouds broke and the fields sparkled in a splash of sunlight. A thunderhead rolling in from the south, and the distant tenor of the Cistercians chanting the prayers at Terce. A proper Welsh morning, Gregory said to himself, and if it is God's will, I shall yet have a few more.

He went back inside, closed the door behind him and put another lump of coal in the fireplace. He stoked it until a flicker of flame rose from the bed of embers. Next to the bed sat his pack and all his gear. Just the sight of it made him tired, for in its cases, pockets, and folds lived the work, the mission, the writs, and commands upon which this entire journey was based. In particular, a letter remained unopened because around it was affixed a second roll with a terse message—do not open me until after Exeter. Gregory had no idea what this could be, but indeed, he had come and gone from Exeter. Now was the time to see what else the king had in store for him. He sat on the bed, his back against the wall and his knees drawn up. He broke the wax seal and unrolled the parchment.

If you are reading this, and you have already hanged Richard Strode at Exeter, then you have done as you have been told. Norwich, Canterbury, Faversham, Sandwich, Ponthieu and Devon. You would have completed a host of important errands that will surely keep my name in the good graces of my people. If you are reading this and you have already hanged Richard Strode at Exeter, then you have surely risked your life, and endured your share of depredations, in service to the crown. As you must know, the realm is infested with those who would rather it be that my father still sat on the throne. Old allegiances are difficult to maintain, even when they are handed down from father to son, from one rightful heir to the next. A king must embrace his nobles, but the nobles must also embrace their king. My realm, the one that nurtured you and gave fruit to your labor, is rotting from within. But if you are reading this after having hanged Richard Strode in Exeter, then you are not part of the spoilage. You are of the new world I wish to create, one that pays homage to our august past, but one that does not repeat, and find comfort in, the sins and transgressions of a prior age. There are many in the kingdom who want to do just that, and cannot fathom that I, Edward of Caernarfon, Lord of Ireland, Duke of Aquitaine, Count of Ponthieu, Prince of Wales and King of England, would suggest otherwise. They say of me that I am strange, that I am not like my father, and that my friends and brothers are not worthy of the admiration I bestow upon them. They appreciate my love of horses, hawks, and hounds, but see no value when I row my boat along the River Thames, or eat and drink with stonemasons, or turn cards with ploughman in the shire. That is why I selected a man such as yourself, a lowly Gascon who made something of himself, even if he came from nothing. Orphaned when you were young and brought to your majority by people who didn't love you, still you emerged from the desolation in which you were wrought. A loving wife and children, commerce that keeps silver in your strongbox, and patronage from Richard Beaufort, the Earl of Southampton. Indeed, the list of your blessings is long and well earned. But if you must know, Southampton is one of the many who speaks of me beneath his breath, who questions the life I live and those I live it with. And you must believe me, for I know what he has said and who he has said it to. It has been sometime since you worked for him—another of your blessings, and one that you would be wise to keep. Alas, I have allowed the injury of gossip to cloud what I have to say. This letter is about you and what you can do for yourself by serving me, and only me. If you are reading this and you have already hanged Richard Strode at Exeter, then you are the kind of man I need. And by validating my trust, I assure you the rewards in coin and title will be beyond what you have ever imagined on one of your sleepless nights in your little merchant's hall on Royal Street in London. Go to Ireland and serve me there, and upon your return, you will have all that you desire. Your lord and king, Edward of Caernarfon.

Gregory set the roll on the bed, paced across the room, and undid the latch to the window's shutter and pulled it open, welcoming a refreshing burst of cold. He rested a forearm on the sill and looked into the brooding sky. The sprinkles from the coming storm were just now dripping from the roof, the fields glittered, and a distant roll of thunder promised havoc. Ireland. Cold and wet, impoverished and untamed, the graveyard of many an Englishman. And the letter itself, cloaked in the king's menacing narcissism, made Gregory sick with concern. He had felt this way not too long ago, in November, when the king's men had arrived unannounced at his door. But this was worse. Service and betrayal as loomed the rebellion. He poured himself a cup of watered ale and watched the storm, a big gray shoulder pushing through the universe, enveloping helpless Glamorgan.

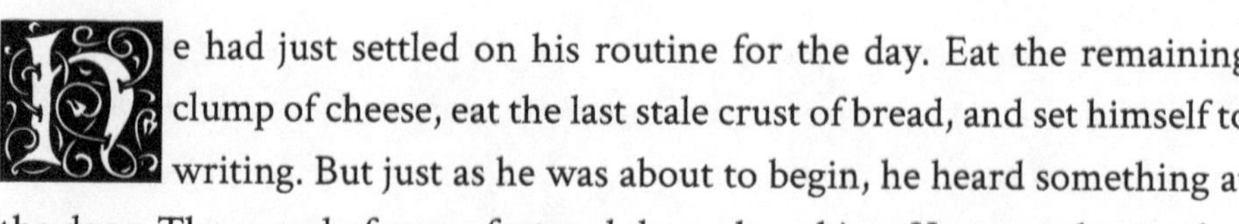

He had just settled on his routine for the day. Eat the remaining clump of cheese, eat the last stale crust of bread, and set himself to writing. But just as he was about to begin, he heard something at the door. The sound of many feet and then a knocking. He opened up and to his surprise saw a group of lay brothers, in their rough woolens, laden with all manner of foodstuffs. With nary a word, he invited them in, gestured toward the table, and allowed them to do what they had come to do. They brought him poached fowl smothered in a broth with onions and leeks, a loaf of white bread, a hunk of soft goat cheese, a fried fritter with honey, and a bucket of ale. A tub of butter and a bowl of cream and a side of smoked beef. Eggs to fry on the griddle at the hearth, a shoulder of salted pork to carve with his knife, and a sack of dried cherries. The table well stocked with food for days, Gregory could do nothing but clap his hands and smile. He spoke briefly with these country lads, these Welsh peasants tied by duty to this bounteous land. It was they who had drained the bogs, cut back the brush, unearthed the stones, and who had plowed the fields and laid the seed. It was they who had built the barns, who sheered the sheep, and who made the boats, barges, and wheels that carried Neath's commerce to market. These unknown boys and men, sneaking out of the hushed hamlets and ironclad manors where they were born, to work here, for food and lodging, and to make of this a prosperous place where once there had been nothing. True, the old nobles who stood at the top of this operation, the Cistercians themselves, were a shrewd and industrious lot, but it would all be for nothing without these broad-shouldered, weed-tough ploughmen who butchered the pigs, mucked the stalls, fired the kilns, and dug the graves for the dead. And standing there in this humble cottage, with a few of them inside and yet more outside, Gregory was overcome by this show of Christian generosity.

"Is it to Abbot Carmarthen that I owe this feast?" he said.

One of the lay brothers, who apparently knew English, turned to the others and, in Welsh, repeated what Gregory had said. When he was done, all of them laughed. The lay brother turned back to Gregory and said, "Were it up to Abbot Carmarthen, all you would have is bread and water."

Gregory's mouth dropped and his eyes grew wide.

"So why do you defy him by bringing such plenty?"

"It is said that the dean does not like you," the lay brother said. "If that is the case, then you have many friends here at Neath."

Gregory shook his head and chuckled.

"Immediate enemies," he said. "I have been through similar such instances many times in my life. They are the same wherever you go."

Gregory asked for the layman's name. Deykin it was. And when Gregory looked into his eyes, he saw in them the vast reach of time, generations of ignorance, poverty, and regret, yet also in them the dawning glimmer of hope, a rugged hope that had been tested, yet not destroyed, by the hoof and spur of power. This Christian face, coarsened as it was by a lifetime of trouble and toil, brought a beautiful peace to Gregory's heart. Before he could utter a phrase of thanks, Deykin said, "We must go. But you will see us again."

As they left, each of them approached, laid a hand on Gregory's shoulder, and kissed him on the cheek. He counted, seven of them. Bewildered but heartened, he watched them disappear just as suddenly as they had arrived. Back to their winter chores but leaving much love behind. Gregory did not fight it. He turned to the table, cluttered as it was with more food than he had seen in months. He took a seat, filled a cup with ale, grabbed his knife, and made of himself a glutton.

Sated by God's victuals, he took a nap. When he awoke an hour later, he was groggy but soon found his spark. He cleared the table, sitting the remaining edibles near the hearth. He dipped the ladle into the bucket and poured a cup of ale. After a sip, he dug into his bag and retrieved his parchments, ink and quill, level, pumice stone, and erasing knife. While traveling, he always brought with him a small panel of finished wood and an oblong leather sack stuffed tight with linen. He propped the panel up against that sack so that it rose at an angle from the table—a writing surface, not ideal but serviceable. He sharpened his quill, dipped it into the well, and with a small parchment set atop his makeshift desk, began to write.

Dear wife, queen and keeper of my heart, empress of my realm, and bosom of my family, know that this letter does not find me well.

I am in Wales, listening to the rain upon the thatch, feeling the draft in my bones, and, as does the fox, predicting the hunt and plotting the foil. Our lord the king has ordered me to Ireland, and to here and there before I head across the sea and back. I do not know when I will return, but my promise to you is that we will see one another again, and that we will bask in the light of the child we most recently and lovingly made while I was in London. Even if my pursuits are troublesome, I will hold you first in my heart, and if the times are more than I can endure, the thought of you will cause me yet to prevail. I will procure the most beautiful thing I see while I am gone and deliver it to you upon my return. A gemstone, silver or gold, or a sprig of heather from the ground where I make my stand.

I am presently at Neath Abbey, a most spectacular Cistercian estate near the Severn Sea. The bread is good, as is the ale and cheese, and the lodgings are comfortable enough. The lay brothers came to visit me today and cheered my heart with their Christian charity. Welsh lads, straight from the fields, but their kindness was quite noble. They came to me to spite their dean, but I surmise there is more to their visit than the simple deceits of the cloister.

At last I have been able to rest, something of importance considering my exploits in Dartmoor. The miners are a rough lot, and the moors are rife with peril. But you must know of what I speak as you are from Devon. Indeed, I made short work of the moors and left with my prize. And now I find myself in Wales, hunched over a table and writing a letter to you.

I would like to tell you more of what I am about to do, but I should not commit too much to writing for it could come back to harm you, and that would be to my greatest detriment, if you were ever hurt on my behalf. Remain loyal to our alliances, our business, and to all the commitments we have shared through the years. They have served us well in the past and they will serve us well now.

Give Gregory and Herlève a kiss on the cheek and tell them their father loves them. If you feel a kicking in your womb, determine a name for a girl and a boy—and find those names in your family line. If it is God's will, I will be back in time for the baptism at St. Martins.

Your devoted husband, Gregory

Since his arrival at Neath, he had chosen to personally care for Lady Tatenhill. He usually had her stabled, let the grooms do the work and arrive only when it came time to mount and leave. But not this time. It was just a feeling he had. He wanted to have her close, to further strengthen the blooded bond they already shared. Much riding, and fighting, was yet to be done, and now with Ireland on the horizon, Tatenhill was poised to be the decider. She had gotten him home once before and she would have her chance to do it again. And it was with that *mélange* of emotions—his love for her, his fear of what lay ahead, and his pride in what she had done and might still do—that he doted over his friend and servant.

She needed new shoes. Her coat was diminished with the mud and turf of Dartmoor, and her rig needed repairs here and there and a good polish. A few pounds light, her mane unkempt, and a healing scrape on her right hindquarter. Still, there she stood, silver throughout with tout chestnut points, a white whorl down her forehead, and that high and haughty Arabian tail. The perfect blend of old Moonbeam and Black Saddle. Long and lean but stout in all the right places. But even as Gregory saw in her the mother and father, there was no doubt she was her own horse. Tatenhill had won her own battles and races, had killed her own contingent of unfortunates, and though she had not outrun the Blue Stallion three years ago in Gascony, when she was still a filly, she had certainly outlasted him. And with that feat of heroics, Gregory had been able to return to London an incredibly wealthy man. Gregory owed her, and he knew it. He scratched her forehead and looked into her big brown eyes. She pinned her ears forward in a show of happiness, gently neighed, and in that moment, when the two of them evaluated their chances, he knew they both had a lot left to give.

He sat down on a stump near the barn and, with a clump of straw between his feet, weaved together a wisp. A braid, folding in and folding over, layer upon layer until he had a dense brush nearly the length of his arm. He had seen it done, but had never done it himself, so it took time, with Gregory murmuring his frustrations, abandoning the task, pacing away, but returning until he finished. Tool in hand, he pulled it over Lady Tatenhill's soiled coat, across her withers, back, and loin, along her flank, croup, and thighs, teasing out the mud and dust, soothing her aching muscles and, finally, bringing out the deep, platinum shine befitting of a warhorse such as she. He went to his pack, retrieved a much smaller, softer brush, and worked it over the entirety of the horse, combing out the mane and transforming the shine into a mesmerizing metallic luster. He took her to the stall and replenished the water and oats. Self-satisfied, Gregory rewarded himself with a few cups of ale, watched the salmon sunset creep over Wales, and then tucked himself into bed for a good night of sleep.

Leading Tatenhill by a tether, Gregory arrived midmorning at the blacksmith's shop. A long stone hall covered by a vented, peaked timber roof, this place, paved with flagstones, showed the worn patina of heavy use. The hammer-and-anvil heart of the secular side of the abbey, the smithy provided what prayers could not—axes, pitchforks, hoes and ploughs, nails, door hinges, locks and keys, bits, clasps, buckles, and horseshoes. The ringing of iron and steel, the crackle of fire, and the deep exhale of the bellows, the smithy had its own language, one that only a few could speak but that all understood—a place to come to get what one needs. And here at Neath, the needs were plenty. Still under construction, the brooding abbey consumed iron and steel with its unending appetite, swallowing shutter latches and chisels, chain links and lanterns, and the lives of those who toiled in the forge. And so stood Gregory, horse at his side, peering into the soot-stained workhouse of benches and tongs, of sledges and punches, and its deep furnace glowing with coals. When one of the four smiths inside acknowledged him, Gregory pointed to his horse, held out a hand in a gesture of request, and was pleased when the farrier nodded in agreement.

He came out. As he sized up the horse, a respectful smile came to his face. He gathered his tools and returned. Without a word of preamble, he started his work. Standing to the side and backward in relation to Tatenhill, he grabbed her left cannon, pulled it up between his legs, and held it between his knees. With his clinch cutters, hammer and knife, he pulled out the nails, tapped off the shoe, cleaned out the foot, and shaved the hoof until he reached new tissue, white and clean. He then filed it smooth. One hoof after the next, quick work by the hands of this master, and Tatenhill was soon shoeless, standing on the smithy's cobbled landing. Gregory, sitting on a stool and nibbling on the dried cherries given to him by Deykin, nodded his approval.

The farrier went back inside to lay the iron billets into the forge. That's when the dean, accompanied by a group of younger monks, all of them sour-faced and confrontational in their demeanor, appeared. Gregory spit out a bad cherry, popped another one into his mouth and, chewing on the fruit, stood to confront his nemesis. Gregory swallowed. In a show of nonchalance, he picked at a back tooth, where a cherry skin was lodged, and made sure he took his time with this little act of dental hygiene. The dean, accustomed to his presence being acknowledged quickly and respectfully, soon grew impatient with Gregory's antics. With an expression of faux concern, and in a voice as equally and purposefully false, he said, "Leaving soon?" his eyes darting to Tatenhill and back to Gregory.

"I always leave," Gregory said. "And when one is on the king's business, one cannot afford to linger. Besides, it has been nearly a fortnight."

"And where will you go?"

"I have made arrangements to travel to Jerusalem on pilgrimage."

The dean detected the heavy note of sarcasm and shook his head.

"Where are you really headed to?"

"I am sworn to secrecy," Gregory said. "The king does not want just any person to know of my whereabouts, and that would include you and your abbot."

"But you are a guest here," the dean said. "Perhaps it would be best if you repaid our generosity with a bit of truthfulness."

The farrier returned with a hot horseshoe and planted it on Lady Tatenhill's front left hoof. The hot iron seared into the hoof, and in a puff of smoke, the musty scent of burning hair wafted through the air. He pulled the horseshoe back, read the burn line, and returned to the forge to hammer out the final fitting.

"Shouldn't you be overseeing a construction plan, or better yet, saying your prayers?" Gregory said. "It is, after all, the hour of Terce."

"Do you mock me?"

"I do because it seems you are more interested in my whereabouts than you are in your duties as Dean of this magnificent abbey."

The dean folded his arms across his chest and huffed.

"I hear some of the lay brothers have brought you victuals beyond what was approved for you," he said. "You should not have allowed their hospitality. By doing so, you have aided them in their disobedience of the rule. When they are found out and their cases properly heard, they will be banished from here and sent back to the dung heaps from which they came."

"You would destroy men's lives over a side of pork and a sack of dried cherries?" Gregory said. "Surely you have more important things to do."

"Yes—Gregory of Bordeaux—perhaps I do," he said.

The dean and his fellow monks turned and left, heading back to the inner precincts of the abbey. The farrier came out from the forge, nailed in the first shoe, and worked his file over the curve to complete the perfect fit. The process was repeated three more times, each to the craftsman's spotless standard. Well before the hour of Sext, Tatenhill had a new pair of shoes and was ready to run.

hat night, an urgent knocking came at the door. Gregory woke with a start, unsheathed his knife and rose from his bed.

"Who is it?" he called.

"A friend," came the reply, and in those two words he heard the voice of Deykin. He opened the door, slightly, peering out. Indeed, there he stood, and his expression was dour.

"Riders," he said. "Coming for you!" He grabbed his belongings, slung them over his shoulders and ran out of the door. He turned to the stall to dress Tatenhill in her kit. To his heartening disbelief, a lay brother was just now finishing the job. Rigged out in all her gear, including her spiked face mask and her ankle boots, Tatenhill stormed out, turned so that Gregory could mount, and waited patiently as he loaded the bags and climbed into the saddle. He looked down at Deykin, valiant in his act of rebellion, and reached out to him. They clasped hands, sharing a fleeting moment of kinship. By impulse, Gregory plunged his free hand down into his pouch, fishing out a trinket, a bronze dove, its wings filigreed in gold.

"If ever you are turned out from here, this will pay for your passage to freedom," he said, and thrust the ornament into Deykin's hand.

"God bless you, Gregory, God bless you," he said.

Gregory worked a spur and snapped the reins, signaling the utmost urgency of the moment.

A comet that black night, Tatenhill surged across the field, stopping only when Gregory wheeled her to a halt within the stand of beech. Looking back, his neck craning from behind a tree, he watched the squad of demons arrive at the cottage he had just fled. A dozen of them, weapons drawn, torchlight glowing in their roundels of armor, their fleet steeds blowing thick jets of fog. In that circle of light, a hazy orange orb, Gregory discerned the shadowed face of Henry de Thornhill, a look of disgust framed in an open-faced helm. One of his henchmen kicked in the door. Several of them flooded in. As they ransacked the room, de Thornhill looked out across the field. For a moment Gregory could have sworn that he had been seen, twitches of torchlight reflected in the knight's searching eyes. A man rode up beside him, and the two of them appeared to be talking. Gregory laughed to himself, the grim, amazed laugh of a man who discovers something he'd rather not know. De Thornhill's accomplice was none other than the dean, in his robes and tonsure, at home with this band of ruffians. The cottage burst into flames, and the lot of them rode back in the direction of the abbey. Gregory waited until they were out of sight before turning his horse and heading east.

As he rode, he thought about Deykin and the lay brothers. He knew they would pay the ultimate price if their presence at the cottage were ever discovered. The dean was probably on his way back to the dormitory to find out who was not where they were supposed to be. Gregory would never know why someone would risk so much for a stranger when there was nothing to receive in exchange. Perhaps it was simple Christian love. The true brotherhood of man. And if that were the case, then Gregory would be content with just that. If later he felt an unexpected pain in his conscience, he would say a prayer for the souls of those men who had helped him escape. But for now, he had no time for such considerations. Tatenhill full tilt, her new shoes tearing into the turf, rambunctious and free as she galloped to Cardiff.

THE WAR HOUNDS OF STAFFORDSHIRE

Gregory wanted nothing to do with Cardiff, a lonely, dripping city where he knew no one. A dreadful night at the inn, its cellar empty of wine, its larder depleted of pickled fish, its loaves hard and stale. A vermin house of squalor, of rude gestures, and cold courtesy, and Gregory could not wait to leave.

In the darkness before dawn, just as the gulls fluttered up from the marshes and dunes, he went to the port. He secured passage on a barge heading up the River Severn on the morning tide to Gloucester. Loaded with barrels and sacks of who knew what, Gregory found himself in the company of wind-bitten river men and a lone merchant who, with a small dog nestled in his lap, sat guardedly next to his cargo. The barge glided up the swelling river and all was placid this cold morning, until there came the growing roar of turbulent waters. Along with everyone else, Gregory turned and looked back down river. A white-crested wave, the great Severn Bore, raced their way. The river men, with shouts and calls, dug into the water with their oars, powering the barge forward. Not to be left out, Gregory grabbed a paddle and joined them in their rhythmic toil. Silt and foam, debris and fish, the wave crashed over itself and formed anew, its girth stretching from shore to shore. Even as he rowed, Gregory looked over his shoulder. Taller than a good man, the rolling whitecap moved with the grace and fury of God, and just before it reached the barge, Gregory just knew that he and his horse would soon be swimming.

"Row, lads, row!" one of the river men bellowed.

The crew responded with a coordinated series of strokes that were of such skill that the barge, rather than being overcome by the wave, landed squarely at the front of it. Now pushed by this immense coil of energy, the barge shot up the river, past villages and through bends, gushing onward and upward into the guts of Gloucestershire. The thunder and the spray, and the stupendous, sustained roil of energy, charged Gregory with a thrill the likes of which he had never felt. Overwhelmed, he dropped his oar, held his hands over his head, his fists clinched, and let loose a primal yell of joy. The crew, and even the dour merchant, joined in, the lot of them cheering and clapping, the dog barking. Gregory removed his hat. Perched at the forward tilt of the wave, the barge moved so fast he could feel the wind in his tuft of hair. On the horizon, barely visible behind a clump of trees, the silhouettes of a steeple and a bell tower. With the skyline of Gloucester in sight, Gregory knew he had made a full day, and perhaps even two, on de Thornhill if indeed he was in pursuit.

"Lads, this is God's work," Gregory said, to which the river men heartily agreed.

An uneventful week on the road. Rain and sun, bitter mornings and sweet afternoons, ramshackle inns, bland food, and thin English wine. And Gregory couldn't be happier. Out of Gloucester to Worcester, Wolverhampton, Lichfield, a proper night's rest at Burton, and then into Warren's domain at Tutbury. He blunted his excitement by telling himself that Warren might not even be there, that he was off doing business for one of the many superiors who he must obey. A long journey for naught, a waste of time when that was the last thing he could squander. But here in the bosom of Staffordshire, a rolling land nestled at the bottom of the Pennine Hills, he sensed the presence of friendship and bid farewell to his doubts.

He took a well-kept road, the one the locals told him to follow, north out of town. Tatenhill at a heavy trot, Gregory thinking of the reunion, a welcome respite in these uncertain days. His reverie was interrupted when ahead he saw two riders, neither of whom appeared pleased to see him. An archer, a bow strung across his back and a gutted deer draped over his horse's withers, and a helmed man-at-arms in a mail shirt and a sword at his hip.

The man-at-arms glared out from his open-faced helm,

"Who is it who trespasses on Lord Warren's estate?" he said.

Gregory sized them up. Both of them young and poor, the man-at-arms surely one generation removed from common stock, and the archer, a crude backcountry Welshman. Intimidating to be sure. These were the kinds of men who plunged headlong into peril because it was better than what they had left behind. It being two to one and he a stranger, Gregory knew he had to be careful. Still, if they were guarding Warren's estate, then that meant they were Warren's retainers.

"I," he said, "am Gregory of Bordeaux."

The man-at-arms and the Welshman looked at one another, exchanging boyish looks of surprise, then looked back at Gregory. The man-at-arms cocked his head in challenge, as if to regain his composure, and said, "*The* Gregory of Bordeaux?"

Gregory gave the boy one of his dreadful vacant stares.

"Is there another?" he said, his tone suggesting that he had been insulted by the mere thought that someone else had his title. The man-at-arms softened considerably, and for a blink, a smile nearly crossed his face. But he held his demeanor and continued.

"The Gregory of Bordeaux who wrote a chronicle during the reign of the old King Edward, and who skewered the Dominican order?"

"Yes."

"The Gregory of Bordeaux who sprung a trap on Lord Baldwin of Essex, and who shamed him at the Stourbridge Fair?"

"Indeed."

"And the Gregory of Bordeaux who arrested Alphonse of Bayonne? And who likes wine, and to feast, and to sneak out through the city long after the curfew bell has rung?"

"It seems you know me well," he said.

He smiled, the ungainly, toothy smile of a boy who is just about to become a man.

"I do—Master Gregory," he said, with a sudden note of heartwarming reverence. "Follow us. Lord Warren will surely light the fires this night!"

The three of them pressed their steeds down the road, Tatenhill veering around the others and taking the lead. Tutbury castle, more a residential fortress high on a slope, came into full view. As they rode into range, the man-at-arms began to call out to the household.

"Master Gregory is here! Master Gregory is here!"

Soon thereafter, a bell rang, shutters opened, and the portcullis lifted. They thundered through the gate and into the bailey, pulling in their horses. The householders piled out of the domestic buildings lining the inner walls, and before Gregory could dismount, they showered him with greetings. Gregory doffed his hat in reply, but he searched the crowd for Warren.

He emerged from the hall, beaming and jovial. He shouldered through the crowd, grinning as he did. Just as Gregory stepped down from his horse, Warren corralled him in one of his bear hugs, lifting him up off the ground and bouncing him in his arms. The greeting wasn't the most dignified of affairs as Gregory's hat fell to the ground, and as he was held so tight he could barely speak. But the love was undeniable, and once Warren put him back down, the two of them hugged once more, exchanged kisses on each cheek, and gazed long and admirably upon one another.

Warren, in his lord's robe and cloak, still wore his hair in a braid, and to match, a groomed beard and drooping mustache. Comfortable in the trappings of his status, he looked as he was, a blooded noble who had earned his title through feats of arms. Vanquished, the vestiges of his humble origins, replaced with the easy authority of a man with an estate and a forty-pound annual income. It all looked good on him, the adoring crowd of householders, the stone-and-timber sprawl of the manor, the luxuriant green wool and the fur mantle, the drips of silver and gold. But most of all the sparkle in his blue eyes, the handsome set of his chest and shoulders, and the dignity of a fighting man who also knows restraint. From the boots on his feet to the feathered hat on his head, Gregory could only come to one conclusion.

"Lord Warren, you have made good on the promise you showed as a kid," Gregory said, and when he did, his voice betrayed a bottomless pride, an unvarnished joy in the fact that this terrible world had not yet gotten the better of him.

Warren recognized the sentiment. Putting a hand on Gregory's shoulder, he said, "Master Gregory, it is to you that owe what I have. Let us go to my hall and rejoice in this reunion. I did not know when this day would arrive, but I have waited on it for a long time."

Immediately upon entering the hall, Warren stopped, held out his arm in an introductory manner and, as Gregory followed the gesture, saw a woman, radiant and brunette and swollen with child, sitting in a cushioned chair at the far end of the hall. Surrounded by her ladies in waiting, swathed in the silk and wool of her station, and crowned with a red veil topped with a silver ringlet, this could be none other than Warren's new wife, Lady Cecily of Shrewsbury, the second daughter of a cadet branch of a middling family—the best prize available to Warren.

She brought a healthy fifteen pounds per year to the marriage, and from what Gregory had heard, and from the pregnancy he now witnessed, she and Warren had gotten to the business of producing an heir. Gregory felt a pang of guilt. He had not been able to make the wedding. Joan had been sick with the cough, he was waiting on a big shipment of finished textiles from Bruges, and the invitation had come late because the first courier had died on his way to London. Still, he could have dropped everything and dashed to Tutbury, where the nuptials took place. Instead, he had stayed in London, sending an apologetic note and a small sack of silver to help defray the cost of the ceremony. A month later a note arrived from Warren saying that all was well and that he had been missed, but that they would make up the time on another occasion. With all of that in mind, and after Warren's formal introduction, Gregory doffed his hat, bowed down low and said, "Greetings, Lady Cecily. I did not believe Warren's talk of your beauty—until just now."

"Surely you flatter me, Master Gregory," she said. "But if Warren has told me true, flattery is one of your many talents."

"Indeed, it is," he said, "but in this case it is not a talent I employ. My lady, you are the sun at dawn, or the mist on the field, and if you are neither of those, then you are a twilight mountain climbing into the horizon."

Lady Cecily at first seemed perplexed, but as her ladies in waiting giggled, a slow smile crossed her face. Seeking some type of answer, she looked at Warren, who also began to laugh. At last she could not resist, and perhaps she had finally detected the touch of humor in Gregory's voice, and with a hand to her mouth, shared their mirth.

"Dear Warren, he is as you have described," Lady Cecily said, and with that utterance of approval, Gregory knew it would be a good visit to Tutbury.

Later that night, after the feast had been eaten, the reminisces told, after Lady Cecily and her court had retired, and after even the servants had fed themselves and gone to sleep, Gregory and Warren sat at a small table near the fireplace, a tankard of mulled wine between them. In the shadows on stools nearby sat the man-at-arms and the archer, themselves sharing a bucket of ale. It is hard to go to sleep that first night when old friends find themselves together again, and thus it was that Gregory and Warren discovered a new tranche of conversation, a moment to share, something agreeable that would necessitate another log on the fire, another pour of wine, and another exchange of laughter, or of sorrow, or of speculation, or of truth.

Staring into the fire, his shoed feet crossed at the hearth, Warren put a cupped hand to his mouth and coughed before beginning.

"A courier arrived at the manor not too long ago," he said. "I did not know him. He does not work this circuit. He was new. But I think he was sent just to spread word about you, Master Gregory. Indeed, you are the only person of which he spoke. From what I have heard, there are others who have done the same in other parts of the realm."

Gregory glanced at Warren and raised a brow. The tone had changed, without theatrics but definitively nonetheless.

"Continue, as it seems you have something important to say."

"You could not possibly know what they are saying about you," he said.

Gregory sighed, fortifying himself for what was about to come.

"How bad is it?"

"You will have a lot to answer for when you are back in London."

"But that tells me nothing," Gregory said, adjusting in his seat. "What are the details?"

"Hmm," Warren began. "When you were in Norwich, it is said that you negotiated a losing deal for the king. That you lost him many marks on an old tax dispute with the merchants there."

"Under duress," Gregory replied. "Had I not agreed, it would have been the end."

"—And that your horse killed several men."

"As they tried to confiscate her," he said. "The version of the story you have been told is lacking just a few important facts."

Warren switched his feet, putting top to the bottom and bottom to the top. With a subtle nod, the archer rose from his stool, fed fuel to the fire and adjusted it with the poker.

"But Norwich is the least of it," he continued.

"Oh, there is more?" Gregory said, topping off both he and Warren's chalices.

"Much more," Warren said. "When you were at Chilham Castle, it is said that you strong-armed the local lord, that you threatened him with ruin if he did not agree to your terms—over a shipment of ale? That you commandeered all of his malted barley and burnt all of his wood so that he had nothing to serve his thirsty guests during Christmas. He has filed a complaint and has asked it to be read at Parliament."

Gregory's mouth fell open.

"That was a shipment of ale requested by the king, and it was his desire that it be brewed there," he protested. "Under the circumstances, I had no choice. But tell me, is there yet more?"

Warren took a deep drink of wine. He set the chalice down and put a hand to his mouth, a gesture not of deep thought, but of signaling, to forewarn Gregory that he would not like what he was about to hear.

"They say you incited a riot, that then turned into a massacre, at Abbeville in Ponthieu. I know you could not have done this, but it is what they say, and it is being said by important and powerful people, so it will be believed. From what I hear, a merchant named Julien de la Vallée is in London as we speak, pressing a claim against you. Not only does he accuse you of what I have just mentioned, but he also says you stole a bell."

"Again, on the king's orders." Gregory said. "But let me guess, I was not just a witness, but a participant, in a brutal act of piracy out in the channel."

"Yes, Master Gregory, that is what people are being told."

"And is there yet more?"

"Unfortunately, yes," he said. "At Exeter, two royal officials died while you were there—an assayer and a warden. And you deeded mining claims away to a German rather than remit them to the king. Those very claims are in the process of being overturned and reauthorized. The messenger told me that the German and his men will soon be rounded up and banished from the realm, and if they protest, will be rounded up and killed. Master Gregory, you should have known that King Edward would never agree to such terms. The mines are under royal authority. But perhaps the German was too ignorant to understand what he was doing—but you weren't."

"I did what had to be done to arrest and execute Richard Strode," he said. "And by the tone of your voice, I take it you do not understand or approve."

Warren turned and looked Gregory straight in the face.

"No, I understand, Master Gregory. We have ridden together too many times. I myself have sacrificed the less fortunate in pursuit of my ends and the ends of others. I am with you and will always be at your side. I just want you to know that your exploits have made you a villain, perhaps even an outlaw, and the very king you serve is the one who deems it so. It has been a few years since Gascony. I know things have been quiet and fruitful for you. But now your name is being spoken by people who can take everything away from you, and from me, without remorse or pity. They are blackening your reputation so that later on, if it suits them, they can use it to their advantage. You are disposable, and now you cannot win—unless there is something I do not know about."

The basking hound at Warren's feet yawned and stretched. The fire hit a wet pocket in the wood and popped. Gregory rose from the chair, propped his right hand against the fireplace shelf, and with his left, cradled the chalice.

"I was the one who accused Henry de Thornhill—in sworn testimony before the Earl of Southampton—of killing the crew and sinking the ship, which was owned by Earl Arundel. In exchange for my testimony—as I serve and betray the king—Southampton and his allies will support my candidacy for a lordship and manor in Kent, a lordship and manor also sought by Henry de Thornhill, who nearly captured me in Wales. All the while, the king has plans to appoint me mayor of London, which if successful, would result in my ostracism from all my friends and family! Did you know those details?"

Shaking his head in disbelief, the slack smile of amazement hanging in his face, Warren sat up in his chair.

"Master Gregory, as strange as it may sound, you are in a great position!"

"Indeed, it matters not what they say about me—and yes, even as an outlaw I can win!"

Warren reached out and scratched Tatenhill on the muzzle, and then leaned in and kissed her on the forehead. For an ordinary man, a good way to lose a nose or an ear. But not for Warren. He had bred this horse, had broken this horse, and had ridden her for a good year before giving her to Gregory that terrible day in Bajamont. And though it had been years since she had seen him, she remembered Warren. In a rare show of submissiveness, something usually reserved only for Gregory, she pinned her ears forward and greeted him with a warm neigh.

"You have kept her well, Master Gregory," Warren said. "Even with all the horses I have bred, she is still the best of them."

"She refuses to grow old," Gregory said. "It's as if time has stood still since Gascony."

"She knows what glory feels like, and that is what she will not relinquish."

"My guess is that she has heroics in her still."

"There is no doubt with that."

They were at the stables, a long timber enclosure lined with a dozen stalls on each side and cut with a wide middle aisle paved with flagstones. The construction was new. The scent of timber mingled with the waft of hay and manure to create the rich, intoxicating aroma of lordship, the dank smell of money coming from where it mattered most, horsepower. Stallions and mares, colts, fillies and geldings, all of them peering out from their enclosures. Gregory looked down the line, marveling at the quality of what he saw. Blue, black and white, roan, chestnut and silver, chargers and coursers, but none of them working stock. Here, only horses of the hunt and of war, the racers and the fighters. Statuesque in their physiques, elegant in their lines and markings, and each of them eager to be the champion.

These were the spoils of war, the spoils of Gascony. Warren had come back with both the Blue Stallion and Devil's Work, his reward for his role in ousting Alphonse of Bayonne and delivering Castlenaud back into royal hands. Both horses had died within a year of their arrival in England. But before that happened, Warren had stood them as stud, the exotic bloodlines breathing life into the county stock in and around Staffordshire, and over time, throughout the Midlands. This quality piece of business brought Warren into ongoing contact with nobles from near and far and planted his name securely in the ferment of that great body of men and women known as the gentry.

"I like your horses," Gregory said.

"I figured you would. Now, let us tour the estate. There is much to discuss away from the eager ears of my manor."

They rode out on two of Warren's young horses, testing the blood of the farm. Juveniles, both colts, and just as fast and skilled as Gregory expected them to be. Trailing them were the man-at-arms and the archer, both riding their dedicated mounts. Together, the four of them toured the estate, stopping off in hamlets, trotting along the edges of wheat fields, circling around orchards, meandering down winding paths, up over the hills and down through the dales. An egret, its large wings flapping as it took flight from a marsh, thrushes singing in the trees, and the old crows sitting on the shingled ridge of a parish church. The birds serenaded them as they passed, these four men and their beasts that came and went in pairs.

"Did you know that the earls and their supporters arrived at Parliament—armed?" Warren said. "Southampton was among them. The earls are angry at the way the king treats them, and they want his favorite banished from the land."

"Is the realm on the verge of rebellion, as I might have heard?"

"It is, Master Gregory. And as we said the night before, the game we now play is more dangerous than ever before."

They cut down a steep path, riding beneath a canopy of budding branches. The path opened up to a large green, and at the far end stood a leaning barn and a thatched home. Upon seeing them, an old man sitting near the front door fetched a bucket and limped over to the well.

"We were swept away last night by your predicament, so you never told my why you are in Staffordshire," Warren said. "Surely the king did not send you here. Or did he?"

"No, this visit is of my own doing," Gregory said. "But from here I must go to Nottingham—and then to Ireland."

"So, does the king send you to those places?"

"Indeed, he does, and dark business in both places."

"And have you come to recruit me?"

"I at least thought I'd ask. Traveling alone, as you know, is not as pleasant as one would like it to be."

They rode their horses up to the house, where the old man had filled the trough with water from his well. The horses drank. Warren turned in his saddle and put his hand on Gregory's shoulder. His rugged lord's face softened, with just the slightest of wrinkles at the corners of his eyes, and in that gentle expression, Gregory saw the dutiful lad from Lichfield.

"I would never let you go to Ireland alone," he said, in that voice of earnestness that Gregory so loved.

"That is the answer I had hoped to receive," he said, and clasped Warren's hand.

"It is the only answer I could give," he said. "But I must tell you one thing. Once you go to Ireland, you will always want to go back."

"I don't see how that could be true, but for now I will accept your word."

The day of preparation—the gear and weapons oiled and polished, holes patched, tears mended, the horses pampered, and the provisions packed in linen sacks. As best he could, Gregory replenished his parchments, ink, and quills. He went to chapel, too, reading his devotionals, making the sign of the cross, and lighting a candle for the world's unfortunates who needed God to shine down on them. He prayed for Joan, Gregory, and Herlève, and said the names of the others who awaited his return—Alan Spicer, the band of burly porters who always unloaded his ships, and the four Williams—William Purchase, William Pepper, William Stokes, and William Hawkins.

Warren spent the evening with Cecily, and knowing that he did, Gregory felt the guilt of a man who takes another from his family. But what needed to be done could not be done without Warren. And, selfishly, Gregory reminded himself that it was he who had helped make Tutbury possible, that the life Warren lived would have never been so had it not been for his intervention. That debt must always be paid. The justification did not put him at total ease, but it was enough to quell his doubts so that he could sleep.

They assembled before dawn, Gregory, Warren, the man-at-arms, and the archer, all of them mounted, all of them armed and armored, and all of them wearing black jupons and black capes. Gregory even wore a kettle helm, a simple dome and brim of hammered steel. It was too big for him, so he wore it snuggly over his beaver skin hat and mail coif. He looked at Warren and his men and knew that he looked very much like them—a fanged war hound with not the trace of remorse in the twinkle of his eye. Gregory turned in his saddle to Cecily, who stood on the flagstone at the threshold of the hall.

"My lady, I will return your husband in good time," he said.

"Time is not my concern, Master Gregory," she said. "It is the *return* on which I am keen. Bring him back, and I will forgive you for taking him from me."

They rode out through the gate and into the frosty darkness to Nottingham, the only fanfare the chirrups from the skylarks nesting in the grasslands.

THE HONORABLE AND MURDEROUS LADY CLIFTON

With the ringing of bells, the crack and thud of fulling paddles, and the anvil cacophony from Smithy Row, Nottingham awoke from its long winter nap and shrugged off the pious prohibitions of Lent. Perched on a knot of stone overlooking an oak and birch valley, the city seemingly erupted out of the great Sherwood Forest surrounding it. Tucked behind its walls, nourished by the River Trent, and guarded by its splendid hilltop castle, Nottingham, a city of hardship and prosperity, a nucleus of disheveled hope and ornate despair. It was this city, arriving by way of the Derby Road, into which came the war hounds of Staffordshire, that black mob clattering through the gate on their snorting, prancing horses. Glowering out from his hat and helm, making sour faces at the locals, Gregory was unsure if they yet knew who he was. If they didn't, he told himself, they would soon find out.

ncluded on his list was the task at hand, escorting Lady Clifton from her manor to the one at Burton, where she would prepare for her marriage to Lord Shirle. Dynastic matters, the uniting of two houses, the accumulation of land and titles, the consolidation of power. Except that's not what was going to happen. Lord Shirle's family had fallen out, publicly and outrageously, with the new king for reasons no one quite understood. For petty spite—or perhaps a justified response to an egregious breach of protocol on the part of the Shirle family—Edward had ordered Gregory to escort Lady Clifton not to Burton but to Dublin, where she would be placed under house arrest at the castle there. This act would not only wreck a wedding that had been in development since the betrothal two years earlier, but it would also shake the very earth beneath the feet of the nobility. Kings always meddled in the marriage market. It was their way. But so soon into his reign, and so soon after an ugly squabble with one of his vassals, Edward courted an unnecessary outrage. Gregory didn't know exactly what kind of result the king wanted to achieve. He presumed Edward sought to marry Lady Clifton to one of his men, thus enriching an ally while jilting an enemy. Or perhaps this was for a simple ransom, a quick way for Edward to put silver in his coffers while humiliating both the Cliftons and the Shirles. Whatever the reason, it mattered not to Gregory. This was the second to last errand assigned to him, and he was resolved to see it through, not out of desire but of necessity.

Of all the errands I have assigned to you, this one is the most important. Fittingly, the penalty for failure will be the most extreme. We will destroy your wine trade at the root. We know how to usurp La Réole, and we know how to burn that city to the ground. Show no scruples in your dealings with Lady Clifton, lest she take you in the wrong direction.

hey rode to the market and from there headed down Pepper Street to the cluster of tall houses and taverns near the northern road to York. They pulled their horses to a halt in front of the Spotted Toad, so named due to the large sign depicting such a creature hanging from brackets above the front door. A four-story timber structure, each white-washed level corbeling out from the one below, its windows teaming with the faces of occupants, shouts and music sounding from within, and from somewhere near, the aroma of roasting pork, the succulent reminder that Lent, indeed, was over.

Warren glanced at Gregory.

"What do you think?"

"It is perfect," he said.

They dismounted, tied their horses to the hitching post and one after the other—the archer, the man-at-arms, Warren and then Gregory—ducked inside this boisterous place. While the music didn't stop, a lonely ballad on the bagpipes, the conversations went quickly hushed. The taverner, sloshing a ladle of ale into a large leather cup, stopped serving as he watched them walk into the room. The jokes did not reach their punchlines, the coquets did not finish their flirts, the new candle was not lighted, and the toxic lie, the one that could destroy a man, woman and child, was not told. In command of the room, Gregory turned to the taverner and said, "There are four of us, but there could be more."

He pointed to a table in the back. The locals sitting there grabbed their cups and found other seating arrangements. The four of them invaded the vacated space, situating themselves conspicuously, and purposely so, with their gear and their weapons. Once embedded in the Spotted Toad, Gregory reached into his robe and pulled out the Langley Credential. Open for all to see, he put it on the table. Warren pulled his knife and plunged it into the wood, the gilt pummel glimmering with candlelight. Now that it was impossible to ignore them and their sinister intent, Gregory cleared his throat.

"I am looking for Lord Clifton, but I have not been able to find him," he said. "I am Gregory of Bordeaux, and I certainly would like to make his acquaintance."

Captured by the theater of it all, the crowd transfixed, it was obvious when the amateur, looking over his shoulder as if no one could see, slunk out the front door. Gregory saw it but did not betray his pleasure in knowing that the bait had been so easily taken. Instead, he kept a straight face, dangled a small sack of coins above his head and said, "Taverner, decant a half pipe of wine and tap the bunghole on another cask of ale—for everyone."

The crowd cheered, the joviality returning at a higher level than before. Under the din, the four of them could speak without fear of being overheard.

"Did you see him, Master Gregory—the man who snuck out?" said the man-at-arms.

"As plainly as I see you now," he said, a sly smile parked in the bottom corner of his mouth. "Enjoy your drinks, for we will ride soon."

"Yes," said the man-at-arms, who joyfully grabbed a brimming cup from the wench who served their table.

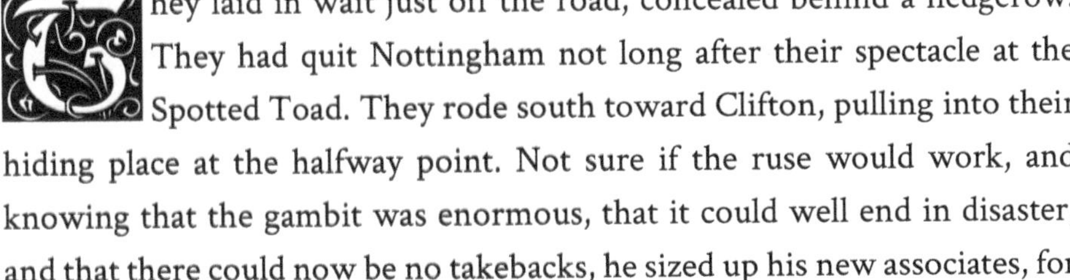

They laid in wait just off the road, concealed behind a hedgerow. They had quit Nottingham not long after their spectacle at the Spotted Toad. They rode south toward Clifton, pulling into their hiding place at the halfway point. Not sure if the ruse would work, and knowing that the gambit was enormous, that it could well end in disaster, and that there could now be no takebacks, he sized up his new associates, for they could be the deciders.

The archer, simply known as Archer, had had his tongue cut out years ago during the Welsh rebellions but had escaped the cruel fate of having his string fingers removed. Balding, his hair otherwise gray, his face sunken by the world's tribulations. War, famine, pestilence, fire and floods, and snow and ice, Archer had endured all of it. Since he could not talk, he communicated with Warren through rudimentary hand signals or instinctually doing what his master would have him do without need for direction or explanation. A place to sleep. Food to eat. A lord to serve. Gregory had not seen it yet, but Warren had told him. Archer's bowshots were thunderbolts, the aim true for as far as the arrow would fly. He had arrived at Tutbury a vagrant, only showing his value when, at his mute urging, Warren allowed him to join the householders during target practice. Warren procured a piece of unblemished yew wood. Archer made his bow as well as his poplar arrows and secured his place in Warren's retinue.

The man-at-arms was a teenager called Beverley, named after the town in Yorkshire where he was born. Just one generation removed from the plough, all he could hope for was that a lord would hire him and that he could advance through service. Warren met him at a tournament, where Beverley begged several noblemen to bring him into their employ. All of them refused—too young, too close to common, too long, and too skinny. Until he met Warren, his fourth option. He took him on to see what he could do and was surprised with what he found. A gifted horseman, strong as iron, and in possession of those outsized, impeccable manners that evolve into honor.

Both of them were kitted out like their lord in open-faced conical helms with a nose guard and plumed at the front with greased crow feathers. The grim set of their faces, the unblinking eyes, the motionless silence as they awaited the command—Archer and Beverley were serious and terrifying men, and Gregory couldn't be more pleased that they were the ones who obeyed Warren's word.

At last, the approaching thunder of many hooves could be heard. Louder and louder, movement in the ground, and on came the mighty cavalcade. At least thirty strong and at full gallop, these perturbed men on their way to settle things in Nottingham. And all of them fools, their buffoonery increasingly on display as they charged further into the charade.

Once the *posse comitatus* had come and gone, Gregory, Warren, Archer, and Beverley raced breakneck to Clifton, their mounts coursing down the road at a magnificent pace, Tatenhill in front by a full length. They soon arrived at their destination, and Gregory could not believe what he saw. The gate to the Clifton estate had been left open. Archer and Beverley pulled up to guard the drawbridge while Gregory and Warren swept into the bailey, riding up to the front entrance to the great hall. Gregory dismounted, and with his fist balled up in a black, mailed glove, beat on the door. And to his disbelief, it creaked open. He turned and exchanged a concerned look with Warren before stepping inside. A shaft of light beamed through one of the windows, illuminating an area at the foot of the stairs, where stood a teenage girl and a much older woman—and both of them were armed with crossbows. The girl shot, Gregory flinched for his life, the bolt thudding into the door sill. And then the woman fired. Gregory watched this bolt, propelled with the force of a hundred deaths, as it sailed toward his head. He ducked just so and watched the bolt as it passed, turning his sights toward an unexpected horror. The missile whistled through the doorway and caught Tatenhill, who stood just outside it, square across the forehead—and shanked off her faceguard. On the ricochet, the bolt cracked against the brim of Warren's helm before falling to the ground.

His mouth open, his hand shaking with adrenaline, Gregory turned to the assailants.

"Please, do not try and kill me, or my horse, or my man ever again," he said.

The two of them ran upstairs. From the commotion of it, Gregory knew they had locked and barricaded the door behind them and would likely reload their crossbows. He walked across the hall to the bottom of the stairwell.

"There are strange men in Nottingham asking about my father," came a voice from upstairs. "Do you know who they are?"

"Yes, I know them very well," Gregory said. "But none of that matters right now. I am here to escort you to Burton for your nuptials with Lord Shirle."

"Burton? You are early for Burton. And you are not the man who we were told would be my escort."

"Yes, things have changed now that we have a new king," he said.

"I will not go with you. I will wait until my father returns, and if you are here at that time, then you will be off to the gaol."

"No, I have no plans to be here when your father returns. But you must know, I have a royal order to take you to Burton. Had you not tried to kill me, I would have shown it to you."

"Your order will not sway me."

"But perhaps this will. There are other men out there, men who your father cannot disobey. If I do not take you to Burton, then they will take you to the garrison in Dublin. I'm sure you understand the difference between the two. And I'm sure your father has told you that these days, anything can happen."

"Dublin? Surely you lie."

"No, Lady Clifton, on this I am as honest as I have ever been."

An hour later, once the dread of Dublin had fully seeped down into her, she agreed to come out. Gregory was disgusted with himself for lying to such a young lady and for playing with her mind. He cursed the damned king and his games. All of this for his entertainments. As bad as Abbeville had been, Gregory justified it due to the vanity of Julien, the arrogance of Peter. Out in the moors, he counted on Halberstadt's greed. And at Norwich, the merchants always feuded over whose pot had the most piss in it. But here at Clifton he only felt shame. He thought of his Herlève and how one day she would be the same age as Lady Clifton. How would he like it if armed men broke into her hall, made ominous and false statements, and whisked her away to a life of uncertainty? Even if this wasn't his idea—*damn the king and may he one day rot in a damp place*—he was doing it to further his own ends, to keep the good graces of the king so that his life could continue as planned. He told himself, and felt it down deep in his soul, that this was a sin for which he must atone.

Lady Clifton, an embroidered ochre veil around her neck and chin and over her head, peered out from the top of the stairwell. Her plump cheeks sprinkled with acne, her eyes bleary from having cried, a sixteen-year-old burdened by the decrepit hierarchy. Upon the second look, Gregory saw the pluck of her, the woman within the child, the empress that she could become. Indeed, she had endeared herself when trying to kill him.

"You are two weeks early," she said. "I have not had time to pack."

"We will see to it that your belongings follow you to Burton. But for now, haste is of the utmost importance."

She came down the stairs. Gregory looked back, out through the open front door, to see that the estate's staff had come out of hiding. Standing in knots, pensive and concerned, they were clearly alarmed by the strangers in black who had so audaciously taken control of the manor. Gregory knew that time was about to run out. Lord Clifton's return or a sudden outburst from these householders. There were plenty of ways for Gregory to meet his end this day. He pulled out the Langley Credential, held it up for Lady Clifton to see, and once she had signaled her acceptance of the document, Gregory walked out into the bailey and held it high so that all could see. That royal seal and tassel, that beautiful sheet of parchment. It struck awe into the onlookers, searing into them a fear so terrible and true, the promise of retribution, the king's punitive justice.

"Lady Clifton is leaving for Burton today, and it would be wise not to hinder us," Gregory said, as Warren glared here and there.

The householders were compliant, but when one of them began to sob, and then another, and when three of them consoled themselves with a group embrace, it was evident they knew their Lady Clifton was not bound for Burton, that something sinister was at hand. After kissing her elder on both cheeks, Lady Clifton came out and waved to the crowd.

"I will see you again, when I am Lady Shirle," she said, but no one seemed to believe her.

"Your horse, Lady Clifton," Gregory said, gesturing toward the spare they had brought with them for this specific purpose.

"You do not expect me to ride that, do you?" she said, referring to the shiny blue colt who looked as if he had sprung from the loins of Satan.

"But you must," Gregory said.

With a footstool, she climbed up and arranged herself side saddle. The colt didn't flinch.

Gregory mounted, shot one last look of warning to all those in the bailey, and drove Tatenhill toward the gate. Warren, his horse tethered to the one ridden by Lady Clifton, fell in behind. Once over the drawbridge, Archer and Beverley joined them, the five riding southward into a gloomy dusk.

Gregory didn't say anything out loud, but he certainly talked to himself. The manhunt. The repercussions. Dealing with guilt and shame, he just couldn't shake the most basic of questions—*what have we done?*

Warren caught his worried eye.

"I know what you're thinking," he said, on a baleful note.

The next morning, they arrived at a junction in the road where they could either continue south to Burton or head west to the coast. Gregory pulled the entourage to a halt, making sure they went in the right direction when they began again, but also giving himself one last chance to abandon the endeavor. Go onward to Burton, allow the marriage to move ahead as planned, and let King Edward deal with it as he must. The punishment he had promised in the event of failure seemed farfetched. Surely the king knew that La Réole was a stronghold of some repute, and that any attempt to defile her, even if by the king's men, would be met with tooth-and-nail resistance. But the king already had plenty of men in Gascony so the order could be issued quite easily, and to men who would eagerly do the bidding of their sovereign. He couldn't help but think of uncles Hugo and Helias and the time he had spent with them. Down at the quay or at the market square, dining in their vaulted home, and everywhere people who sounded like him, and who resembled him, and who saw the world in the same way. He could not give the king an easy excuse to harm such a place, the ancestral home of all that he was.

Lady Clifton, swathed in a flowing blue cloak and hood lined with deer fur, sat tall and proper in the saddle, the train of her cloak draped over the horse's rump. The hood pulled up over her head, she peered out from the shadow it cast, reading the emotions competing in Gregory's face. The sight of her, and the maturity in her demeanor, startled Gregory.

"Burton," she said, pointing south with a ringed finger, "is that way."

"Yes, but we are not going to Burton," he said. "When I told you that *other* men had plans to take you to Ireland, I should have said that *we* were the ones with such designs."

Tricking him with a smile, she trotted her horse up next to his. And then she pulled a dagger, from deep within the folds of her accoutrement, which Warren had missed when he had searched her. Yanking the weapon upward, she stabbed down with all her grunting might, her teeth clinched, a vein pulsing, the hood falling away from her head. The blade gashed through Gregory's cloak, jupon and robe—but scraped off the coat of mail below. Otherwise straight through his heart. He grabbed her hand and shook the dagger loose.

"I asked you not to try and kill me again," he said. "Warren, keep a better watch over this girl!"

He worked the reins and a spur. Tatenhill bolted west, tearing down the road that would eventually lead them to the sleepy port at Liverpool. He looked over his shoulder, a face full of such anger and regret that even his own men feared him.

"Follow me now or you will have to answer to King Edward!"

They needed rest. After three days of hard riding, the horses were fatigued, everyone rattled, sore and famished. While Warren looked after Lady Clifton, and while Gregory collected firewood, and while Beverley tended to the horses with water and oats, Archer laid a net across a stream, snared a hare in a trap, and with his sling, took a pheasant. Combined with the provisions they'd brought with them, they enjoyed a feast of poached trout, spiced and roasted meats, cakes of unleavened bread, and dried strawberries mulled in honey and wine. From their skins they guzzled ale, sat near the fire, enjoying this stolen moment of bounty and respite. Lady Clifton joined in as if she were not a hostage but one of them, eating at everything on offer and gulping her share of drink.

Her last bite swallowed, she looked across the fire at Gregory, still sopping at the mulled strawberries with a corner of bread.

"You are not like my father's men," she said. "They take pleasure in enforcing his will. But you? You do not like what you do. For all your talents, and I must admit you that, there is also hesitancy."

Gregory licked his fingertips and then wiped them clean with a wetted linen cloth. He dabbed at the corner of his mouth to remove a crumb. Resting on an elbow, lounged out with his feet kicked up on his pack, he wanted nothing more than to look into the stars and fall to sleep. But he was responsible for this girl, the keeper of her virtue, and the thought did not lend itself to slumber. And she had tried to kill him, twice, and could very well make a third attempt, so she deserved his attention. "You declare yourself wise, but you are young yet," he said. "Perhaps you think you know more than you do. But if I am to agree with what you say, then I must ask, why is it so? Why do I differ from those strays who found service with your father?"

"They would rejoice in doing what you have done," she said. "But they are not good like you."

"Am I to presume that you see something honorable in your captor?"

She smiled, the same disarming smile that had shown on her face when she had pulled her dagger.

"I see honor in decline, and I will make its demise complete," she said. "I will go to Ireland without protest, knowing it will haunt you that you did such a thing to me. If I cannot kill your person, perhaps I can kill your conscience. Over the reach of time, a thorough victory, wouldn't you say?"

"Indeed. Salt in the fields and poison in the well."

"Lady Clifton, I think it best that you remain quiet for the rest of the night," said Warren. "While he may have honor enough—even in decline—I can tell you that there are men in this camp who are not so blessed."

With that reprove, the evening wound down. It was Archer who kept watch. He really knew how to sleep with one eye open. And it was that sad, dreadful eye, its pupil lit by the dying embers in the fire, that kept Lady Clifton from her third try, or from stealing a horse to make an escape. Angering Gregory was one thing. Angering the old Welshman was quite another.

The ship bobbed along as it crossed the Irish Sea. England no longer in view, nor *Hibernia* on the horizon. Just the water, the wind, errant gulls circling off the stern and a silver sunset forming in the sky. All the passengers were below deck except for Gregory and Warren, standing near the aftercastle, pulling their cloaks tight against the chill. They had come up for fresh air and a *tête-à-tête.* Nothing planned, but a spontaneous recognition that certain words needed to be said.

"Master Gregory, if we take her to the Dublin garrison, she will be ruined," Warren said.

"I agree. There is nothing there but filth and danger."

"And what would you do if someone abducted Joan, or what would I do if someone ransomed my Cecily?"

"Do not make me have such thoughts," he said. "But I have already served the king, so now it is time to betray him. Do you have anything in mind?"

A big breeze filled the sail, pulling the cog over a cresting a wave, and it was at that height that they saw the silhouette of Ireland, the silver twilight pierced with a trident of burning gold and red.

"There is a convent north of Dublin," Warren said. "I saw it when last I was here. In County Meath."

"Then that is what we'll do," Gregory said.

Warren turned to the captain.

"If it is not too much to ask, would you set your rudder for Drogheda?"

"Yes, my lord," he said, and the ship soon turned north.

Five pearls, three emeralds, a silver groat, a gold bezant, and a fat sack of pennies. Almost all that Gregory had, and with it his ability to influence and to bribe. A terrible loss, and he made a show of it, too, suggesting that this was a one-time offer, that the convent at Lismullin would never again see a lump sum such as this.

"For maintenance and upkeep," he said. "As well as for your discretion."

The abbess nodded her approval as one of her assistants took possession of the loot.

Before Lady Clifton was taken into the convent's grounds for safekeeping, she looked at Gregory with that same beguiling smile, that enchanting, murderous smile of lunacy.

"Gregory of Bordeaux, an *honorable* London merchant of some renown. Is that correct?"

"Indeed, Lady Clifton, that is how I am known."

In Clonard, a Clover Comet

They rode into Dublin over the bridge crossing the River Liffey. At the crest of the span, the skyline opened up, its bell towers and castle keep, its walls and dense whitewashed rows. A fleet had recently arrived, the quay jammed with ships and freight, the singing of the porters, the harangues from all manner of mongers, the stress and joy—and the curdling stink—of commerce. It seemed as if all of Dublin society were in attendance, the crowd so thick they moved shoulder to shoulder, their collective voice, filled as it was with straight talk, gossip and gibberish, the deafening chorus of new beginnings, the boisterous hope of spring. A pocket of London, a parcel of Bordeaux, or a slice of Paris, this Dublin, snugged up near its namesake bay, flourished out on the edge of the world.

And so it was that Gregory entered the city for the first time, pleased with what he saw and heard, comforted by the way it made him feel. The four of them, riding in single file, past Ormonde's Gate and St. Eoghan's Church, and down raucous High Street to the stables near the castle.

Many people with many accents were there, a frenzy of horse trading since the fleet was in town. Gregory and his men had come to sell Lady Clifton's horse with the hopes that the offering would be enough to replace, at least in part, what had been handed over to the convent at Lismullin. The spare horse wasn't the best one there that day, the full Arabians were, but he was good enough. In little time a sizeable group of buyers formed in a circle around him. They judged in totality, his teeth and eyes, his shoulder and back, the croup and thigh, the height and length, the depth of his breast, and the set of his tail. A splendid courser, this black and blue colt, a natural for racing or long travel, of war and the hunt. As his quality emerged, so too did the price increase. Warren, pointing here and there, upping the bid with cajoling and flattery, drove the sum to a sumptuous ten pounds, payable right then and there in coin or gemstone. Done with this black-market deal they headed back into the innards of the city, to Wine Tavern Street, where Gregory hoped to find a warm reception with an associate of an associate of an associate. They found him, Jean-Michel, down in the stone-and-timber labyrinth near Christ Church. In the back room of a hidden house at the end of a hidden road, they settled around a table.

"Jean-Michel, tell me what you know of Lord Mabank."

"How much should I tell?"

"This much," Gregory said, opening up a pouch and dumping out the proceeds from the horse sale.

An Englishman named Gerard Mabank held the castle at Clonard. He had come to Ireland under the old King Edward to help keep the Irish under control. It didn't last long. He soon fell into the ways of the Irish, taking an Irish bride and aligning himself with various clans as he worked to carve out his own tiny kingdom. Lost along the way were the taxes he owed the crown, the duty he owed to his liege, and the very Englishness that got him appointed to Clonard in the first place. Farm the taxes and send an allotment back to Westminster. Obey the rule but make rules of your own. Hold the land in the name of the king but take land as you will. Above all, make war on the Irish swine, and let their blood, not ours, nourish that barren and forsaken land. He did just enough militarily to placate the overlords back in London and remitted just enough in coin to keep his name off the doomsday list of reprobates. But that had been under the old king. The world had turned, young Edward sat on the throne, and Mabank, aligned with the men who by solemn oath he had sworn to oppose, had aged into that class of unfortunate men who had outlived their usefulness. When and if he paid what he owed, he would be done. And due to his Irish proclivities, he would never be accepted back home if he were ever to return. His only choice, Gregory knew, was to remain and to defy, to live out his years as the bastard lord of Clonard.

The debt had been called at an astounding 1,345 pounds and eight shillings, a career of profligacy tidied up in one account receivable. Gregory had the note in his pack and knew that it must be redeemed.

Do not return to England before making Lord Mabank pay what is owed. If you do, I will levy the amount against your interests. I will bring a case against you in court that you will not be able to win. If you do not hold Lord Mabank responsible, I will make an example of you. Your friends and associates will see what happens and they will become acquainted with fear. Burn him out, if you must, but do not fail to rectify Lord Mabank's account.

They drove their horses at full gallop, the sun shining, the long silvery grass swaying in the breeze, bleached hilltops and shimmering glens—the lush, lonely embrace of Ireland. These four, charging into the unknown, shared the joy of the chase, urging their horses to even greater feats of speed. They topped a hill and on the crest of another saw Simon Aude and his plodding caravan. This merchant, driving a four-horse wagon, the cargo teetering, was on his way to Lord Mabank's stronghold, delivering the spring stores as he always did. Jean-Michel had told no lies, the exchange in Dublin an exorbitant fee well paid.

Gregory and Warren headed straight, whereas Beverley and Archer veered right, moving into a wide arc that would put them ahead of those they had caught up with. As they closed the gap, Simon Aude and his men turned in the direction of the ruckus. Gregory and Warren pulled their horses to a halt. As the commotion settled, Gregory peered into the eyes of Simon Aude, effecting his practiced glare of London rot, the look that promised calamity. Simon Aude was certainly unsettled, and his men, their hands on the hilts of their swords, were frozen with indecision.

"Your letters of trade," Gregory demanded. "Please show them to me."

"And do not consider yourself cunning, merchant, or this day will only get worse," said Warren, who had already drawn his sword.

As an exclamation to their arrival, an arrow thudded into the wagon. When the merchant and his men turned to see from where it had come, they saw Archer, standing next to his horse with another arrow loaded, and Beverley trotting his horse up the road toward them. Simon Aude, his face creased with the stress of his circumstance, turned again to Gregory.

"What is this?" he said.

"Show me your letters of trade," Gregory said. "If they are not current, I must seize this cargo, deem it contraband, and send it back to the king's lieutenant in Dublin."

"But I have my letters," he said, fishing a weathered parchment from a fold in his robe. "They were issued during the reign of the old King Edward."

"But his son, the new King Edward, now sits on the throne. Surely you knew."

"Yes, but he has not been king long, and surely *you* must know, Ireland stands in line after England—and if you demand letters from me, then I should demand letters from you."

Gregory pulled out the Langley Credential and held it out at eye level so Simon Aude got a good look at it.

"Issued at Martinmas just last year by the king himself. The *new* king."

The rank established, Gregory pressed forward.

"My informants in Dublin tell me this delivery is meant for Lord Mabank of Clonard?"

"Yes," he said, his voice conciliatory.

"You do know that he is in arrears, that he owes the king an enormous sum in taxes."

"I had heard as much."

"So, you do business with a man who has shirked his duty to our beloved king?"

"I buy and sell, and I trade this for that, but I do not worry myself with things that don't concern me, like what Lord Mabank owes the crown," he said. "And he has not paid for this yet. If you confiscate this chattel, I will be ruined."

Gregory made eyes with both the men-at-arms, and then trained his sights on the merchant.

"That is not my intent," Gregory said. "Tell me, what have you spent?"

"Nineteen pounds, three shillings, and four pence—if you are to take it, I would ask that you give me full recompense, including the wagon and horses."

"Full recompense? Warren, what are your thoughts?"

He turned the sword in his hand and scowled, as Beverley pulled in beside him.

"We should let them leave with their lives, and not a farthing more," Warren said.

"Merchant, you should like to deal with me, for as you see, my man does not like equal trades. So, what will you take for this wagonload of contraband?"

"Something, anything so that I do not return to Dublin a beggar."

Gregory felt the pang of remorse. The merchant was an innocent man, caught in the middle of a conflict he had not caused, or maintained, or otherwise perpetuated. He bought at one price and sold at another. Just as Gregory had done. But here he was, under the threat of arms by highwaymen, and watching his world crumble before his eyes. This stretch of road, one of the easiest in the whole of Ireland, but not on this day, when his fate was consumed by the fates of others. Although he did not show it—his lips remained pursed in warning, his chin out-jutted with the menace of royal authority—Gregory had genuine pity for the man. The merchant did not deserve to lose it all, and Gregory did not have the heart to take it from him. But he didn't have enough to make the merchant whole. A promissory note would have to do.

"Go to Clonard in a few days," he said. "Your wagon and the exchange will be hidden in the woods closest to the castle."

"Are you mad! It will be looted and gone before I get there."

"And we will take your letters of trade, your bill of lading, and your men's horses, too," Gregory said. "If you walk away, you can make Dublin by the rooster's crow tomorrow morning. But if you tell of what happened to you this day, and speak of it within the fortnight, then you will see me—and my men—soon enough."

Dumbfounded, Simon Aude climbed down from his wagon. His men-at-arms dismounted. Under the careful watch of Archer and the threat of his bow, they headed back to Dublin on foot.

Before sending him on his way, Gregory and Warren had interrogated Simon Aude. Lord Mabank, he told them, had a retinue of a dozen armed men and a household of a dozen servants. The castle's warden, a knife-happy Irishman named Dónall, would receive the delivery and be meticulous with the bill of lading. The gate would be open to them and they would deliver the goods to the storehouse next to the hall. If the bill was accurate and met Dónall's approval, scrutiny would be lax. Delivery day was a day of celebration. Honey, dried fruits, salt and pepper, and above all, monastic ale and Gascon wine, were always the first to run out. When those precious items were replenished, Clonard rejoiced. The servants would form a human chain, passing goods from one set of hands to the next, unloading the wagon in a festive flurry. With spices on the meat and the tankards brimming, Clonard would once again indulge. Due to his wife's preferences, Lord Mabank kept his chief residence in the top floor of the tower, a private area jealously guarded against everyone. It was even rumored that his wife, Finnseach, practiced magic there, as from time to time a strange green light shone from the tower window. Mabank's oldest son, Gerard the Younger, kept a pack of large hounds, and at the slightest hint of trouble, would command them to attack. Simon Aude said he had seen it happen just a year ago during one of his deliveries, when a royal messenger, in possession of a writ of seizure, was mauled and left to die from his wounds. Lord Mabank himself could be a saint or a tyrant, depending on the day. Simon Aude had seen men hanging at the gallows inside Clonard, and it was well known that Lord Mabank enjoyed keeping rivals stuffed in a dank hole beneath the tower. But if he were in a good mood, he could be generous and witty with banter. Once the goods had been offloaded, the wagon would be piled high with wolf pelts, as these were one of Lord Mabank's chief sources of revenue. If the weather was poor, Simon Aude would sleep in the hall until conditions improved. Otherwise, he made his delivery, took possession of the exchange, and headed back to Dublin.

"Clonard is not a place where one dallies," he had told Gregory.

They pulled the wagon into a secluded area off the road and unloaded it. Leather goods, a pot of pepper, star anise and saffron, linen and wool, silk and finished fur, rope and tools, dried fruits and cheeses, ale, wheat, wine, salted pork, pickled herring, and a large vat of pitch. Deep within the cargo was a wooden chest, knee high and an arm's length wide, the key inside the lock. They opened it. Gregory gasped at what he saw. Bound tomes, a veritable library, an extraordinary cache of manuscripts. Gregory leafed through a few of them, written in Gaelic, a language he did not know. Its margins adorned with images of exotic beasts, fantastical landscapes, and diabolic symbols, these parchments shouted with hatred and rage, and so too did they summon with the enlightenment of forbidden knowledge. Gregory looked up from the page, breaking with its allure, and into the faces of Warren, Archer and Beverley.

"These manuscripts belong to Finnseach," he said. "It's the work of the devil and we will use it to our advantage."

They emptied the chest, the manuscripts in a stack. And then they put Archer to work. He squatted down and ran his fingers all along the joints and panels of the chest. He fetched a mallet from the stash of tools on the wagon and pulled a square of resin from his own pouch. He gently tapped one of the trunk's sides, up and across and then down again. The panel, deftly bumped from its joinery, fell free. A sly smile spreading across his gummy, toothless mouth, he rubbed the resin along the panel's seams, and then slid it back into place. He tucked a wad of wool, saturated in pitch, inside his jupon. He kissed the cross hanging at his neck and climbed into the trunk, his knees pulled up to his chin. They covered him with a layer of books, closed the lid and locked it. They put everything back on the wagon and disguised themselves with the outer garments they had taken from Simon Aude and his men. Warren and Beverley even mounted the inferior horses they had taken from the men-at-arms.

Gregory snapped the reins. The wagon lurched forward. Soon thereafter the lonely keep of Clonard came into view. A simple mound and tower surrounded by a courtyard and curtain wall, this was an old stronghold, built ages ago when the English were new to Ireland. A sagging fortress, too, its stone patchwork of repairs evident even from a distance. But time had done nothing to diminish its menace. The pall of smoke hanging over Clonard, and the surrounding ditch and palisade, spoke succinctly to its potential, that it was a venerable seat of conquest, that at any moment it could belch out a phalanx of horsemen, as it had done countless times, to punish the land with steel and fire.

Warren, riding out in front with Beverley, turned in the saddle and said, "Master Gregory, are you ready?"

"I am ready, Lord Warren," he said, but with little conviction.

He dug into his robe and pulled out the sash of checkered yellow and gray he had taken from Simon Aude. He raised it over his head and waved it back and forth, giving notice to the guards that the victuals had arrived. A horn blew and a bell rang.

On the final approach, as the wagon climbed a small incline, the drawbridge lowered, like a tongue sticking out from the maw, ready to swallow them up and shit them out. Warren glanced over his shoulder one last time, giving Gregory a nod of assurance. He and Beverley then trotted their horses over the bridge and into the castle. Gregory, his head down so that his face was all but concealed, soon followed. The clack of the hooves and the grind of the wagon wheels echoed up into the stone reaches as he passed beneath the gatehouse. On the inside, the disheveled splendor of Clonard.

While many such places had a village outside the walls, at Clonard, the village was inside of it. More than the lord's outpost and administrative hub, here the inner courtyard was crammed with cottages of thatch, turf, and timber, stretching from the gatehouse to the tower mound on both sides of a narrow lane, forming a street just wide enough for the wagon to go through. And as the wagon rolled forward, the excitement grew. Whoops and hollers, the singing of songs, and the thud and drone of drums and bagpipes. Warren and Beverley had already arrived at the barn. Warren was in conversation with someone, probably Dónall, dressed in the kit of officialdom.

While Gregory trusted Warren with his life, he had wanted to do all the talking himself. And then there was Beverley. He did not carry himself like an ordinary man-at-arms. He sat tall and proud in the saddle, his lanky physique betraying the truth about him, that dull subservience was not his way. Seized by a spasm of urgency, Gregory slapped the reins one more time, eager to arrive at the talking place before too much more could be said without the benefit of his ear. He pulled the wagon to a stop, lifted up his head for the first time, and showing an assurance he didn't truly feel, looked into the face of the man in front of him, and said, "Dónall, is it?"

"Yes," he said, and frowned. "You are not the normal man."

"I am not," he said, gesturing to the leaning stack of cargo on the wagon behind him. "But the goods I deliver are what you have requested."

In his peripheral vision, Gregory saw what could only be Gerard Mabank the Younger, sitting on a stool near the entrance to the hall, whittling on a piece of whale bone as his pack of hounds lounged about. He looked up from his work, feigned indifference, and returned to his tinkering. But the mere fact that he had given a look, that he had allowed their arrival to interrupt what he was doing, was enough to send the intended message—he knew they were here, he knew they were strangers, and he knew what to do should things go awry.

Here at Clonard, everyone looked the same. Gregory could understand if this were among Lord Mabank's family, but even the armed retinue and the household servants resembled their lord and one another—sandy blonde hair, bushy brows, bulbous brown eyes, upturned noses and shallow chins. Subtle differences were aplenty so that none of them appeared to be twins. Still, Gregory found the uniformity disturbing, and fought the tendency to gawk at these incestuous people. His stomach turned once more when it occurred to him that this host might in fact be Lord Mabank's kin, that this wayward Englishman had managed to sire his own Irish clan.

The beat of the drums intensified, the bagpipes continued to drone, and from deep within the castle grounds there came the low, relentless murmuring of many as they surrounded the newcomers. Simon Aude had told Gregory that this was to be expected. As he counted heads, he looked up to the tower for an unknown but compelling reason. In the window, a woman's face, an old face that had once been young and beautiful, framed in a faded emerald veil. Finnseach. She put one hand to the sill and one hand to the shutter, almost as if she were going to pull herself out through the window and leap into flight. She caught Gregory's eye, and when he looked into hers, he nearly wretched. She noticed his discomfort and greeted it with a malignant grin.

"Tell me, where is Simon Aude?" said Dónall, mercifully breaking the spell Finnseach surely had cast.

"He ate a surfeit of bad eels and has sat shivering in the latrine ever since,"

Gregory said, as he had rehearsed. "Here is his credential."

He handed over Simon Aude's letters of trade. Dónall snatched it from his hands, glanced at it, and handed it back.

"And the bill?" he said, his face contorted in a confrontational glare.

Gregory handed him the bill. Dónall snatched that away, too, holding it close to his face as he read the content.

"Every bit of it must be accounted for, or we will throw you in the hole and keep you there, and I will enjoy carving you up as the days go by," he said.

As hoped, the household servants formed a human chain, and in little time the wagon had been offloaded, the cargo out of sight and in the barn, kitchen, or hall. The trunk in which Archer lay hidden was the last to go. Just as Gregory had guessed, two men hauled the chest off the wagon and went straight up the stairs to the tower, where they disappeared through an oaken door. Gregory glanced back up to the window, but Finnseach no longer appeared there. He watched as householders stacked the wagon high with the agreed upon exchange, wolf pelts, cowhides, fox, marten, and badger, enough fur for many cloaks, mantels, and mittens. To make a show of it, Gregory poured over Dónall's bill, counting each fur, inspecting the quality of the pelts, and otherwise pretending to be unimpressed with what he had received.

"It appears the wolves have gone hungry in Ireland," he said to Dónall, "for these skins are mere scraps compared to what I have seen on the piers in London."

"You will be happy with what you've got," Dónall said, and spit. "Now be on your way, you English pot of shit!"

Gregory was more than eager to obey, and as Dónall bore down on him with a stare of scrutiny, he turned the wagon and drove it toward the gatehouse. As he passed the hall, out stepped Lord Mabank himself, shirtless, potbellied, creased with battle scars, and already deep into one of the tuns of wine that had just been delivered. Laughter and song echoed from the hall, and a high note shimmered from the plucked string of a lute. Lord Mabank raised his cup and burped, to which Gregory politely nodded.

"Merchant," Lord Mabank called.

Gregory pulled the wagon to a halt, turned in his seat, and faced the man who he had come to destroy. In that very moment, when the old nobleman studied him with an alarming level of interest, Gregory cursed himself for thinking that all of this had been too easy. Warren pulled to a stop as well. If Lord Mabank were an observant man, he would see that the two of them were much more than merchant and man-at-arms. He would see in them the peril, the heroism, and the soul-stealing guile with which they had made their way. He would find in them the beating hearts of ruthless men, and he would be disturbed that they were inside his citadel. The hounds would pounce, the garrison would come running with arms, and that gate, sitting open, would close soon enough.

"Yes, my lord?" Gregory said.

Lord Mabank drained his cup, and once the wine had been gulped down, he gasped with satisfaction.

"The wine is good," he said.

"Indeed," Gregory said. "I selected it myself. It is a *Nérac* shipped straight from the quay at Bordeaux."

"Bring more of this next time," he said.

"Yes, my lord."

Gregory, Warren and Beverley rode out through the gatehouse, leaving Clonard jubilant as it gorged on its folly.

They camped out on the hilltop stand of birch where they had left their horses. From there they had a sweeping view of Clonard. They got back into their own kits and became themselves again. They checked their horses and went over their gear, tightening this and that, refastening a hook here or a buckle there, and otherwise restoring their Staffordshire array.

"So, what is about to happen?" Beverley said to Warren.

He turned to Gregory and then back to Beverley.

"We do not know yet. Maybe nothing. Maybe everything."

Beverley sat next to his horse, sharpening his knife. He looked up from his work.

"Master Gregory, you seize a man's goods, take them as your own, deliver them under false pretenses, at great risk, and do so with nary a slip of the tongue or a tremble of the hand," he said. "How is it that a merchant is in possession of such daring?"

"Because," Warren interjected, "he is not really a merchant. That is what he does to feed himself and his family, and it is what his father taught him to do and what this world tells him he must be. But Gregory is a fighting man so clever his enemies do not know he is one. They do not know they have been opposed until they have lost. What you saw at Clonard, and what you will yet see, is the way of war without swinging a sword."

"But the sword is always needed, Warren," Gregory said.

"Yes, but its stroke is most effective after the trick has been played, not before," he said. "Beverley, you have learned much from me, but there is plenty still to learn from Master Gregory."

"That is as I had hoped," Beverley said, as he sheathed his sharpened knife and then reached for his axe.

They didn't know exactly what they were looking for, only that it would be obvious when and if it ever appeared. They waited, biding the time with muted small talk, their horses fidgeting as a ripple of Marigold washed across the western sky. Night fell with ten million stars, and from time to time they heard laughter and singing rolling in on the wind. Even as they waited and grew impatient, from the looks they shared it was evident that they felt that something was about to happen.

And then it did.

A flicker of flame, a twisting tongue of devilment, sprouted from the top of the tower. The three of them exchanged sideways looks of amazement. The flame grew higher and higher, and then it spread, consuming the timber reaches of the roof, burning blue hot and beyond containment. And then came the shouts of panic, the commands of desperation, and the shrieks of confusion and fear. The very heart of Clonard was alight, but this was but a preamble to what happened next.

The flames sucked in on themselves and all but disappeared. Then, a silence, as if the world had gone deaf and dumb. Out of that creeping moment of stillness came a tectonic clap, much meaner than low thunder, seismic in its force, the very earth a drum on which pounded Lucifer himself. Then, a clover comet launching from the top of the tower, sizzling into the heavens before bursting into a popping, bedazzling mushroom of embers. They shielded their eyes, the horses whinnied and reared, the light of such strength that for a blink, night turned into day, the dark castle seared under a dome of unholy sunshine. As the embers rained down on Clonard, flames soon rose from every corner of the castle.

Recovering from the sheer stupendousness of what he had just seen, Beverley turned to Gregory and Warren, themselves agape and dazed, and said, "I was not expecting that."

For a time even Gregory did not know what to do. He just sat and stared, gazing into the smoky haze hanging over Clonard, still feeling the quake of the explosion rattling in his bones. But he recovered from his astonishment when he noticed Lord Mabank and his householders evacuating through the gatehouse, leaving the castle unmanned.

"Now!" said Warren, the three of them riding breakneck to the gate.

Tatenhill broke to the front, gaining many lengths on the other horses. Urgent she was, coursing with intent, aware that this moment had to be won. Gregory glanced over his shoulder. Beverley and Warren lagging farther behind—and a detachment of Lord Mabank's mounted men pulling into pursuit. The pack of hounds also banked into the chase, surpassing the horsemen, cutting across the turf and gaining ground. Gregory had the sinking notion that Warren and Beverley could be caught, but he could not wane in his work. Driving Tatenhill even harder, they reached the drawbridge and crossed into Clonard.

He wheeled her to a stop, covered his face with his cloak to keep from choking on smoke, and looked long and hard from left to right. Smoldering ruins everywhere, the stench of inferno, the soot and ash of the catastrophe he had made. But in the wreckage, he saw Archer and motioned to him. He dismounted, scrambled to the gatehouse door, and dashed up the spiral staircase to the room housing the crank and chain for the drawbridge. Archer soon joined him. They peered out through a murder hole. The hounds had all but overtaken Warren and Beverley. The best among them sprung from the pack, and in a burst of impossible quality, tucked in on the left flank of Warren's horse. He then lunged, and just as it was to sink its teeth into the horse's rump, Warren turned in his saddle and swung down with his forearm.

The dog, as big as the wolves it was trained to kill, bit into him and tugged. As the horse kicked and whinnied, Warren's face the grimace of doom. The dog drug him from his horse, but as he fell, Warren pulled out his knife. As the blade flashed up and down, he and the giant hound rolled through the muck. Warren gained his feet, the gutted dog laying limp and dying. Beverley, the last to arrive, pulled in and covered Warren as he collected himself and entered the grounds. With his axe, he killed one hound and then another—they began to attack in waves—before turning his horse and tearing across the bridge. With Beverley clear, Gregory and Archer turned the crank.

The bridge rose and clunked into place just as Lord Mabank and his men arrived at the ditch. Gregory and Archer, both of them gasping with exhaustion, clasped one another's shoulders in a gesture of relief. And so it was that they took Castle Clonard. Now, it was time to retrieve what they had come for and make their escape.

Beverley gave Archer his bow and arrows. From his position atop the gatehouse, he could make easy targets of Lord Mabank and his men. But before taking his post, he pointed toward the tower. With a series of articulate and animated hand gestures, he intimated to Gregory and Warren that something special was to be found there. But the tower now stood on the brink of collapse. The explosion had blown the top off and had opened a seam down the entirety of its eastern face. Blocks of stone and smoldering cross beams littered the mound, and even as Gregory and Warren pondered their predicament, the third floor gave way with an earsplitting crack of charred wood and roasted masonry.

"It will be the death of us, Master Gregory," Warren said.

"Let us hope you are not right," he said.

They went to the tower mound. When they had nearly reached the summit, a plume of toxic smoke consumed them. They had to turn their faces away. Coughing and gagging, they found relief after cutting kerchiefs from their cloaks and holding them over their mouths and noses. Thus protected, they continued their ascent, climbing, and at times crawling, through the rubble to the hole along the tower face. They pulled themselves up onto the foundation as it remained intact, and from there they could see inside. All four interior stories, made of timber joists and crossbeams, had given way, collapsing down into the cellar. A terrible jumble of destruction, the tower an empty husk, the low belly twinkling with coals and audible with dying whispers. Still hot enough to broil a man, and as they stood and stared into the pit, Gregory felt the heat in the stone coming up through the soles of his boots. Gregory and Warren looked at one another and shook their heads. If the treasure they had come for was down in there, God help them. Still, Archer's suggestion, signaled with utter confidence, inspired them to be long and careful with their inspection, to endure the fumes, to choke back the stench of burning flesh wafting up from the dungeon way down below, and to balance themselves on the edge of this yawning furnace.

"If Archer saw something," Warren began.

"Then it most probably was on the top floor," Gregory ended.

"Which means if it is in this pile of burning shit," Warren began.

"Then it could still be on top," Gregory ended.

They looked again with rejuvenated spirits, that spasm of excitement sharpening their senses. It all looked the same, charred ends, large cuts of blackened stone, and the infinity of rubble. But then came a subtle gust of wind. It caught inside the tower shell, whirled into a circle, and for a moment, carried the smoke away. And that's when both of them saw it, what appeared to be a coffer plugged into the very heart of the hellscape, too intact to be wood, and too ornate to be stone. Once they took a good look at it, there was no doubt. Lord Mabank's hoard, likely hidden between the floorboard of the top story and the ceiling of the story beneath it, had been revealed.

But now how to get it.

To go down into the pit was to burn oneself at the stake, and neither Gregory nor Warren wanted to martyr themselves this day. But they did not have the luxury of waiting for things to cool down. Even now, Archer with his bow, and Beverley with a crossbow found in the gatehouse, manned the walls against a numerically superior foe, depleting their store of bolts and arrows as they drove them back out of range.

"What do you suggest?" Gregory said, knowing that if the coffer were to be gotten, then Warren would be the one to do it.

He looked upward in thought, and then scanned the surroundings. He settled his sights on the only structure that had not been damaged or destroyed, the gatehouse.

"What did you see in there?" Warren said.

It had all come and gone so fast. The arrow loops, the chain crank and the drawbridge, the urgent dash up and down the stairs. Gregory hadn't thought to take notice of what was inside the building, but now that he was being asked, he considered the inventory as it related to the circumstances. A trestle table and stools, a large pot, a stash of crossbows and projectiles, a heap of siege stones, and a half-empty hogshead of animal fat. He gave Warren the list. An idea showed in his face. They descended the tower mound and ran to the gatehouse, ignoring the gaggle of the old and infirm, huddled and watching from the door of a turfed cottage.

Inside the gatehouse, they found Beverley, crouching, aiming a crossbow through a murder hole, and jeering Lord Mabank as he did. He pulled the trigger, stood up and prepared to reload.

"Where is Archer?" Warren said.

"He is out on the wall—he has gotten two of them and I have gotten one," he said.

Gregory and Warren ransacked the gatehouse. They collected much of what Gregory had told him of, but added to that a discovered wedge, hammer, and hook. Warren then climbed up into the guts of the gatehouse. There he looted the pulley system attached to both of the portcullises, thereby gaining the benefit of chain, rope and pulley blocks. Thus encumbered, they returned to the tower mound. Reaching the summit huffing and gasping, they dropped their assortment of gear and caught their breath.

At Warren's command, Gregory fetched the horses. He returned to find Warren down on one knee, tying knots and calculating lengths, silent in his work and thoughtful. Coils of rope and chain at his feet, he looked up and said, "Are you ready to loot Lord Mabank's trove?"

"I sailed from England for the chance," he said.

Warren called for Beverley. A length of rope over his shoulder, he walked around the curvature of the tower and went in through the entrance. Standing at the edge of the landing, he took another long look at the crackling bed of coals below. He looked across to Gregory, stationed with Tatenhill at the tower breach. Warren gave some slack to the rope, weighted by a sack of stones tied at its end. With an underhanded motion, he twirled the rope in circles, once, twice, and then a third time. On the fourth rotation, as the underhand motion came upward, he let go of the rope with a deft flick of his wrist. Weighted as it was, the rope lobbed over the pit and landed on the outside of the breach, at Gregory's feet.

"Now grab the rope and hold it tight," Warren said, and Gregory did as he was told.

Beverley arrived, and after a short consultation with Warren, positioned himself on the landing with his end of the rope anchored around his waist. Warren ran the length of chain, affixed at its end with the hook he had found in the gatehouse, through the pulley block. He attached the pulley block, itself suspended on a hook and swivel, to the rope pulled taught between Beverley and Gregory. The landing was at a higher point than where Gregory stood, so the rope slanted downward across the pit. Once the pulley block was attached, it slid down the length of the rope, only stopping when it caught on the knot Warren had tied for that very purpose. And in that way, a hook and pulley hung over the coffer. Gregory, looking across at good Warren, beamed with pride, for this idea had not occurred to him. But Warren was having none of it. He handed the end of the pulley chain to Beverley and returned to Gregory's position. He tied that end of rope around Tatenhill's shoulders.

"Perhaps we'll finally get a good day's worth of work out of her," he said, before returning to the landing.

Positioned on the extreme edge of the pit, where any misstep would be the beginning of his end, Warren took possession of the pulley chain. He lowered it down. The hook came tantalizingly close to the handle loop on top of the coffer, but it was a foot off. Warren ordered Gregory to move Tatenhill a step farther to her left. Once that was done, the hook dangled directly above the coffer—and one of the flames in the bed of coals, finding something new to burn, licked upward toward the rope. At Warren's command, Beverley moved the cross rope from side to side, ever so slightly, so that the hook began to swing, pendulum like, above the coffer. And it swung, back and forth, up and down, again and again—until Warren gave an inch in the chain, sinking the hook on its back stroke, and cinching it into the coffer's handle. The rope caught fire as Warren, his strength quintupled by the torque of the pulley, grunted and heaved on the chain. Embers and debris cascaded away in a shower of sparks as the coffer, glowing with heat, was hoisted from its resting place.

"Pull, Gregory, pull!" Warren said. "And make sure she gives you everything she's got!"

With his willow whip, Gregory slapped Tatenhill on the rump, yelling, "Yaayy!"

She went forward with a muscle-ripping, heart-heaving, hoof-digging, spittle-spewing pull down the tower mound, as Beverley gave slack from his end. The rope skidded under the pulley hook until it caught with the second knot Warren had tied earlier, launching the coffer forward as Warren finally gave slack in the chain. The coffer slammed into the breach, toppling a weakened tower stone, before thudding to the turf and coming to rest sideways up against a smoldering beam. Gregory raised both arms in triumph, as did Warren and Beverley, and the three of them whooped with cheer as they exchanged expressions of disbelief.

"Now, Lord Warren, how do we get out of here?" Gregory said.

"I was hoping you would figure that out."

The three of them couldn't help but grin, a moment of mirth they knew would not last long.

Dawn broke. With the new day came a new set of problems. During the night, Lord Mabank had put out his call for reinforcements. Throughout the morning they trickled in. An assortment of bumpkins and ploughmen, the lot of them, but they had spears, knives, and slings. Most importantly, they brought ladders and ropes—the hard goods needed to retake Clonard—and had fanned out to cover a large section of the wall. Archer, having enjoyed free reign, now faced a new reality. When he appeared on the battlements to fire an arrow, a hail of projectiles came screaming back at him. Barricaded in the gatehouse with no victuals and but a quarter bucket of water, Gregory exchanged worrisome looks with Beverley and Warren. Without a word amongst them, they all reached the same conclusion—they were trapped.

"At least let us see what we have come to die for," Gregory said, motioning toward the coffer sitting in the middle of the room.

They had drug it up the stairs and into the gatehouse the night before. And even in the dire circumstances in which they found themselves, the mystery inside this chest claimed title to their curiosity. And, depending on the contents, what lay inside might give them something with which to bargain should they fail to figure out an escape. At least that's what they told themselves.

Warren went down on one knee. He worked his axe blade in a prying motion down the seam between the lid and the box, cracking the coffer open as if it were an oyster shell. He opened the lid, and to their pleasure, there shone a solid, lustered sheet of melted silver. Warren tapped the back of his axe up and down all four sides of the coffer, and with Beverley's help, turned it on its side. Out fell a giant silver ingot, encrusted with gold and a galaxy of gemstones, almost like a fruited pork-fat gelatin recently tipped from the mold. When a shaft of eastern light shot through the arrow loop, it collected in this splendid hunk of aggregate, filling the room with a dreamy citron hue.

"That is a fine sight," said Beverley, as he cocked his crossbow and readied to load. "Master Gregory, what do you think?"

"Oh, it is more than I imagined," he said, trading a stunned look with Warren.

Beverley crouched up to the arrow loop and prepared to take another shot. But he stood back, looked at Warren and Gregory and said, in a tone of grave concern, "One of you should take a look!"

Warren went first. His jaw dropped in amazement. He turned to Gregory. "You will not believe it," he said. "Look out and tell me what you see."

Blazing in from the east came a valiant host, a cavalcade of galloping stallions, their riders draped in glinting mail and heraldic jupons. Pennons whipping high above them, an arcing tail of turf and mud rising in their wake. From spur to helm, all of them fighting men. Their leader, atop a blistering white courser, gliding across the dew-laden field, a cloak of purple billowing from his shoulders, a spray of ostrich feathers sprouting from his Bascinet. Squinting, Gregory made out the insignia on the livery. The three lions of England. These were not Lord Mabank's allies, but the king's royal lieutenant in Dublin. Looking deeper into this oncoming retinue, Gregory put a hand to his mouth and gasped. Among them rode none other than the merchant Simon Aude. At last, it had come—that which Gregory had once feared—but now welcomed.

Their arrival sent a ripple of panic through Lord Mabank's entourage, and many of them scattered. The lieutenant and his men wheeled their horses to a halt just a few feet on the other side of the ditch, giving Gregory a good look at those who had come to capture him. He was pleased to see that Henry de Thornhill was not among them, but that is the only solace he found. These were rotten men, deep in noble pedigree and embellished with all manner of ornament, but as foul as old ale piss in the bottom of the bucket. And this posse of English adventurers, as nasty as they themselves were, were not the worst of it. Among them was a unit of Gallowglass, professional Irish warriors feared for their prowess in combat and their bottomless cruelty. The mere sight of them, and knowing they were here for him, made Gregory say a prayer.

"What, in the king's name, has happened here!" said the lieutenant.

In that instant, Gregory knew who this man was. The Gascon accent, one which Gregory himself had, gave him away. This was not just the king's lieutenant, but the king's infamous favorite, Piers Gaveston, the dreaded Earl of Cornwall. Effeminate in face and manner, yet revered for his ability on the tournament fields, where he had won many accolades and had made many enemies. Consumed by vanity and reckless in his vengeance, Gaveston reigned as the most hated man in all of England, which is why he was in Ireland. Serving out his latest sentence of exile, he was just biding his time until the king, reputed to be his lover, made arrangements for his return. A bad seed from the beginning, Gaveston had sown much discord among the nobility with his aggressive upstart ways. A pretender to his titles, the profligate taker of what was not his, Gaveston nurtured his ill repute, basking in the compromised glory of the tyrant. And here he was at Clonard, backed by thirty men, adorned with royal authority, and brimming with wicked conceit.

Gregory knew this would not end well, but try, he must, to craft a conclusion that suited him.

"I have royal letters," Gregory said, speaking through the arrow loop.

"That must be him," said Simon Aude, pointing upward. "That must be the man who stole my chattel!"

"Show yourself and show your letters," Gaveston said. "I assure you, if you force us to break in, the penalty for your defiance will be severe—but you will live long enough to feel it."

Gregory walked up the spiral staircase to the gatehouse roof. Looking out from behind a battlement, he produced the Langley Credential, holding it high so that all could see.

"I am here at the behest of King Edward," Gregory said. "I am a clerk in the king's wardrobe, and my business here is *his* business."

"You had better have more proof than you have already shown," Gaveston said. "For at this moment, I am here to arrest you for highway robbery, and if you are found guilty, then you and your associates will be hanged at the gallows in Dublin. Open the gate—now—and present yourself."

"Will you grant me and my men safe conduct?"

"Open the gate!"

Gregory went downstairs, where Warren, Beverley and Archer prepared to leave. They put the ingot back inside the coffer and lugged it down. In the passage beneath the gatehouse, they mounted their horses, primping themselves to make sure that their accoutrements were obvious, that the sword and knife hilts protruded, that the axe blades caught the light, that their helms were snug, and that their black capes and jupons hung properly across their mail. As this happened their faces hardened, and in the silence of their preparations, they found their resolve.

Warren removed the stop block. The gate fell open, sucking out a noxious waft of pollution that caused Gaveston and his men to cough. As they were consumed by this gush of smoke and fumes, the War Hounds of Staffordshire clattered out through the gatehouse, Warren, Archer, and Beverley in front, and Gregory, with Tatenhill dragging the coffer behind her, in the rear. They halted on the drawbridge and, as Gaveston had ordered, presented themselves.

In a diplomatic fashion, Gregory handed both the Langley Credential and Lord Mabank's writ to Beverley, who then handed them to Gaveston's clerk. As he read them, a curious smile crept over his face. He leaned in, speaking into Gaveston's ear. The change in Gaveston's expression suggested that he had just heard something of great magnitude, something that gave him an advantage, an unexpected boon he could wield as a weapon.

"My clerk tells me your letters are good," Gaveston said. "And if my guess is right, Lord Mabank's treasure sits in that coffer."

"That is correct, my lord," Gregory said. "The contents should be more than enough to settle Lord Mabank's arrears, with perhaps a bit left over to compensate you for your trouble."

Two of Gaveston's underlings dismounted, went to the coffer, cut the rope and hauled it back to Gaveston, setting it beside his horse.

"You should take it out," Gregory said. "It is a treasure the likes of which you have never seen."

At Gaveston's acknowledgement, the underlings opened the coffer and dumped out the ingot. Even Gaveston and his men could not resist the beauty of this prize, their granite faces softening, if only for a blink, at the sight of this twinkling slab of magnificence. Gregory could not have dreamt of a better response. He hoped it would be enough, but as he read Gaveston's face, he saw that something else was yet to come.

"My clerk tells me this is the last of the errands that our dear king has given to you," Gaveston said. "You have been to Canterbury and to Ponthieu and back, to Norwich and Dartmoor, and now Ireland."

"Yes, my lord, the king's list was long."

"I must say, when I came here, I thought I would arrest a simple man, a frantic outlaw regretting what he had done. But I find myself face to face with the extraordinary Gregory of Bordeaux."

"My lord, extraordinary is not the word I would use to describe myself."

"Oh, but you are," he said. "You humiliated Lord Willoughby in front of his peers at Chilham. The king lost a fortune at Norwich due to you. You instigated a riot, which turned into a massacre, at Abbeville, and then you confiscated a bell after having first been dishonest about your intentions. And it was you who testified that Henry de Thornhill sank one of Earl Arundel's ships. You even gave away the king's mining claims at Dartmoor! And while you were there, an assayer and a warden died suspicious deaths."

"All in the king's service, my lord."

"Yes, you have served him well," he said. "But there is one thing you did not do."

"And what is that, my lord?"

"Lady Clifton," he said. "We know you abducted her, as requested, but you did not bring her to the garrison in Dublin. If you are here, then she should be there."

"You are correct, my lord."

"Then where did you take her? The king wants to know."

"That, I cannot tell."

Gaveston sighed, giving voice to his displeasure.

"Lady Clifton. She is nothing. A roadside flower at best. She is just part of the game my dear king likes to play. And I would say the same of her father."

"Forgive me, my lord, but I could not see her spoiled."

"I find it hard to believe that a man of your reputation has such scruples," he said. "But indeed, Lady Clifton never made it to Burton, so in the end the king still gets what he wants."

"Yes, the betrothal is all but moot."

Gaveston's face turned smug, and in that expression of joy, Gregory saw the depths of the man's depravity. Throughout the conversation Gaveston had looked directly at him, almost as if the others did not exist. But with a subtle back-and-forth dart of his eyes, so fast and easy that Gregory almost did not catch it, he stole a glance at Warren. Gregory took a deep breath and exhaled through his nose. In the time it took to do that, he figured all of it out. This Gaveston, this extravagant stranger, was nothing of the sort. He not only knew *of* Gregory but knew a lot *about* him. He had read Southampton's chronicle. He had read Gregory's account of his travels in Gascony. He would have heard all manner of hearsay over his years as the king's associate and sycophant. Which meant he knew a lot about Warren. Upon arriving at the realization, Gregory swallowed hard and braced himself.

"I know you like deals, Bordeaux, so here is mine," Gaveston said. "I will forget about Lady Clifton. If the king ever asks about her, I will make him forget it, too. But in exchange—and for my trouble, as you say—I would like to take the horse."

"What horse, my lord?"

"Your horse."

The gravity of the moment turned to Warren, just two lengths between him and the Earl of Cornwall. It seemed as if the whole world went silent, as if it waited for Warren to speak. When his words finally came, they were not hard to hear.

"That is Master Gregory's horse, and you cannot take her," he said.

"Lord Warren, I would ask you to repeat yourself."

"Lady Tatenhill belongs to Master Gregory, and she will never be yours."

Reddened with petulance, having been denied the quick prize of Warren's honor, he glanced over his shoulder at one of the Gallowglass, giving him the command with a slight jerk of his chin. The mounted warrior spurred forward, his drawn sword a slanting crack of lightning. Before it struck home, Warren leaned in across his saddle and unleashed a maul of an overhand right, his mailed-and-leathered fist breaking the Gallowglass's face. He went limp as the conical helm tumbled from his head—but the sword continued. With an impossible act of contortion, Warren avoided it. But he had yet to win, for even in this moment of devastation, when the Gallowglass's helm bounced against the drawbridge, when his mouth hung on the side of his chin, and when an eye popped loose from its socket, he threatened to recover. Warren backed his horse two steps, drew *Fionnaghal*, and rolled the hilt over his hand. He reared the horse, and as it came down lurching forward, Warren harnessed its power, uncoiling into an attack of such immense force that he cleaved the Gallowglass from shoulder to groin. As the gushing corpse slid free from the blade and fell from the saddle, Warren turned his horse in a clattering circle of victory, and then sheathed *Fionnaghal.* He reached out and grabbed the Gallowglass's horse by the bridle before pulling in beside Beverley. Gaveston, unable to hide a dark smile of astonishment, soon effected an air of great respect.

"It is settled then, you can keep the horses," he said. "Now leave Ireland and be quick with it."

Warren, Beverley, and Archer rode off the bridge and through the horsemen who had parted to let them pass. As Gregory left, Gaveston ordered him to stop. He returned the Langley Credential and Lord Mabank's writ.

"You earned your safe passage today, Bordeaux, but we will see one another back in England."

"It would be my honor, my lord."

Gregory continued on, but then he stopped and turned his horse. For the sake of theater, he tilted his head and paused before speaking.

"Lord Gaveston, I believe our grandfathers would have known one another," he said. "My father's father worked the Garonne from Auvillar to the Gironde. He knew everyone north and south of the river—even as far as Béarn where, I believe, you are from."

In silence the two of them looked upon one another for some while, young Gaveston absorbing what had been said, old Gregory confirming it, before he turned and rode away. He and Tatenhill joined the others, and they were soon headed to Drogheda. Before Clonard disappeared from view, all of them stopped and took one last look. A cloud of vomitous green still hung over the fortress, a sprinkle of ash and embers still falling from the sky. It appeared as if Lord Mabank was trying to explain to Gaveston exactly what had happened the night before, when that comet had blasted into the sky, and when life had changed in quick and fantastical ways. Gregory looked over at Archer. Since he was mute, the story of what really happened up in the tower with Finnseach would never be known except to him. Perhaps it was better that way. Mysteries, Gregory knew, always got better with age.

"Lord Warren," Gregory said, "I should wish to leave Ireland and never return."

"Master Gregory, that is what you say now, but that will change."

"Oh, it will not change, old friend. It will never change."

THE IRISH GOD OF THE SEA

They boarded at Drogheda. Marching their horses up the loading plank, they took their places on deck just as the ship was to take the tide and the wind. Aboard were a merchant and pilgrims, itinerate workers and a troupe of musicians. In a corner near the aftercastle, a huddling clutch of migrant women and children. All of them looked away, sensing that those who had just boarded were terrible men who had done terrible things. If they had left trouble and corpses behind, then surely trouble and corpses were ahead. The soot and stain of Clonard, the bedlam eyes of having seen something hideous and unforgettable, and all about them the clinging odor of arson. A committee of strange vultures, these men, come to roost where they were not wanted.

Gregory produced the Langley Credential, rudely shoving it out in front of him.

"We are commandeering this ship," he said. "Now take us to Chester."

The shipmaster paused as he mustered his courage. And even when he did speak, he dared not look Gregory in the face, lest he offend.

"But we are bound for Liverpool, my lord," he said.

"No, you are bound for Chester."

On day three of the voyage, it first appeared as a dark spot on the southeastern horizon. Gregory didn't give it much thought. There were many ships in the channel as there always were, so he dismissed that sinking feeling as a bout of paranoia. The journey had caught up with him, he reasoned, the fatigue and anguish finally coming due. But as the day progressed, and as the waters began to course with an anger gurgling out from the abyss, that dark spot, which he looked for again and again, grew larger. Peering into the distance, his hand cupped over his squinting eyes, he noticed that the ship had turned north, heading their way. He looked back toward Ireland where a storm gathered.

"Warren, what do you have to say?"

"It is not good, Master Gregory," he said. "Look at the passengers."

Indeed, they were streaming below deck, and urgently so. By Gregory's guess, they were sheltering before the storm, now a black and brown thunderhead with vast circling clouds and bursts of blue light.

"I was not referring to the tempest," he said, pointing southeasterly. "Look."

Warren gazed long and hard in that direction, Gregory studying his expression as he did. What began as basic curiosity evolved into a look of undeniable concern.

"That is a big warship, Master Gregory, it is *Hastings Whale*, and they are flying the fleur-de-lis," he said. "Archer, take the horses down below! Beverley, fetch our shields!"

A sheet of blinding rain punished them. Then arrived the wind, a gale of the howling dead, and with it a swelling wave rolling over the channel. The hulk, moaning from this furious shock of energy, sped over the dark waters, the sail at the brink of splitting, the mast bending, sea spray jetting from the hull. And so it went, the storm whisking them eastward to England as *Hast-*

ings Whale, thrown forward by the churning, angry vortex above, closed on them. It looked as if the two ships would ram, and as the narrow distance between them dwindled, Gregory began to see the faces. Henry de Thornhill, his long chin and nose, the gnashed teeth of the famished animal, and those eyes, blue drops of rage, a noble pastiche glaring out from the black basinet. And his men, dripping wet with rain, their armor glimmering in the dark day, all of them lined along the gunwale.

A web of firebolts illuminated the clouds and then a drum of hell's approbation. Gregory recoiled from the tumult. When he regained himself, he saw more faces, that of Lord Corby and Le Gaunter, Marcus of Burwell and the Bishop of Lincoln, Lord Baldwin of Essex and the Dominican Priest, Clementia and Claudine, Gilbert Le Blanc, Fumel's Clerk, the nameless townspeople of Abbeville, the Assayer of Dartmoor, the grocers of Norwich—and even Alphonse of Bayonne. All of them armed with bows and crossbows, slings and spears and swords and axes, rocks and hooks and knives and clubs, anything that would help them gain their revenge on the man who had wronged them. Mesmerized by the sight, shackled and unmoving in a cage of memories, he watched them ready their weapons as *Hastings Whale* made its pass. And then it all went black. He opened his eyes and found himself curled in a bunch beneath the wall of shields held up by Warren, Archer and Beverly. He heard the fusillade, the clank, whistle, and thud of flying steel, the success of the defense, and the vehement exchange of insults. The deck, a porcupine of spent arrows and bolts, littered with axes and stones. And lobbing over the starboard side, a lit and fused pot of pitch. It crashed against the deck, unleashing a sash of fire. Gregory stood. Through the flames he saw *Hastings Whale,* hurtling toward Ireland, and de Thornhill, standing on the aftercastle shaking his fist, his harangues drowned out by the wind.

The hulk, still careering across the channel, crashed through a swell. The deluge of water splashed over the deck, dousing the fire just as it threatened to engulf the sail. As the four of them shared a look of relief, they heard a frightful roar, out from the abyss, as if Lir, the Irish god of the sea, himself had awoken. Stricken with awe, Archer pointed in the direction from whence they had come. They turned, only to see a wave, as tall as a cathedral and as wide as infinity, shrouding out the horizon. It caught the ship, the hulk rising to the crest. From this magnificent height, they could see the coastline of England—and a toothrow of rocks jutting up near the shoals.

The captain lay slain, shot through with arrows. Clambering up the deck as the ship shot down to the trough, it was Beverley, with all the sinew of his strength and honor, and grinning as he did, who put both hands on the rudder post and pulled. The hulk veered and tilted, its rivets about to burst, its planks shrieking under the strain, as it glided past the rocks, the stone below grinding against the keel. Plummeting, a brace of hail pelting the deck, the hulk barged through the surf, plowed across the beach, cutting a trench through the sand until it came to rest against a dune. The sudden stop tossed the four of them overboard.

On his knees, one hand on the ground and the other clearing sand from his eye, Gregory looked for the others. Like him, they worked to recover. Then came the violent crack of wood. And then again. The hull blew open, the planks springing out to form a breach. Out trotted Tatenhill, followed by the other horses and all the passengers. With the musicians and a parish priest leading them, the pilgrims, the itinerate workers, and the women and children continued on their way, rejoicing with what they thought to be a miracle. Only the shipmaster and the merchant remained, dumbstruck as they surveyed the wreckage. Yet even in their dismay, people came to assist them.

Gregory mounted his horse.

"You can sell your cargo at mitigation," he said to the merchant. "But my apologies for the ship. If ever you must, tell them this was the doing of Gregory of Bordeaux. Perhaps then you will obtain a fair recompense."

THE GOLDEN STRIPE ACROSS CALM WATER

Call it the revenge of Finnseach. The creeping nausea that came upon Gregory after the return to England finally reached its zenith. He turned in his saddle, hanging his head, and coughed out a gelatinous stream of vomit so foul, its stink so overwhelming that it was as if he'd defecated from his mouth, the ordure an oozing green caterpillar of righteous retribution, his penalty for masterminding the ruination of Clonard. As he wiped a drip of froth from his chin, it all became clear. When he had seen Finnseach in the tower window, when he had felt that spasm of revulsion at the mere sight of her, it was then that she had placed her hex, planting her malignant magic inside of him. He dismounted, and then fell to his hands and knees.

"I am about to die," he said, and wretched again.

They took him to an abandoned cottage on the outskirts of the hamlet of Tarvin. They made a pallet of his cloak and laid him down, his head resting on his gear, a folded cape a pillow. The frankincense and myrrh burning in the tray. Sinking deeper into delirium, Gregory had a moment of lucidity before collapsing into the cavern of despair. He thought of Sister Gertrude of Poor Clares, the nun and medicus who had preserved Warren's life with an elixir of her own concoction. She had told Gregory of every ingredient, made him watch every step, to teach him the art of healing, to give him the guarded secret to salvation.

"Bean flour," he began with a croak. "Equal parts galingale, ginger, and sanicle—and a tear drop of opium boiled in a broth of bone marrow and *Jurançon* wine."

Through the crack in the cottage door, Gregory watched them speed away, Warren and Beverley, taking the spare Irish horse with them. He closed his eyes, only to hear the screaming of the banshees, the babbling of the insane, the chaotic arguments of the disillusioned and the damned. He cupped his hands over his ears, but the voices did not go away. He curled into himself, but the pain did not abate. So situated, he found neither rest nor succor, only the misery bequeathed to him by his dear Finnseach.

Archer sat out front on a stool, carving on a piece of whale bone, a hay stalk dangling from the corner of his mouth. His big knife stabbed into the ground at his feet, his bow and quiver propped against the cottage. Nearby stood his horse, that fleet-footed stallion that had no name. At his age, this was Archer's last tour of the gauntlet. Even now he could collect what lay for the taking—splendid horses and all of Gregory's weaponry and gear, sell it in one place or the other, take the treasure back to Wales and call it a life. But here he sat, his chin jutting out from beneath his sunken gums, bound by duty to Lord Warren and, by extension, to Gregory. Indeed, no one was getting to the great merchant while he lay on his deathbed. All he had to do was stay alive.

They returned in a cloud of dust, the commotion of the horses stirring Gregory from his tormented sleep. Warren and Beverley came through the door, urgent and purposeful, their manner charged with the dignity of service. Warren knelt down, cupped Gregory's head in his palm, and showed him a corked leather bottle.

"I will not tell you what we did to get this or how much it cost, but you will know this much—it is time to drink," Warren said.

With Archer and Beverley looking over his shoulder, Warren titled the bottle into Gregory's mouth. As he drank it down, Beverley snapped his fingers three times and recited the *Paternoster.*

"It is done, Master Gregory," Warren said. "Now go into the darkness and search for the mourn."

And oh, did the darkness come. So black and bleak, so endless and cold, nothing of the world Gregory knew. Another place, out on the edge of the universe, the hard spade of solitude digging beneath his sanity, unworking his stone and mortar to make the damage permanent. Try as he might to resist the force of this dementia metastasizing down in the depths of him, he found himself falling farther into the hole, looking about but seeing nothing.

Until he did.

A shimmering ray of benevolence, a warm comfort that fortified him. The vision grew, completing itself, the shape taking definition. Gregory put a quivering hand to his mouth and took a deep breath when at last the hallucination presented itself in full. There in front of him, sitting regal in her throne of commerce, was wife Joan. Arrayed in the full regalia of the merchant princess, she twinkled with pearls, the Dijon veil lined with brocade of gold, the flowing lapis robe and the mantle of silk and ermine. Her fingers ringed with silver, a strand of emeralds about her neck, and a brooch, a swan carved of ivory, its eye a fine-cut sapphire. Even her shoes, poulaines of supple leather, were painted and adorned with bright buckles. But she had not come to flaunt her riches and it showed in her face, patrician and fierce, the green eyes set with mettle and shining with iron pride. Indeed, she had come to make war on Finnseach.

For a time, she said nothing, instead allowing Gregory to absorb her immense presence, to know beyond doubt that she had joined the battle. Satisfied that he had given her full account, she began.

"Dear husband, if there was a gift you could give me at this very moment, what would it be?"

Gregory, unprepared for a question and quite perplexed, pondered the query. Nothing immediately came to mind, the request so seemingly out of place that he became flustered. But then he figured it out. As she sat, she had everything that could possibly be bought. What she wanted was something from within him, something he had made, something unique that no other man could have created.

"There is a poem," he said. "I wrote it for Margery—but I now give it to you. Dear wife, you are the only one."

"Continue," she said.

And he went.

She is the sun piercing the clouds on a somber day. She is the field yielding bounty when all others fail. In her heart rises the bread of love, and in her mind turn the gears of the wheels rolling over fear. The dew on the grass is bright in the morning light but is pale compared to her tear falling honest in the night. The doe in the glen and the hawk in the tree, the rose in the wind and the blue of the sea, dusk on the hill and dawn in the vale, the wheat growing gold and the laughter of tales, wind in the leaves and rain on the thatch, truth in sheaves and wits to match. Joan's song I will sing as I go, over mountains and rivers and deep through the snow.

"Dear husband, your gift is well received."

She stood, leaning into it, one foot in front of the other, a hand on her hip, the other balled into a fist, her forearm out in a stance of defiance, a stance of devotion, a lavish bulwark of unyielding loyalty, of undying love. Joan, the first light at dawn, the golden stripe across calm water.

"Dear Gregory, do not die here in Cheshire," she said. "I forbid it, and my forbiddance is my command!"

When he awoke, he found himself in a puddle of excrement and urine, vomit and mucous, sweat and tears, the rancid stew of Clonard having drained out of him. They stripped him down and doused him with buckets, scrubbed him with brushes, and sent his clothing to the local milkmaid for washing. Sitting before the cottage hearth fire, wrapped in a linen blanket, and nibbling on a chunk of roasted hare, he felt his strength returning, in both body and mind. He took a quaff of watered ale, a swallow of normalcy he relished with a weary smile. Looking across the fire, he set his eyes on Beverley, who watched over him with great attention and care.

"How long was I gone?"

"Nine days, Master Gregory," Beverley said, and then reddened with a grin. "From now on I will think of you as the master of sleep."

The four of them chuckled at the joke, the laughter heralding Gregory's return.

"We will give you one more night, Master Gregory," Warren said. "But when the morning comes, we will ride hard for Tutbury. The time we put between us and Henry de Thornhill has been lost. If we remain in Tarvin, we will perish in Tarvin."

"I will be ready," Gregory said. "It is Lady Joan's command."

The Miracle of St. Thomas Beckett

Tutbury, and Ireland behind them for good. They swept through the gatehouse and into the bailey, pulling in their horses near the water well. The householders stopped their chores and greeted them, a noisy, festive reunion with their beloved Warren. Lady Cecily appeared in the doorway to the hall, leaning against the sill. Plump and radiant with child, as if she could become a mother at any moment, she beamed with joy at Warren's return. He dismounted, took her in his arms, and smothered her with a hug and a kiss. Blushing from the overt show of affection, swooning with admiration, she looked out from Warren's embrace and caught Gregory's eye.

"I am pleased that you remained true to your word," she said. "You have brought Warren back to me in good time and in good health."

"My lady, you give me more credit than I deserve, but I will surely accept your gratitude," he said.

fter a full night and day of rest, they settled into a festive evening, eating comfortable food, drinking good wine, and reliving the recent adventures in Nottingham, Ireland and the return trip home. Lady Cecily and the householders, awestruck by what they heard, awaited each and every word, shaking their heads and murmuring in disbelief, their eyes wide with wonderment. And each of them took their turn, Warren telling of what he had seen, Beverley adding details of his experience, Archer nodding in punctuation, and Gregory handling the main thrust of the narrative. To the accompaniment of a droning bagpipe, these courageous travelers, their faces and gestures lit by the glow from the fireplace, held the crowd in thrall. They repeated certain passages when they were asked and provided more context upon request. What they didn't do was exaggerate. The events leading up to, during, and after Ireland were so extreme that they had no need for inflation. In the telling, the four of them shed their anxieties, enjoying the first easy night in weeks.

And then it all came to an end.

"Lord Warren," said one of the men-at-arms as he walked into the hall. "A messenger has just delivered this, and he said it was from Sir Henry de Thornhill."

He handed Warren a small, rolled parchment. Warren looked at it, but before untying the strand of gut and opening it, he handed it to Gregory. Holding it near the fireplace, he deciphered it to himself before reading it aloud. It had been hastily written, in French, and it included many errors. He read it one more time, correcting it in his mind as he went, so that when he read it aloud, it flowed as menacingly as intended.

I have already been to Dunstable and the secret is out. When I was there, I spoke with the Earl of Southampton. I know he is sponsoring your candidacy for the lordship at Winwick—at my expense. But I will not let you take what is mine. When I met with Southampton, I proposed a simple remedy to our problem. If you arrive in Dunstable, then what you want is yours. But if I stop you, and if I present proof of your deceased person to the witnesses there, then your claim, and any substitute claim made in your name, will be abandoned. Southampton has agreed to these terms. But this does not concern him. Nor does it concern our blessed king, the organizer of our dispute. This is between us. This is about honor and who will prove the better at protecting it. I rescued you at Abbeville, only to be betrayed later when it suited you. You eluded me in Wales, much to the detriment of my time and coffers. I tried to apprehend you on your return from Ireland, but I was thwarted by the fury of the sea. The king's lieutenant mocked me when I arrived at Dublin and ordered me back to England at the first tide. Such an embarrassment is difficult to accept, and I assign the ignominy of the ordeal, and the besmirching of my family name, to you. I will cleanse my reputation with your blood. I will restore my status with the destruction of yours. Above all, I will claim my lordship by denying it to you, your widow, and your heir. And you should also know that there will be recriminations for your accomplice. It is known that Warren of Lichfield was party to the abduction of Lady Clifton. Even now her father is mustering his forces and will have his vengeance at Tutbury. While we quibble over Dunstable, Lord Warren faces a much larger conundrum. He is a common dog. His title, which you helped arrange, is a counterfeit. Warren will be reminded of that when Lord Clifton storms his estate. Bordeaux, I know all about you, and I am pleased that it is my task to bring it all to an end. On the brink of your ascendance you will be laid low. Your demise will be discussed in every guildhall from Newcastle to Cornwall. And then you will be forgotten.

Gregory looked up from the letter.

"It seems as if our predicament has worsened," he said.

And then came a shout from the wall. They ran out into the bailey and up the steps to the battlements. From there they saw the reason why Warren's men-at-arms were alarmed. Out in the distance many fires, the hamlets and cottages on the Tutbury estate in flames.

"It has already begun," Warren said, as his men took positions along the wall, as torches and cauldrons were lit, as buckets of pitch were uncovered, as bundles of bolts and arrows were retrieved, as men so recently at leisure were pulling into their mail coats and donning their helms, and as the grooms dressed a half dozen warhorses in tack and saddle.

"Master Gregory, it is time for you to go," Warren said, looking out at the distant blazes. "Lord Clifton is now my issue, and you have yours in Dunstable."

"And you will soon be a father," Gregory said. "That you should remain is not a question."

"No, it is not—but Archer and Beverley will go with you."

"You give me your two best men?"

"Gladly, because it is you. Dunstable must happen if you and are I to survive all of this. If we lose Dunstable, we lose Southampton. If we lose Southampton, we lose it all."

Warren swallowed hard, and from his tortured look, Gregory knew he wrestled with the many things he wanted to say. But as was his way, he kept it simple.

"Henry de Thornhill is no match for you," he said, his voice dour with respect.

"And on your end, neither is Lord Clifton. Hit him hard if you must. But you should be prepared to make a deal. After all, his daughter is safe at the convent at Lismullin, with a gold bezant as guarantee."

"Yes, I will propose an agreement," he said. "But in your case, bring nothing but war."

In the hard stillness of farewell, they embraced, a somber moment in their brotherhood, an exchange of unspoken oaths and impregnable promises. Gregory mounted and made his adjustments, pulling the mail coif over his head and tightening the strap on the helmet, putting on his gloves, fitting his boots in the stirrups, and patting Tatenhill on the neck. Falling in behind Archer and Beverley, and not looking back one last time, he rode through the secret gate and out into the night. The three of them skirted the edges of wheat fields, cut through orchards, meandered down the thin trails that only Archer and Beverley knew, and up over the hills and down through the valleys. They came upon the first ambush, four riders at the timber bridge over the stream. But they did not notice because they had not heard a sound, allowing the trio to simply ride by as their backs were turned. They crossed the stream where they knew to be a ford, leaving the riders waiting on what had already come and gone. When they reached the road, they were no longer within the Tutbury domain, the horses full on the hoof and well on their way to Coventry, their first milestone on the way to Dunstable.

From Nottingham to Liverpool to Ireland and back again, Tatenhill had bested the other horses, always keeping a few lengths between them and the tip of her tail. But no longer. The nameless steeds had found themselves, and they now ran neck and nose with her. The race was always on, and as they worked to beat her, rising to her level rather than the other way around, Gregory and his men made unimaginable time. Hamlets came and went in a blur, flocks of squawking black birds took to flight upon their approach, and the peasants, preparing the fields for planting, stopped and stared as the three of them rode by. And so it was one dawn, the horses at the top of their tilt, when Gregory and his men crossed de Thornhill's retinue. In bivouac near a clump of trees beside the road, the second ambush was in disarray as the men were just then shaking off their sleep, relieving their bowels, or nibbling on bread and cheese. Inwardly, Gregory laughed. They had arrived here much sooner than de Thornhill had expected. And knowing that to be the case, Gregory could not resist a dig. With one hand, he ran his fingers up his neck and flicked them out from his chin, making an ugly face as he did. The obscene gesture enraged de Thornhill, but at the moment all he could do was stammer and yell because Gregory, Archer, and Beverley were already on down the road, their sights set on Coventry.

The city, surrounded by a massive ditch and palisade, soon came into view. Coughing up its requisite share of smoke and ash, the bells ringing sext, Coventry was clogged that day, a line of people and livestock stretching from the gate. Exercising his royal authority, Gregory flashed the Langley Credential, and he and his men were allowed to bypass the crowd. As they neared the gate, Gregory looked over his shoulder, and as he expected, de Thornhill and his riders raced through the suburbs. Passing through the gate and into town, Gregory pulled Archer and Beverley to a halt. He looked this way and that. He had never been to Coventry, but it bore the hallmarks of the many cities he had visited. He read the streets, watched the people, and in short order knew in which direction they needed to go. They went to Pepper Lane, the beginning of the long market district down Gosford Street. Trotting their horses deeper into the thin canyon of stone and timber—of shop signs and storefronts, of cellar doors and corbeled awnings—Gregory found a good spot, right in the middle of street. There he did his best to make a spectacle of himself. With de Thornhill and his retainers appearing at the top of the street and picking their way through the crowd, Gregory cleared his throat and spoke loudly.

He used the merchant's cant, that mélange of languages always heard down in the entrails of the cities, from Edinburgh to Seville. He spoke of the weights and measures of grain, the quality and quantity of ales and wines, the price of silk and that of finished and unfinished wool, of skins and furs and from whence they came, of timber and finish stone, of anise and cinnamon, the guild and their philanthropies, the craftsman and the masterpiece, grades of leather and linen, the cut and polish of amethyst and amber, the barrels and the wheels, parchment and vellum, the mayor and the aldermen, taxes and tariffs, ships and barges, the market and the fair, of Ghent and Bruges, and on and on—until he got their attention—until they knew he was one of them. And out they came to greet him, the coopers and the weavers, the cordwainers and the saddlers, the girdlers, glovers, and grocers, the drapers and the shoemakers, the smiths of silver and gold, the coopers, the vintners, the bakers, the brewers, and the butchers.

"Merchant, what is it that you want?" said one of the drapers.

Gregory looked to his right. De Thornhill and his men, twenty in total, were much less than a stone's throw away and moving closer by the moment.

"Block the road against *them*," he said, pointing in their direction. "They are outlaws and reprobates, and they are the kind of men who seek dominion over you!"

The draper turned his head, looking at the line of horsemen, knee to knee and two deep, athwart the road. Up close, the details of their hazard were quite apparent—the absurd assemblage of weaponry and armor, the dead eyes, the mouths that had rarely smiled, and the collective air of men who rejected love. Though their ancestry made them the rulers of the world, they were in fact the dregs. They knew this about themselves and did not care. And it was their remorselessness, and the satisfaction they found in it, that made them what they were, the eternal nightmare.

"Do not listen to what he says," said de Thornhill.

"And if I defy you?" said the draper.

"Then it would be the last act of a foolish man."

"Foolish? In Coventry, the city of my birth where I know everyone?"

The draper raised his hand and turned it, a signal to action.

"Do as the *merchant* says!"

The townspeople hastened to his request, and before de Thornhill broke through, they barricaded the street with wagons and carts and barrels and tables, and above all themselves. Thick with knives and hooks and rocks and clubs, they raised their fists and sounded the booming, bloody cheer of Coventry.

"Draper, if ever any of you make it to London, ask for Gregory of Bordeaux."

They drove their horses down Gosford Street and out through the eastern gate, taking the last leg to Dunstable. The afternoon remained good, the three of them sharing confidence in their pace and in their lead, knowing that if Coventry had held, and if things remained the same, the chase would be theirs for the winning. But a curse remained to be made that day, and as it was, Archer's horse lost a shoe. Starting to lag, Gregory and Beverley pulled down, and eventually came to a stop. Observing the shoeless hoof, the conclusion was obvious. The horse would never make it to Dunstable, at least not at speed. And they neither had the tools nor the know-how to make a repair. Despondent that they must forfeit the lead they had so dearly made, in silence they exchanged sullen looks. At a loss as to what to do, absorbing this acid disappointment, Gregory shook his head.

"Damn," he said, and spit.

And then they heard the horses of the pursuit.

"Master Gregory, ride ahead," Beverley said. "Archer and I will stop them here. But you must continue."

"There are too many of them."

"No there are not."

Archer dismounted and prepared his bow, the only show of emotion a slight nod in Gregory's direction.

"Ireland was good," Beverley said, and grinned.

"And you steered the ship."

The two clasped hands.

"Yes," Beverley said. "And now I will go kill those bastards in your name."

He and his horse charging toward the retinue, Beverley began his descent into both death and glory. Gregory went ahead, as he was told, but only at a trot since he was unable to keep from watching. As Beverley closed in, there came the pull and pluck of the string, the whisper of the launch, one after the next, Archer's thunderbolts arcing into the retinue and thinning them out, this harrowing assault the work of a dark yet loyal heart. And Beverley let loose with his axe, the weapon looping through the air until it caught one of them crossways on the chest. He then pulled his sword.

"For Bordeaux!" he cried and angled into the cavalcade.

He somehow maneuvered through the bodyguard and brought his sword against de Thornhill himself. He parried. Beverley swung left and felled one and swung right and felled another. He raised his weapon for a second attempt on de Thornhill, and it was then that he was swarmed. And then he went down, perhaps thinking his glory had gone unfulfilled.

But he had stopped them.

The arrows surely resumed as Archer continued his massacre, the riders falling in piles, clutching at the poplar shafts, crying for their mothers and yelling at God. Arriving at his last arrow, Archer aimed and let it fly at de Thornhill—the only one who remained. Because he wore the best armor in the world, that fantastic Welsh bowshot, the one that should have sent him groveling to purgatory, ricocheted off his chest plate. At that moment, when Gregory realized Archer would also die, he arrived at an impossible epiphany. He knew Archer's name. He reined Tatenhill to a halt.

"Caerwyn," he called, his voice breaking with lament.

He turned. Caerwyn smiled, that old toothless face shining through the melancholy. He slowly raised his hand and waved. And then he confronted his fate, yanked out that terrible blade of his, and charged de Thornhill on foot. Gregory could not bear to watch anymore, so he wheeled Tatenhill and gave her the spurs. He heard the anguish of battle, the finality of the kill, and made the sign of the cross. As hard as it was to do, Gregory left it all behind, Caerwyn and Beverley, telling himself he would grieve when the proper time came due.

He and Tatenhill went down a wide path shaded under a canopy. Coming out on the other side of this woodland tunnel, the land opened up, rolling hills, fallow emerald fields stretching everywhere, a hamlet and parish church silhouettes against a towering blue sky. Up ahead he saw something peculiar, a horse and rider so swift and effortless it was if they levitated down the road. Gregory and Tatenhill closed on them. More ethereal than flesh, more heavenly than mortal, a shimmering vision of something that, in a thunderclap of awareness, he recognized from the past—he and Black Saddle on one of their charmed sprints, on their way from hell to heaven as the angels and demons made their bets. The black and chestnut points, the cloak flowing, the brim of the beaver and peacock bent upward by the wind. He did not know if Tatenhill saw it, but he figured she did, so he leaned in over an ear, still goading her with the willow whip, and whispered, "Go catch them, Tatenhill. Do us a favor and best your father."

She gave it a go. The belly grunt, that reassuring tug, the champion's lust for heroics. The ten lengths between them soon dwindled to four, and at four is where it remained. Strange, running against himself, competing with the past as he hurtled toward his future. And frustrating. Their lead, as slim as it was, seemed insurmountable as every elevation in Tatenhill's effort was matched by the slightest improvement in Black Saddle's. And so it went for furlong after furlong, Tatenhill tucked in on Black Saddle's hindquarters, gritting her way through the exhaust of divots spewing in her father's wake.

Down a slope and across a muddy bottom, orphaned fields of rye and blue wildflowers. Up ahead, an abandoned village, emptied by a forgotten plague in a forgotten year. Past the vacant stables and the sagging barn, the burnt-out inn, the leaning parish church, and the row of deserted thatch-and-plaster homes. And it was in this village of bygone dreams where Tatenhill made her move. She took the turn out of town a bit sharper than did Black Saddle, and as they passed the rotted water mill and the grain silo, Tatenhill gained two lengths. Gregory heard the crack and split of wood, the creaking cacophony of failing timber. He looked over his shoulder, only to watch the entire village collapse in a cloud of dust. So fast was Tatenhill's pass, and so full was the gust in her train, that it swept that cloud into a swirling, rising funnel of poison, with nails, pegs, and splinters spitting out and showering the pestilential ruin. Emboldened by the destruction she had wrought, Tatenhill charged even harder, and by the time the narrow stone bridge over the ravine came into view, she had pulled even with the great stallion.

But there was only room for one at a time, as a plodding horse and wagon clogged the arched expanse. Gregory turned to look at the very image of himself, crouched over the withers and hissing at his steed. But this doppelganger did not acknowledge him, looking only ahead as Black Saddle maintained his astounding, endless pace. Lurching breakneck toward the bridge, all of it in the balance, the final push ensued between colt and filly, for both had found the years of their youth, the pair leaning in on each other, gnashing their teeth and snorting as they fought for the lead. And Tatenhill found it with a greathearted jump-cut at full stretch, enough to break her at the bone, to burst her at the sinew. Swerving in front of Black Saddle, she claimed first passage over the bridge.

With the shoes of Neath Abbey pounding over the stone and cracking them in places, she shot past the wagon. Her appearance was so sudden and her going so disruptive that Tatenhill spooked the docile wagon horse. Sounding a shrill whinny, it bolted and reared, sending the carter, the wagon, and its freight spilling across the bridge. Gregory looked back, expecting to see himself and Black Saddle in close pursuit. But they never appeared, and Gregory knew that having served their purpose, they had vanished back into the depths of his imagination. But even without them as competition, Tatenhill showed no signs of relenting.

The road beyond the bridge tapered over a plain, running parallel to the ravine and offering a clear view back from whence they had come. And there on the road, between the bridge and the village ruins, came de Thornhill and his horse. Gregory watched them as he went, his opponent moving at frightening speed, and when they crossed the bridge, they leapt over the pileup and continued in stride.

"We are not yet done," Gregory said to Tatenhill, as she crested an incline and accelerated down a sunken turn. For another furlong she went, galloping into that moment of resplendence when the world stops for all but one, when God looks down on a wretched place to yet witness a feat of rare beauty. And then she came to a crook in the road, a tight downward turn lined with mossy stones. The reliable front left hoof, that of the hard stick and pull, slipped out from under her. What followed was the dip of her shoulder, the sinking of the flank, and a sorrowful snap at the knee. She plunged until her chin cracked against the ground, the girth of her a silver heap, her tail and limbs flailing, turning as she scraped against the ruts and crags, roots and rocks, and a tangle of thorns and nettle, coming to rest as a shattered jewel lodged against a hedge near a sash of blooming daisies.

From the saddle, Gregory watched the collapse, all of it unfolding in an instant hour of agony and dismay. Just as Tatenhill crashed, he leapt from the stirrups, himself tumbling with such force that when his head collided with a tree, the impact knocked the hat and helm from his head, and when he tried to stop by planting his foot, his ankle bent into a terrible sprain. Abrasions at each elbow and knee, a deep bite in his lip, and a knot on his head, he lay flat on his back, gazing double into the canopy. He took a deep breath, closed his eyes, and stole a moment to collect himself.

Clutching at his ankle, he sat up, put a hand to a tree, and with considerable difficulty, gained his feet. Limping deeply, and wincing as he went, through the underbrush he returned to the road. Looking upon his dear Tatenhill, he shook his head in despair. The fine horse, so recently gallant and giving of her lion's heart, lay motionless in indignity, her chin and teeth flat against the ground, the left leg bent upward at a sickening angle. Gregory hobbled to her, hoping to catch the final breath so that he could speak a word of love. He knelt down, stroked her neck, and leaned into her ear. But Gregory could not bring himself to speak, instead trembling and swallowing back the anguish of losing her, of losing the last of the three murdering warhorses that had made a hero out of him. He collapsed into the crook between her head and shoulder, and as the quiet was only broken by the singsong of a finch, clutched at her lush silver mane.

And then he rose, collected his hat and helm, and using a branch as a cane, walked back up to that bend in the road. Craning his neck, he peered around the corner and saw what he hoped he would not—de Thornhill closing in. Not knowing what to do, Gregory wrestled with a moment of panic. Impaired by the injury and stranded, he was helpless. And de Thornhill would show no mercy.

Growing ever more morose and resigning himself to the end, he heard an unexpected quartet of sounds—the thud of a hoof, the jingle of a bridle, the creak of leather and, finally, to his breathless disbelief, a splendid neigh. He turned, his head jerking. Even as he wobbled on a swollen ankle, he scampered back around that bend in the road. Though he had left a scene of wreckage, that's not what he found upon his return. Between the ruts stood Tatenhill, her front left leg skinned and bloodied, dried froth at her mouth, and a strawberry scrape slanting from croup to thigh. She blinked, her big walnut eyes an enchantment of life. She penned her ears forward. And those little specks of ruby, the ones Warren had soldered onto her bridle years ago in Gascony, the ones that were hidden beneath miles and months of dirt and dreck, somehow caught the sun and dazzled bright, bathing she and Gregory in a flash of crimson light. He started to laugh. The laugh of joy, true, but so too the laugh of relief, of incredulity, a laugh that remained so long it became something other than what it was, beginning as a common burst of sound and ending as a soul-turning shout against surrender, a belligerent boast to any who would listen that on this day, the merchant and his Tatenhill would have their way.

A million explanations as to how this could have happened, of how both of them yet lived, gushed through Gregory's mind. But only one of them made sense—this was the miracle of Saint Thomas Beckett. When he had visited his shrine in Canterbury, he had asked the saint to help him make it back home. He had not expected the assistance to arrive in such fashion, but Gregory was in no mood to quibble. He tightened his belt, straightened his helm, and pulled the fingers tight on his gloves. Knees popping in a fanciful show of pedigree, Tatenhill pranced in a circle to his side. Climbing into the saddle, he could not contain a tear of pride, even if that's not what Saint Thomas would have wanted. Once seated, he wiped it from his eye and took hold of the reins.

"Give me what remains, good girl, and let us take this road to Dunstable," he said, and Tatenhill rumbled forth in a trot.

As they resumed, de Thornhill veered around the bend, his horse leaning into the turn, churning through the daisies, and then regaining the road. Taking the high ground between the ruts, that cursed thing showed no signs of fatigue. Judging the diminishing distance between them, Tatenhill still struggling, Gregory knew they would be caught. De Thornhill pulled his sword, his courser pulling even. He readied his blade. In that lash of a moment that he had to take, Gregory reached over, grabbed de Thornhill's horse by the bridle, and tugged with all the strength his desperation would allow. The horse faltered, as did de Thornhill's strike, the sword at half strength skipping off the shoulder of Gregory's mail. But when he tried to pull his hand back, he found it stuck in the bridle. De Thornhill noticed, and with the manic smile of triumph at last exploding in his face, he swiped downward. But Gregory worked his hand out of the glove and tucked in his arm just before de Thornhill lopped it off.

And it was then that Beckett's miracle turned to the second phase. Tatenhill began to pull away. Her trot turned into a gallop, and before Gregory fully appreciated what had happened, she was again the ruby shooting star, dashing over the sheep-dotted hills as she strove to win her second race of the day. Up ahead he saw something that heartened him—a ribbon of white smoke, a civilized swath of smoke, a lingering wisp from some great oven or kiln. Dunstable, Gregory said to himself, smiling as he leaned over Tatenhill's withers. And that is how they finished the last seven furlongs, de Thornhill, abusing his mount with whip and spur, and Tatenhill, ahead by five lengths and counting, refusing to concede.

Thundering in from the north, they entered Dunstable, themselves a circus, becoming the top gossip, the irresistible rumor, the latest addition that could not be ignored. Already festooned with the kaleidoscope of the tournament, Dunstable, on this very day four times its normal size, greeted their arrival with a besotted shout of gratitude, and then came the note, sounded at once by every drum, lute, harp, bell, bagpipe, and whistle, a faltering note with no key, but a round belch of merriment that rattled the rafters and shook the cellars. Within the din of this jamboree, Gregory and de Thornhill sped through the ancient crossroads, past Eleanor's soaring cross and the row of squalid inns, through the penny-and-farthing market and into the long shadow cast by the priory.

In the open end of the High Street, Gregory turned Tatenhill, and nearly choked on the tail of dust that enveloped him. He reared her and then she erupted back in the direction they had come. He pulled *La Bonne Vie* and brandished it forward. The distance between them closing by the double, he was upon de Thornhill before the knight could set his defense. Making the pass, Gregory leaned out with his long knife, letting Tatenhill's horsepower do the work. He caught him across the brim of his basinet, the blade cracking in two as it slammed into the helm, lifting de Thornhill out of his saddle. A foot became caught in one of the stirrups so that his steed, that long black devil with a glob of drool hanging from its mouth, drug him in a circle. De Thornhill, dropping his sword, struggled to set himself free.

And there Gregory sat, straight and prim atop his mount, in possession of the upper hand. He watched as de Thornhill fumbled with his boot, grumbling to himself, gasping with exhaustion, his horse fidgeting. What a fool he seemed, hanging from the stirrup, contorted with the effort it took to remove himself from the trap. Gregory allowed himself the cruel chuckle of victory, that low mocking laugh that only comes when, after many difficulties, the deed has definitively been done.

"Was it me who brought you to Dunstable?" he said. "Or was it you?"

De Thornhill grimaced, glanced up and said, "You whoreson, you know it was me!"

"I am glad you are being honest, for now is not the time to lie," he said. "Since you have clarity, I must ask you one last question. Did you know Lady Tatenhill was the fastest horse in all of England, or were you ignorant of that fact?"

De Thornhill's answer was a spit and sneer, a crestfallen grunt and growl. And then he gave in, the sinking of pride and truculence so extreme that he suddenly looked like a much smaller man, laying there on his back, his twisted leg hanging limp from the stirrup, his handsome horse standing over him.

They came in droves, friars and monks, parish priests and lay brothers, noblemen, merchants, and a reeking throng of peasants. They formed a circle with Gregory and de Thornhill at its center. The craning of necks, the tips of toes, and in some instances, a girl atop the shoulders of her father, the boy at the hip of his mother, all of them murmuring and marveling at the spectacle of this once prestigious knight, he who had just recently boasted in all the taverns of this town, in a pile of defeat. And then they gawked at the horseman who had vanquished him, just a crow of a man, wise and full of sorrow, steeped in mystique and powdered in grime, still clutching the hilt of the shattered knife as he watched from beneath his helm, the black plume dipping in the breeze. The moment turned when de Thornhill, the head wound finally taking its toll, breathed the last breath God had given him and deflated in an exhale.

Now with blood on his hands, Gregory searched the crowd, looking for the familiar face he hoped was there. But just in case it wasn't, he sheathed what remained of *La Bonne Vie* and produced the Langley Credential, holding it high as he stared into the faces of a thousand strangers. A long moment later, he found what he looked for. Amid an assortment of barons and bishops, knights and squires—the cream of the coming rebellion—stood the Earl of Southampton.

"My lord," Gregory said. "I knew you would be in Dunstable, so I came forthwith."

Southampton walked into the circle, stopped and gestured toward de Thornhill.

"Bordeaux, you have delivered yet again," he said.

Gregory sighed. He rolled up the Langley Credential and tucked it away. "I needed a miracle to do it, my lord—but that is another story."

Epilogue: Lord & Lady Winwick of Cambridgeshire

A year later on a fine summer day, long after the iron-gall ink on his deed had dried, Gregory sat out on the terrace near a long row of blooming roses. Trained and manicured, a red and leafy hedge of fragrance and beauty. This was his favorite place to sit, beneath an arbor of honeysuckle, and watch the land rustle in the breeze. Joan enjoyed this place, too, and she often sat with Gregory when he retired to this peaceful nook.

In front of them the yard, its emerald lawn trimmed by a scythe, its perimeter lined with holly. Little Gregory and Herlève tumbled around in this yard, playing tag, riding the hobby horse, and chasing the spotted dog that lived on the grounds. Gregory found joy in their little voices and their brays of laughter, and when he watched them jump about, he forgot his many problems and his many enemies. And recently, he had even more cause for happiness. Infant Joan, the latest addition to the du Mont family, was inside suckling at the wet nurse's bosom and would soon be off to sleep. So enraptured, Gregory slid his hand into Joan's, and there they sat, among the roses straight and prim, Lord and Lady Winwick of Cambridgeshire.

A proper manor, Winwick, complete with a hall, a turret, a gatehouse, and a moat. Ivy climbing up the stone walls, the peaked roof laden with slate tiles, a detached kitchen—manned by a volatile Gascon cook and his army of underlings—and a long barn and stables stretching out in the back. As far as Gregory could see in all directions, he and Joan's estate, with a village, a community of peasants and free farmers, a mill, a brew house, a smithy, and a stout parish church that dated all the way back to the Saxon age. A common green, a stand of oak, a crystal stream, and an apple orchard out past the rolling fields of wheat and rye. In the spring came the swallows and the martins, and soon thereafter, the golden orioles, nesting in their slings hanging high in the poplars.

Inside, the first thing Gregory had done was install a new fireplace, and then he enlarged the upstairs solar to include a second fireplace and a garderobe built into the wall. A new window lined with stone of Caen, from which he and Joan watched the sunrise, and a spiral staircase leading down to the ground level, lined with Oriental rugs, its walls hung with Flemish tapestries, and a long, finished table with two high-backed chairs—his and Joan's dual seat of power. He had already been appointed sheriff for one term, which was to begin after the Feast of St. Benedict. Gregory didn't really want to accept the post, but there was no way he could say no to the king, right? Besides, he would meet everyone in the shire, and with his year of service done, he could hang up his cloak and hat, his boots and spurs, and finally retire, but with a new accolade to his name and with many people owing him favors.

A loud whinny echoed from the stables. Tatenhill calling for her daily jaunt. Across the field, through the woods, over the bridge, around the village, and back again. An easy trot that Gregory rather enjoyed. But for serious business, he now relied on a much younger gelding who, though much inferior to Tatenhill, was actually quite nimble and just fast enough. Ever since her run to Dunstable, Gregory had feared to even breed Tatenhill, thinking he would lose both her and the foal. So, he pampered her, taking her on those meandering excursions through the shire, knowing that the bloodline of Moonbeam and Black Saddle—oh, that imperious line—would in time die with her. The end of an era, whenever it might come, and the thought of it always made Gregory sad. But he was fine with it all the same. Anymore, it was enough that she yet lived and that each day she waited for him, good and courageous Tatenhill, still eager to serve her master.

He had not seen Warren since shortly after Dunstable. After retrieving Caerwyn and Beverley, Gregory returned to Tutbury where the two men-at-arms were buried in consecrated ground next to the chapel. And Lord Clifton? Warren had sued for peace, telling his adversary that his daughter—unharmed and unspoiled—could be retrieved at Lismullin. He gave Lord Clifton three fine war horses as surety, and the angry father lifted his siege, went to Ireland and brought his daughter home. But once back in England she shocked the realm by spurning Lord Shirle and instead marrying into the wealthiest merchant family in Gloucester. Thus, imagine the look Lady Clifton and Gregory shared when, to the murmuring of many, they greeted one another at her wedding. But still, he had not heard from Warren in a year. The king had sent him on a diplomatic mission to Rome as part of the armed retinue escorting a royal embassy. Gregory awaited news of his return, and as the fortnights came and went, grew ever more anxious. Rome, after all, was a long way away.

The kids came and climbed up into the laps of their mother and father. Gregory and Joan kissed them and held them, knowing these easy days would not last forever. In the future they would be fostered in a noble home far from here, and these innocent kids would begin their journey into adulthood, replete with status, competition, alliances, and ambition. And it would be in that time, in the contested coming of age, when they would begin to figure out who exactly their parents were. They would learn that though he was rather famous, that their father had once been an obscure wine merchant on the squalid London waterfront, and that before he was known as Lord Winwick of Cambridgeshire and a member of Parliament, he had simply been known as Gregory of Bordeaux. And their mother, not born into nobility either. Though she held the title of Lady Joan of Winwick, and though she held an important interest in the London pepper trade, they had once just called her Joan the Widow. He hoped his children still loved them when they realized they had come from common stock. Gregory banished the thought. That was a worry, and a real one, he would save for another day.

With Herlève climbing down from his knee, Gregory stood from his seat. He took the pruning shears from the table and went to the hedge. Finding the biggest flower in front of him, he clipped it off, pulling away the leaves and plucking away the thorns. He returned to the arbor, Joan watching as he approached. He went down on one knee, presenting the rose to her, his demeanor playful, but also sincere.

"Dear husband, it pleases me that you give me a gift," she said, taking the blossom and sliding it behind her right ear.

"Dear wife, it is a glorious rose, but not as glorious as you."

He took her hand and kissed the back of it, looking up into those eyes that had burned so bright during the darkness of Cheshire. Across the lawn, the kids laughed and played. The dog barked at them. And a ruby twilight, the kind that heals hearts and gives life to dreams, began to break over Winwick.

In 1961, an American investor and his wife moved to England. They rented a London townhome in Chelsea, biding their time with art and theater, and evening strolls through Sloane Square. While they enjoyed the patina of West London, dotted as it was with palaces, pubs, markets, and boutiques, they were not there for the frivolities of affluence. The couple had come across the pond for something much bigger. An estate, a manor, something out in the country where they themselves could live as modern-day aristocrats.

This investor, who had served in England during World War II, had fallen in love with the country, and from the moment he returned to the United States, thought of nothing else but returning and living in one of the grand country homes he had glimpsed from the roadside during a drunken weekend furlough. On the back of the GI Bill, he raced through his economics degree in just three years, working any odd job he could find along the way. He dumped nearly every penny he earned into the stock market, and when he finished college, went straight to Wall Street. The other brokers said he was a natural, for all his silver turned to gold, his gold to platinum, and if he were to find a stone in his shoe, upon putting it into his palm, it would become a diamond. During college he met his wife, an only child from Cooperstown, New York, who had inherited everything when her parents died in a car crash. She had also been to England, when she was a teenager, and shared her husband's desire to live there. The two of them, he with his financial savvy and she with her inherited wealth, focused everything on the grand isle of *Albion*.

Buoyed for the long term by an encyclopedic portfolio of CDs, bonds, mutual funds, and commercial real estate leases, they cashed out all the stock—Bethlehem Steel, US Steel, General Motors, and Exxon among many others—and the couple "retired" at the decrepit old age of thirty-seven and thirty-five. Once in Chelsea, they hired an agent and began their search. Many of the manors were pristine and unaffordable, even for them, or in ruins, or buried beneath the ancient legal filings of feuding families. On the brink of altering their plan and settling on a London townhome, the couple cheered up when the agent told them about a neglected estate northwest of Cambridge, known simply as "the old manor at Winwick." They dashed up the interstate in an Aston Martin, pulling into the village as the butcher opened his shop for the day. Tourists didn't visit Winwick, so all the local eyes were on the man in the cable-knit sweater and chinos, and the woman who, in her peach sherbet suit dress, white gloves, pearls, and pillbox hat, was a delightful stand-in for Jacqueline Onassis.

They asked for directions, which led them down a winding dirt road that plunged into the heart of a heavenly countryside of streams, meadows, stone fences, and grazing cattle. The road ended in a turnabout. On the far end of the field, cut through with a footpath, sat Winwick Manor. The agent had told them that according to local lore, people had waited out the Black

Plague there, a prisoner had been kept in the cellar during the reign of Elizabeth I, it bore an old wound from a cannon ball fired during the English Civil War, an heir had served as on officer under the Duke of Wellington at the Battle of Waterloo, and, at last, it had fallen into disrepair when the old gentry family that owned it finally died out. And there it sat, steeped in its tattered grandeur, mothballed for generations, and sagging with the roots and vines of Mother Nature.

Compared to what the couple had seen during their search, Winwick was not the biggest, was not the prettiest, and certainly not in the best condition. But, for people who always had a keen eye for the deal, the price was more than right. Without even going inside, they made the offer and got the deed. They immediately had the overgrowth cut back. After decades of darkness, the sun once again shone over Winwick. Over the years there had been plenty of additions, evident by the competing patterns of stone and brickwork, and a succession of architectural styles. But at its core this manor conveyed authority, an authentic expression of power that shown in the weathered gatehouse, the muscular turret, and the big-boned hall. This manor was built when such features were not flights of fancy, or monuments to nostalgia, but indispensable necessities. Winwick, the date of its original construction unknown, was without a doubt medieval. When the truth of the matter became clear to the investor and his wife, they looked into each other's eyes and fell into an embrace, knowing they had found not just a home, but the life they wanted to live.

Weeks later, when the junk was being gutted and the valuables were being salvaged, the couple found themselves rummaging through the attic. They had joked amongst themselves about how neat it would be to find a hidden treasure from history. In a place like Winwick, the thought was not necessarily fantastical. So, when they climbed the ladder and cracked the hatch for the first time, they did so as children embarking on their first adventure. Indeed, their hopes were amply rewarded. The attic was jammed with artefacts. Peeling back the canvas drop tarps, they discovered row upon row of furniture and paintings, sculptures and household wares, all of it seemingly untouched from when the manor went cold in the late 19th Century. A true English trove, too, as the couple, even with their untrained eyes, recognized objects from China, India, Egypt, and Greece—the looted bounty of the old British Empire—mixed in with the bulk of European objects. They looked at one another, frozen in disbelief, and exchanged smiles of amazement. They called the local historian and gave him a brief overview of what they had found. He and a colleague arrived within the hour.

Over the course of weeks, a platoon of art historians meticulously catalogued the hoard, crated it, and sent it to the British Museum, where it would become known as Winwick: The John and Linda Hudson Collection, on permanent display. The find generated international headlines, and for a short while, the arts press corps was camped out in town. But soon enough the excitement settled down, the attic was empty, and the only thing that could be heard at the manor was the thud and whir of renovation. And it was during that time, when the contractor went through the interior down to its nails, pegs and mortar, when Winwick yielded its last secrets. The contractor found a false wall, a piece of stained paneling fitted across the attic's north end. With John and Linda standing near, the contractor pried back the wood, revealing a space in which sat a wooden chest. Unadorned, uncarved, and otherwise unremarkable, the chest was easily many centuries old, and big enough for two grown men to crawl inside. Curiously, the lid was sealed. The contractor turned to John and Linda and said, "I'm not touching it."

Again, John and Linda called the local historian, describing to him their latest find and, mindful of the media scrum they had recently endured, implored him to say nothing and to come as soon as he could. Inspecting the chest, he identified the sealant, tool marks, joinery, and hinges. He then took a long look at the lock, and after so doing, unfolded a neatly kept set of picks, and set it on the floor.

"What do you think this is?" John said.

The local historian smiled and shook his head in reverent disbelief.

"This, sir, is from the Fourteenth Century. And unlike everything else we found, this would be original to the manor."

"Can it be opened?" Linda said.

"That will not be a problem," the historian said, as he held up a razor-sharp pocketknife.

With a steady hand, he ran the blade down the sealant, a waxed and oiled leather strap, beginning at the lock and tracing his way around the entire chest until he arrived back where he had started. He squirted a few drops of lubricant into the lock, and into the hinges, and made small talk with John and Linda as he waited for the liquid to ooze into place. It took some doing, but he found the right picks and sprung the lock. A click and clunk. He pulled down the latch, and with John and Linda's help, heaved open the massive lid. The creak of wood. The squeak of hinges. A great stink lifting in a cloud. All of them turned away and covered their noses as they tried not to wretch. After a bout of coughing and gagging, red-faced and teary eyed, they recovered and again set their sights on the chest.

The historian donned a pair of archive gloves and reached inside. With a soft touch, he lifted out an object of which he hadn't a clue. He held it up near the lantern hanging from a rafter, and turned it in his hands. An enormous black hat with a deep crown lined with crimson silk, a wide drooping brim, a silver rose pendant punched into the side, holding in place the faded eye of a peacock feather. This hat, bearing the stitch work of repair and the fatigue of heavy use, had no doubt been worn by someone who had lived deep in the mists of time. Not an object of art or a stolen valuable, but a living relic that had once been part of someone's wardrobe. In that moment when they realized what it was, they adored that hat, loved for eternity whoever had worn it, and knew that the sight of it, its beaver skin shimmering in the pale light of the oil lamp, would be something they would never forget. The historian gasped, as did John and Linda, as this magical hat, crafted at an artisan's workbench nearly seven hundred years earlier, crumbled away, leaving nothing but a dusting on the historian's shoes. Linda knelt down to retrieve the rose pendant, which had fallen to the floor and bounced to her feet. But it too, was gone.

Astonished by what had just transpired, the historian tried to step away.

But he just couldn't. He again reached into the chest, pulling out a luxuriant textile expanse. He held it up with both hands, letting it fall to its full length without touching the floor—a billowing black cloak, its hood lined with deer fur, its entire outer hem lined with a seam of mesmerizing green silk, its interior shell a swath of blue wool. Like the hat, it astounded them with the blunt beauty of its workmanship. It filled their souls with longing and brought about a profound love for the person whose shoulders this cloak had once hung about. And then, howling sadness as it vanished into waste.

"My apologies, I was too hasty," the historian said, his voice shaking.

"No, it would have happened to anyone," Linda said.

"Agreed," John said. "You have done nothing wrong. Continue."

The three of them, and with the contractor looking over their shoulders, gazed back into the chest, where pulsed a feint heartbeat of golden light. Their faces bright in the ambiance, they discovered bound manuscripts and parchment rolls, stacks of writs, and tied-off heaps of letters. Linda and John gave the historian looks of worry, but he smiled and said to them, "These do not go away!"

They extracted them, one by one, setting them out on the attic floor until the chest was empty. Taking pains to be delicate in their work, the task took hours. Once done, the impressive collection was laid out before them. A library, of a distinctly medieval vintage, the majority of which was secular, not religious. They stayed up through the night, combing through the rich pages of parchment, most of it in Latin and French, and some of it in Middle English. Among the many dull pages of legalese were bound volumes bursting in a riot of color, alive with people doing everything from the mundane to the heroic. Lords and ladies, knights and squires, hawks and hounds and great charging horses. Along with the churchmen and merchants were the humble folk, farmers and shopkeepers, blacksmiths and cordwainers, women working the loom, and kids on the green with dogs at their heels. Castles and cathedrals, city gates and village barns, ringing bells and turning wheels, and ships moored at the pier. Meat on the spit, loaves in the oven, and a pot hanging over a fire. Sacks of wool and bushels of wheat, hogsheads of ale and pipes of wine. And on one page, its margins painted with gold, a woman, her face in profile, as beautiful as the Madonna but without a halo and child, sitting in a throne with a small harp in her hand. These stunning volumes, all five of them bound in gem-encrusted leather, were set aside from the rest of the trove.

The historian went through them one more time, paying particular attention to what appeared in the first few pages of each, and what appeared at the end. He laughed, and by his manner, it appeared that he had solved the puzzle. He put one manuscript to his left, and moving right, placed the second, the third, the fourth, and the fifth. He looked at John and Linda, both of them exhausted, sitting on the floor with their arms across their knees and their backs against the wall. Feeling the importance of the moment, they stood.

"What is it?" Linda said.

The darkness lifted as the first light of dawn shown in the window. Away in the village, a rooster crowed, a lump of coal was turned in the hearth, and the bell at the parish church rang prime. Linda felt the goosebumps racing down her arms and noticed the emotion welling in the corner of her husband's eye. They wrapped their arms around each other, pulling themselves in tight.

"This is the entirety of a chronicle, volumes one through five, written during the reigns of Edward I and his son, Edward II," the historian said. "And if I had to guess, it was written by the man who wore that cloak and hat. Gregory of Bordeaux, he called himself, and as you can see, he lived an extraordinary life."

www.ingramcontent.com/pod-product-compliance
Lightning Source LLC
Chambersburg PA
CBHW030426310726
48979CB00009B/1631/J

* 9 7 9 8 8 9 2 9 9 0 3 1 8 *